TORN FROM A TORTURED SOUL...

On that day, which was the beginning of a singular relationship between my brother and I, on that day there was a spiritual and love bond between us. It is beyond my reach now, and perhaps I shall never again recapture it though I live to be ninety. . . .

———◆———

"The novel resonates with echoes of the Brontës."
—*Newsday*

"Slaughter's characters refuse to leave the mind alone, long after the book is finished. It matters."
—*Dallas Times-Herald*

Carolyn Slaughter

Relations

Previously published in England
under the title:
The Story of the Weasel

PUBLISHED BY POCKET BOOKS NEW YORK

For
Daniel
T.W. and A.T.

Thou hast ravished my heart,
my sister, my spouse; thou
hast ravished my heart with
one of thine eyes, with one
chain of thy neck.

The Song of Solomon

Relations

I

This is the third attempt to put my thoughts down on paper; in my mind they chafe mercilessly. For some reason, events keep flooding in on me these last few days; events I had forgotten, or hidden beneath the blanket of time. Now they become cruelly vivid once more, and vex me with their persistence.

I am in my thirtieth year. It is 1900 and springtime; there is something about the budding bulbs that saddens me today.

My story would be less painful to tell, I dare say, had not my situation changed so radically. The events to which I shall refer were, I am sure, not entirely uncommon to the society in which I lived as a child. We were not a well-to-do family, my parents had little money to squander on treats or trifles. We lived in a small way, depending little on other people or outside influences.

Today, however, my situation is quite different. Vastly improved some might say; marriage has improved my station, as it did my Mamma's. I have married wisely, and remarkably well considering the humble nature of my background. My husband is endowed with good connections, a scholarly education and quite a lofty fortune. And he is a good person, gentle and considerate at all times.

If my story came to light, I fear I should lose all this. I fear it greatly because I have found some measure of tranquillity in this past year; it has escaped me now. The burden of my childhood has descended once more. It is hard to endure, and of late I have begun to observe the effects upon my character and disposition. I feel listless, often close to tears. I am beset by fiendish pangs in my brow; pangs that creep round to the base of my neck, clutching their fingers together, causing me paroxysms of pain.

But I must not deter. Better to get on with the task in the small hope that it may in some measure reduce this torment. Perhaps this pen, this ink, will exorcize the past for me. My mind is on fire, my brow throbs, yet I cannot allow this old wound to fester unchecked. I shall begin; I am resolved to spare no detail, no mite honestly in this. If it is to be done it must be done with all truthfulness.

I was born in January 1870, the third child of Edward and Virginia Roach. My eldest brother, Edward, was born four years before me, Christopher less than two. We lived in Wandsworth, quite near to the common, in a dark house of three storeys.

My mind is racing ahead of me: I can never keep it in check. I think therefore it would be better to confine myself to the time when the story began in earnest. To this end, I shall leap over the years until I am ten years of age.

I was running down the long corridor at the back of our house, it was extremely dark and dusty. Cobwebs lurked like widows' veils in corners. We did not come to this part of the house often; Mamma did not allow it.

I was looking for Christopher. He was nowhere to be found. I called many times: 'Christopher, O come on, do. I don't want to play any more. I am in earnest, please come.'

I was afraid without him. My hands reached out and clutched only the dark. A shadow sneaked sideways through a window. I bruised my foot against the old mirror – blood squirted. I caught sight of myself in the mirror; I thought it was someone else. I didn't like my face. The eyes, the hair: all too black. 'Not a pleasing physiognomy,' Mamma used to say.

I could just detect a small light at the end of the corridor. I thought Christopher must be in there. I held my breath and prayed it was him. I looked round the door with care. It was him. I was indeed glad to have found him. But I pretended to be vexed:

'Christopher. You didn't answer. I called you. Why did you not answer? You know I can't abide the dark.'

'I did not hear you.'

How well I recollect the way he looked; my mind caresses the details now – but enough of that.

His black shiny head was buried over a big wooden box. How his hair shined and gleamed! Often I wanted to put out my hand and touch it. Touch him. I was afraid lest he should reject it.

'Cathy, come and see. See, in here.'

He looked up. His eyes were like black vents in a pale thin face. His brows were heavy with brooding.

Now that it is so many years on, I can think of his face and find things in it I never saw at the time. There was, in retrospect, a fierceness, almost a savagery in that countenance. There was certain cruelty in that mouth.

I looked at the box that held his attention. It was bigger than I had thought at first glance. It was made of wood and it had large locks securing it. Big red dragons interlaced with gold and curious trees were worked into the top of the box. I had not seen it for some time. But I remembered well the day Father brought it back from China...

I heard the bang of the front door, the cold gust of wind sweeping in. I got out from beneath my covers so I might observe Father coming in. He was expected. He had not been home for many months. He had the big wooden box with him and a man helped him place it in a corner.

He loomed large and frightening at the base of the staircase. He was wearing a big black topcoat. He looked fine, but his face had a darkness, an anger about it that alarmed me. He ascended the stairs and entered Mamma's chamber. I listened but I could not hear their conversation. I waited for a while, rubbing first one foot and then the other against my legs to keep them warm.

I did not care for my father. I did not hate him, but he frightened me. He was subject to violent outbursts: he would lash out at us children sometimes for no reason at all. He took pleasure in our fear. An unkind smile would tweak the corners of his tight mouth. So, on this night, I did not go in to see him. I peered instead, very cautiously, round the door, and then moved back swiftly for fear of being seen. I crept back to my room up the stairway – a steep acclivity – and then I heard a sharp, pained cry, followed by a shrill scream. My blood chilled. I could not move. Then there was silence. And a slow, quiet sobbing. I settled into an uneasy slumber, tormented with strange dreams...

'Cathy, you're not looking. Come and help me unlock the box. Pass me that piece of iron over there.'

My brother, I should perhaps say here, had a curious way of commanding me. I would do his bidding without question; although I was not by nature a docile child, and would seldom do as bidden by Mamma or Edward.

I passed him the bar. And remonstrated gently – 'you're not going to burst the locks are you? It was Father's.'

'Well, he's dead so he won't need it any more,' he

replied brutally, his black eyes flashing, and hatred smearing across his face.

Christopher coerced the bar under the first lock. It creaked, it groaned and finally broke away from the wood, leaving an open gash in the box. 'It is done now,' I said.

He tried to break the other lock. It would not give. He screwed up his eyes and clenched his teeth. It still would not give. In sudden fury he smashed the bar down on to the box top: it crashed down on his first finger. The blood belched forth. My stomach toppled. He said nothing. His face reminded me of that of a fiend. When he unclenched his teeth, I observed that his bottom lip was bitten through. Again he applied the bar to the lock. There was a screech as the wood wrenched free and the lock came away. We both laughed with relief. I hugged him, thinking to myself that he was truly brave and clever. Far more clever than Edward, though Mamma thought Edward the clever one as he usually did better at school work.

We crouched down to look inside the box. It contained hundreds of pictures and dark prints; a few old journals and books. They were the strangest pictures we had ever seen. Christopher took one of the pages from a journal and wrapped it round his bleeding finger. He would not allow me to fuss, or call Mamma, though it was bleeding profusely.

Everything within the box was in perfect order. The old prints were carefully backed with stouter paper; some were covered in tissue, some in linen. There were pictures of ladies, naked ladies; they gazed out at us with limpid, expressionless eyes. Their hair was beautifully dressed, they wore white stuff on their faces and their mouths and cheeks had been delicately rouged. Tight corsets encircled their waspish waists; their generous breasts burst forth.

My brother and I looked at these pictures with

little emotion. As I recall I mumbled 'for shame' and then continued leafing through. I remember those pictures very well today, and I know should they be presented in my present, very proper establishment, they would be deemed quite scandalous. There were pictures of girls with girls, gentlemen with gentlemen, doing all manner of depravities one to the other. I remember one old portrait in particular – probably because of the variety of content: I was always eager for variety. It showed a man up the rear of another man, up the front of a lady who was obliging another gentleman with her mouth.

Christopher had gone very quiet. There was a particular picture he had taken out of the box which he kept referring to. It seemed to fascinate him. It was a picture of a naked woman huge with child. The skin on her stomach appeared to be about to split. Her breasts, which were grotesque, had slender leather thongs tied tightly around them. The thongs started at the widest part of the breasts and became tighter and tighter as they neared the nipples. And out of the nipples gushed great rivers of milk. I noticed then that the front of his breeches was standing out. I looked at this protuberance so long and so diligently, that he felt obliged to explain. He informed me that if a fellow had a soft Mr P. (this was our childhood reference) he could not get up a woman. I understood from the pictures what getting up a woman meant. I decided that I wished to see it. Although I had seen it many times before. We always bathed together, and we had slept in the same, small bed since I was three years of age. That was the age I left Mamma's bed, as had Edward and Christopher before me. Christopher, however, always maintained that my birth had deprived him of his full share of this intimate pleasure.

I asked if I might see it as it was at that moment.

I do not recall whether I had actually seen it standing up like that before; all of its own accord; straight out and strangely menacing. I touched the end of it with my fore-finger and leapt back as though it had bitten me.

Christopher regarded me strangely, and moved in my direction. He told me to lie down on the floor. I obeyed unquestioningly. He looked at me darkly it seemed, with piercing clarity, for he knew the exact nature of my thoughts at that moment. I, of my own accord, removed my undergarments, and placed them beneath my head. I had a strange view of him thus; he seemed very tall from my lowly position on the floor. He seemed dominant with the red bulb glowing; but a slight nervousness hovered about his eyes. I smiled at him. He lay down on top of me, and put his member inside my body.

It pained greatly at first. I was not expecting that; though indeed I had no idea what to expect. He moved a trifle, and then the pain was less acute. He seemed to travel so far up the channel of my body that I remember thinking he might emerge from my mouth.

We were not fired with any real earnesty in all this. I got no pleasure out of the act; for my brother's part I think his curiosity was eased. We did not really know what to do with it having got it entrenched. We had seen the pictures, and we made an attempt to follow their example. We laughed a little. And were a little alarmed at ourselves feeling perhaps there might be some wickedness in it.

We put all the pictures away very carefully in the big box and closed it. All except the one with the lady great with child. Christopher took this one away with him, and I never saw it again.

My mind is sore troubled with this recollection. I feel also a small throbbing in my private parts. Although, today, in looking back on our actions, I know we did wrong; still I cannot view it all in that light.

We were complete innocents. We knew nothing of either our own, or each other's bodies. Yet we were filled with curiosity and sexual excitation.

I cannot leave it there though. Because even on that day, which was the beginning of a singular relationship between my brother and I, even on that day there was a spiritual and love bond between us. It is perhaps the memory of this, more than the simple physical nature of our actions, that saddens me so today. And leaves me with only the memory of such complete intimacy. It is beyond my reach now, and perhaps I shall never again recapture it though I live to be ninety.

2

I have read again the last pages. I had left them a few days, due to the constant interruptions of my household – the cook seems unable to take any small decision without constant reference to me.

I ponder now, before I continue, whether the task has been remedial in any way. It is possibly too soon to say. But having begun, my thoughts are all too full of those events of twenty years back; I find myself constantly dwelling on the past, recalling details I thought I had forgotten.

It is fortunate for me that my husband is not of a sensitive nature. My ennui goes unobserved, my frequent retreats into my dressing room have not been commented on.

I will go back to the night that followed the day my brother discovered the box: Pandora's box, one might say.

That night, I recall, Christopher and I looked at one another strangely. In a different way. We had a big secret. I smiled gently at him because I felt he might be fretting. He fretted a great deal.

We were all in the bedroom together. Edward and Christopher and I. Edward was looking loftily at me: we did not get on well. I was about to get undressed, to get into bed with Christopher. We had a small brown bed in the far corner of the room, under the window. Edward slept at the other end of the house, he would not allow us into his room. He was extremely secretive.

Though there was nothing to be secretive about amongst his possessions; as I had discovered to my disappointment after a vigorous search.

Edward that night was not in a pleasant frame of mind. He was observing me taking off my blouse and the old cambric chemise and drawers.

'Look at Catherine, when's she going to acquire such a thing as a bosom?' he declared with some spite.

'Edward,' I replied with as much pomposity as I could muster – 'your ignorance is most trying. Girls do not acquire bosoms until they are at least twelve years of age.'

Edward at this stage of my story was fourteen. He had that strange Irish ruddiness, coupled with dark and heavy features: eyes set too far out, and a clumsiness about his mouth – it seemed constantly to be slipping out of place. I compared him with Christopher; in comparison, Christopher was beautiful. He was not yet twelve; his hair was black and waved slightly. I thought of his eyes as being black also; in fact they were very dark brown, but they gave the impression of black because they were set close together; and his eyebrows almost met in the middle. His skin was fair, his bone structure fine. There was a strange air about him: an air of melancholy, of distrust. It made people anxious when near him. He knew this, and it brought about a brusqueness, almost a callousness in his approach to other people.

Now, he smiled at me: a wan smile. I jumped into bed beside him and cuddled up closely to his thin frame.

'Look at the pair of you – like a couple of babies,' Edward quipped.

We ignored him, as we did not feel like having a bout that evening; so he left the room, smirking in a surreptitious way.

I put my hand under the bedclothes and wrapped it

around Christopher's little stick. It was wrinkled like a leaf. It was always small when we first got into bed; after I had held it gently for some time it would swell and pulse like a heart.

It was raining heavily outside. The big plane tree near the window was smacking its limbs against the panes, as though it wanted to come in. The old house creaked and groaned, and in the darkness I only felt secure because I was close to my brother.

I was thinking of my father. He had left us on a night much the same. Mamma told us he had fallen off a bridge in Ireland and had drowned. My Aunt Sarah insisted that he had thrown himself off it, under the influence of gin. When she said this, Mamma flushed with anger, and denied it hotly. I, however, had no doubts about the matter; I knew he had taken his life, and it worried me not a jot.

I had been frightened of him, and his fits of anger and violence had increased before his death. Christopher hated him, with a vehemence that disturbed me greatly. He had laughed when told of our father's death. In a cold, shrill way; the kind of laughter that is close to tears. Mamma flung her hand viciously across his face, and tears splashed behind his eyes.

Perhaps I should explain the nature of the relationship between my father and Christopher. Father always expected, and hoped, that Christopher would turn out to be very clever. Christopher, on the other hand, with his disregard for my father, had no intention of proving his prowess. He seemed in fact to try to do exactly the opposite of what my father wanted. My father tried to encourage Christopher to write, perhaps because he himself had been a journalist. I recall well the day he had sat Christopher down with some clean sheets of paper and ordered him to write a story. When he returned, after a few hours, my brother had not written one word on the piece of paper. My father's fury and disappointment knew no bounds — he tossed Christopher off his chair and virtually hurled him from the room.

At the time I thought it foolish of Christopher not to have made the attempt — knowing well what the results would be. I know now of course that no one can write to order; and I see also that because of Christopher's hatred for my father it was impossible to write for him. My father's attitude towards him was largely responsible for the fact that he could not get down to the business of writing as he grew older — as he would dearly have liked. My father crippled his fingers: by crippling his mind in so many frightful ways.

Christopher grew up believing that he was not clever; he was constantly told so by Father. I soon discovered that if you told Christopher he was clever — then he was. If you didn't love him and didn't tell him he was clever — then he could not be so.

I heard people say, after my father's death, that it was very bad for boys to grow up without a father. That they would turn out badly as a result, lacking confidence and spirit.

I was thinking of these things lying quietly beside Christopher in the dark that night, with the rain falling heavily and small shivers of cold creeping through the loose edges of the windows. I could see faces in the raindrops as they trickled down. I could see faces in the bumps in the walls.

How those rainy nights frightened me — (they still do). The world then seemed so big and bleak. I'd snuggle down with Christopher and watch his face as he slept. I could never sleep when it rained; I'd watch his face move under the gentle rays from the moon's lamp.

People were animals to me. I thought of myself as a

mole; Christopher was decidedly a weasel. His head was sculptured to travel through small and dark cavities; his nose was sharp and keen. When I watched him sleeping I saw very clearly the definitions of a weasel in his head and form. I kissed the side of his mouth and tried again to sleep.

3

I am sitting writing this at my davenport which is in front of a long window overlooking the gardens. The gardens are too formal – not like the weedy wilderness that stretched out at the back of our London house in years gone by.

The neat rows of hedges irk me. The roses are forced into shapes unnatural to their nature. The bushes are nipped in at the waist like corseted ladies, lest they grow round with contentment. Within this house, these walls, I feel the same – too tightly girthed – separate and alien from my own nature.

The day is balmy. It is springtime. I spied the first violets peeping from corners of the garden; their black eyes darting from the green. The earth is dark with goodness, its odour lingers on my fingers.

I got up from my writing a minute ago; to change the water in the vase of daffodils. As I stooped to lift it I saw my husband approaching. I shuffled the papers together hurriedly.

'What ails you, Catherine, love?' he asked, taking the vase from me. 'You have seemed distant of late, melancholy almost. It distresses me when you shut me out of your thoughts.'

I hurriedly replied that nothing was amiss; but I flinched when he laid his hand upon my head. His sweetness, his gentle disposition was an irritation to me. It worsened my feelings of remorse and guilt; it was a painful contrast to my former life and emotions.

Last night he reached for me in our conjugal bed.

My body stiffened like a corpse, my limbs felt damp. He turned from me in pain, and I spent the remainder of the night in chill unsleepiness, counting the hours till morning, dreaming quick and vivid dreams just before the dawn crept up on the window panes.

In order that this story is put into proper perspective, it is necessary to relate more about Mamma and the way we lived as children.

Mamma came from humble origins. Her father was a pastry-cook, indeed a very good one by all accounts. His services were required in all the top London restaurants, and in a short time he had begun to make a very good living from the trade. At that time, the ladies were all intrigued by the niceties of French pastries, and though their tight stays made it impossible to consume too many such delights, nevertheless they tasted and were well pleased.

My grandfather had risen from a small bread shop-keeper in the East End of London, to a highly sought after French pastry-cook. He improved his accent a little, and adopted a few fashionable French utterances. From what I remember of him, he seemed a kindly old gentleman, who always had a bon-bon in his pocket or a pastry behind his back. He had a great passion for roses, and took frequent evening sorties through the grander avenues of London, arriving home with discreet trimmings. They took root and flourished under his loving gaze.

My grandmother was a heavy and large-limbed woman. Nature had not bestowed on her too many of the sweeter virtues; she was sharp and stern and would tolerate no faults in her children. Hence, their faults went underground – and after they left home, ran riot.

My Mamma left this household as a girl of seventeen. She had inherited my grandfather's talent for cooking, and very soon found herself a good position in a select pastry house in Mayfair.

She told me that by smiling at the owner, and making herself most agreeable to all the rich customers, she soon gained the grand position of manageress of this establishment.

It was in this position that she met my father. He was, as I have mentioned before, a journalist, or more accurately, a struggling journalist. He had a small column in the magazine *Town*, where he had to amuse and excite his audience with witty pieces about matrimony, prize fighting and gentlemens' fashions.

My father's father had climbed into the growing ranks of the middle-classes by owning a goodly chain of book shops, the chief one being in the Charing Cross Road. He had done remarkably well. My father, therefore, having quite some money of his own at a tender age, had begun to collect some of the 'naughtier' magazines. By the age of twenty he had opened a shop which sold a multitude of such dubious articles. In times of such repression, he did a roaring trade. And then he married my mother. She was a respectable girl, and I dare say she did not know of his second trade: the small, scruffy shop in Whitechapel.

It is hard for me to make a judgement on the nature of my parents' marriage. When we were small, I do not recall many disturbances. My father's violence seemed to develop over the years; doubtless because of his frustrations. He was not doing well, he could not get his book published, and the journalism was becoming a strain to him. Consequently, he began to take out his anger on my mother. She had a fierce temper and would retaliate. By the time I was eight their connubial state was fraught with trouble. My father became increasingly violent to my mother, and subsequently to us children. Apart from my brother Edward. Edward was a very cold child: he never got in my father's way, he made sure at all times to keep a good distance from him. He was always obedient to my father's wishes, and as a result he never received any violence; though certainly no affection either. 'A cold fish, is Edward,' my father used to say.

Christopher was the favourite; but it was not to his advantage. If Father was vehement in his love for Christopher, he was vehement in his disappointment and impatience with him too. I cannot tell why Christopher hated my father so much. It could have been because of Father's bad treatment of Mamma – on whom Christopher doted. I think in hindsight, it was because Christopher abhorred any form of violence. And, because his nature was so gentle, and so acutely sensitive, he found my father's form of attachment grotesque and destructive.

But Father's influence on our lives was not to last much longer. One night Mamma and he had a most fearful row – it went on long into the night. I lay with Christopher and we tried to make out what little we could of their discord. Father was abusing Mamma most fiendishly and calling her all manner of names. Mamma cried out a few times as blows fell. Finally, the front door slammed. I thought Father had gone, and breathed a sigh of relief. Then to my amazement, the front door was opened stealthily, and someone began to creep quietly up the stairs. The footsteps halted outside our door; I was filled with trepidation. Christopher and I lay completely motionless. The door opened with the creak of old bones. It was Father. I thought for a moment he was going to kill us in our bed. My eyes shut firmly; my breathing apparatus appeared to have stopped functioning.

Father came to the top of our bed. He looked down on us for a moment; then he rested his hand gently, for but a fraction of a minute, on Christopher's head; I sensed his body so rigid beside mine. Neither of us stirred. Father turned abruptly – left the room and the front door closed once more. Christopher began to weep, silently, bitterly, and I could not comfort him.

We never saw Father again. Mamma never spoke of him, and if one of us mentioned him – which we did but seldom – a quick dart of pain would pass across her features.

By the time I was ten and Christopher almost twelve, we had been without a father for a year. And our life followed a sweeter course altogether. Yet it was a solitary life and we were left to our own devices a great deal of the time.

We got home from the nearby schools at about 4 o'clock each day; I got home a fraction earlier than my brothers as I had less distance to walk. The housemaid, Janet, would let me in, then she'd scuttle off to her quarters. Mamma was very seldom in at this time of the day. I do not know where she went, but she would return home much later, and usually in an elated frame of mind.

It was so quiet and lonely without Mamma. I used to wish so much that she would be there; there was a warmth and goodness about her; she smelt always of fresh-baked bread (though of course she baked very seldom, and only for her own pleasure).

I would go into the kitchen. There was usually a hearty fire burning. Mamma always left a loaf of very fresh bread in the middle of the scrubbed kitchen table for our tea. I always smiled to see it, and if I lifted it up and smelt it, it was almost like having Mamma home. I'd cut up the bread into big slices, spread it thick with butter and honey, or sometimes Janet's home-made raspberry jam.

Then, while the kettle boiled merrily, I'd walk around the house – it was the only time I'd have it all to myself. I was always half afraid there might be someone in the house, waiting to trap me in a dark corner. I had a rich imagination: it was a constant torment to me.

After I'd made sure I was safe by peering anxiously into all the chambers, I'd go into Mamma's, which was rather untidy. She did not allow the maid in there. There was always a pile of used petticoats flung in a heap on the chair. She had fine pink silk stockings with pretty garters, and the most delicate chemises, all bordered with lace. I would try them on, and parade around the room for a few moments fully attired in her garments. Her corsets were a mystery to me; and I was at a loss to understand what became of those voluptuous breasts of hers that I cuddled against as a child. The iron will of whalebone must have flattened them out.

When I heard Christopher and Edward at the gate I'd have to disrobe with all speed, making sure I'd left everything in the same disorder as Mamma had. She would notice any difference.

I'd run downstairs to greet Christopher. I was always happy to see him; indeed I missed him during the school hours. Christopher did not care for school very much. He was often downcast, and it was up to me to put him in better spirits. He was not very accomplished at mathematics, and to make matters worse, the teacher – an insensitive Northern person – did not like him. This was a constant problem on Mondays and Thursdays of the week.

We would have tea, the three of us. We would dispose of the entire loaf of bread. Then Edward would retire to his bedroom, and Christopher and I would be by ourselves again.

I am remembering a particular day. A soft day; the sky an unclouded blue. It was the beginning of the summer.

We walked down to the bottom of our un-kept

garden; Mamma could not be bothered with the expense of keeping it up. Occasionally she had the lawn seen to, but that was all.

Christopher climbed over the fence at the bottom of our lawn and into the garden beyond. He helped me over, hoisting my skirts out of the grasp of the small wire snags.

This garden was a lot bigger than ours. Two elderly ladies lived in the house at the top of the garden. We hardly ever saw them, and they only took small promenades at the top of their grounds. Consequently it was very easy for us to take advantage of the sweet cut grass, and the flowering shrubs that they left for the pleasure of the birds and bees, and ourselves.

The portion of their grounds that we were heading for was right at the very end of their well-trimmed lawn. The grass had been cut that day because the sweet scent of it filled the air. We walked into what was almost a little wood; there was a cluster of trees – beeches, tall and elegant, bending against each other slightly in the wind's sway. I put a piece of grass in my mouth and squeezed the juice from it with my teeth – a most delicious nectar. The grass here was longer – it was cut less often.

I fell down flat in the long grass, not caring about staining my dress. The grass rose gently on either side of me, making a pathway for me to lie in. Christopher was sucking the end of a blade of grass, he looked rather melancholy.

'What's the matter?'

'Nothing, I just wish I knew everything.'

'Like what, Christopher?'

'Like why is everything always so difficult, and why does it signify always to do well?'

'It will always be important to be clever. For myself, I want to know as much as I can, I want to know everything,' I replied.

'Cathy, I woke up last night and my face was wet with tears. I was dreaming about Father, and he kept saying I had to be better, I had to be cleverer. And I just couldn't. It near drove me mad.'

'You don't cry often when you're awake.'

'No.'

'You should cry whenever you want. It is good for the eyes.'

'Who says?'

'The Natural Science mistress at school.'

'What nonsense they put into girls' heads.'

'Come and lie beside me, Christopher. When you're sad I like to comfort you.'

'Mamma says you're too advanced for your age – she is right, of course.'

'It may be so. I'm ten now, but often I feel old. Old as a withered lady.'

Christopher came and lay beside me in the grass. Quiet, quiet as the day. I squinted my eyes up at the sun and then closed them tight. The colours came; just like the old kaleidoscope up in the attic. The colours danced behind my eyes, moving back and forth like the colours of a dream: so real you could almost touch them – so hot they might even burn.

Christopher began to laugh softly. He changed so rapidly in his moods. The laugh was not merry; it was a crippled laugh – odd, almost jeering.

He smiled at me and lifted the end of my dress. It was a lovely dress, cream linen with a heavy flounce at the bottom. Underneath was a crisp, calico petticoat, softly starched. It was shameful to lie on the grass with such clothes on. Christopher tickled my knees with a long piece of grass. Then he pinched me between the thighs.

'Christopher, my clothes will be ruined by the grass stains.'

'Take them off, then.'

I did. The sun crept over my body and kept me warm. He turned me over in the grass and regarded my lying-down-side. His hands moved slowly over the flats and rises. He turned me over again and blew with his mouth pressed hard against my stomach.

I took off his shirt to blow on his stomach, but he would not allow it, as it reminded him of tickling and that was one thing he could not abide. He took off his breeches and said he was the sun god; I said he was the weasel.

A weasel is an animal that lives in the woods. It favours the dark and secret spots. It is shy and keeps away from other animals, preferring its own company. A weasel has a long neck and a very sensitive face. It spends most of its time down small holes.

I bit him instead on the stomach and his hand pushed my head down. I bit, not too hard, the end of his member – what an odd primitive thing it looked. It grew beneath my lips which alarmed me, so I retreated. He lay on top of me, and bit the corner of my ear. He went inside my belly. It did not hurt so fiercely, but I gasped. I wondered as he entered me whether it was doing this that made the cunnies of the ladies in the photograph look so thin and faded.

After a short while, the sensation around my cunny became rather pleasing. Christopher looked very serious and was consumed with concentration. He was moving more vigorously and breathing strangely. He seemed to be willing something to happen; I was not sure what it could be.

It happened; because Christopher at that moment collapsed on top of me like a sack of wheat. His body was in a state of fever, his breathing was most irregular. He rolled off me, and lay face down in the grass. His eyes were closed and I felt a consternation that he might be ill. He lifted his head when I touched him and smiled. He looked very softly at me.

I noticed then that between my legs it was very wet and sticky. I supposed some of this fluid went inside my stomach. He was obviously glad to have got rid of it.

I kissed him on the shoulder. We were both lying face down in the cool of the grass. He reached for my hand, and folded it into his body. I thought something singular had just happened to him; something new. Because he did not utter a word and lay very still, I knew he was thinking. I could almost hear his thoughts thumping and ticking in my own head. He turned over eventually and looked up into the sky. He looked tired and the barley-sugar stick softened and bent in the sun.

I touched him on the mouth with my little finger and asked him what he was thinking of.

He said he was thinking of the lady in the picture with the big, big breasts and the vast stomach.

It made me a fraction sad that he was not thinking of me. And jealous because I did not have big breasts.

A terrible sharp pain – like a quick cut, or the smart of caustic soda – disrupted my thoughts. I did not want to mention it to Christopher, but the pain increased: the sensation was of burning. I did not understand what had happened. Janet always said pain was a visitation from the Almighty. I felt very fearful.

In desperation, I told Christopher, and to my amazement he confessed he felt the same. We became extremely alarmed; more so because we could not detect any reason for the pain. Suddenly Christopher pounced on a small red ant that was travelling slowly down my thigh: one of the biting variety. He must have been either on Christopher's private quarters, or nestling in mine; and when pushed against us he had obviously exercised his biting apparatus!

We laughed at our ignorance and our fear; putting our garments on slowly; brushing the grass off our clothes; Christopher picking strands of dried foliage out of my hair. Then we walked slowly back home together, scarce speaking, smiling sometimes, with complete understanding each of the other's thoughts.

4

It was no easy task to write that last chapter, but I adhered to my resolution of complete frankness; I spared no detail, and am glad of it.

When I first began to write this I did not know how to set about it. But it seems that a tale takes over its own telling. Some force in that portion of the mind from whence dreams come moves the pen. But any venture into that unexplored and forbidden territory would, in our unenlightened times, be deemed certain madness and brain wandering. It might well be so. I have felt often of late that I might indeed be going mad. If this document were to be discovered it is certain that I should be put away.

I am no scholar, but I have read in Plato that in his time people had a broader outlook on all matters; that men could and did copulate together in their own fashion, and that this was even a recognized facet of life. I am not trying to formulate a theory that such things should be permitted; it just seems to me – a mere woman – that it might be more healthy for things that do exist to come to light; rather than be buried beneath a smiling front of hypocrisy.

But what am I saying? My mind is grievous troubled. I would not be so oppressed if I could but feel that my past was wicked and scandalous. If I believed that, I could gladly submit to the institution or the grave. But some buoyant spirit within me keeps insisting that what I had was fine, and contained elements of true beauty hard to capture in any existence. I cannot malign it. I can only tell it as it was.

And what is the purpose of telling it? Do I imagine that there are those who would listen to this tale kindly, smiling indulgently at my past follies? No. Indeed, I am most truly aware that this could only be perceived as hysterical madness. If it is to be written, then it is only written for myself. And perhaps for my brother.

So here I am, a woman of thirty years; years mostly wasted or mis-spent. But chafing, always chafing. Irritated beyond measure not to be able to walk the gentle countryside about these parts without the cumbrance of a maid. To be told constantly that it is not my place to exercise my mind, but confine myself to talk of a domestic nature, or of children. I have none; I want none.

Things all about me are changing. It is an exciting time. Divorce and adultery are spoken of frequently. My husband finds this deplorable, he says it was not the way ten years ago. Certainly it was not; but I think it is a change for the better. Such changes are of course the prerogative of the richer classes, but it is interesting to me that it is no longer unheard-of for a woman to leave her husband and try to survive in the world by her own labour.

I am stuck here in the wilds of Gloucestershire with little outlet to these thoughts and new movements – the *New Woman* is not often come across in Cirencester. It is hard for me even to lay my hands on modern literature, due to the claustrophobic nature of this country household.

But all is not gloomy. I have been reading a most splendid book I found perchance in my husband's well-stocked library. I was amazed to find it there, cheek by jowl with all his musty classics. It is called *The Story of an African Farm* by Olive Schreiner (she was once termed a 'fast' woman in *The Times* and was reputed to have lived an unrespectable life in the society of the Fabians, and other Free Thinkers). I, however, feel she must indeed be a splendid woman, and should do much to improve the lot of the woman in this country. I find myself identifying strongly with the heroine of the book. I feel the same impatience, the same will to succeed – to lead my own life. O, that I might be free of all this!

My husband sits now, at the end of the garden. He is reading the *Saturday Review* – a magazine that irks me greatly.

I walked down to the garden, to tell Thomas that I was going for a little stroll to the top of the orchard.

'Catherine, child, it is nice to see you out taking the air, but you ought to be wearing your bonnet; the heat is intense this morning.'

'I have dark colouring, it should do me no harm.'

'O, indeed, but your skin is very fair, translucent almost. I know your hair is raven, but the darkness has not spread to your complexion. Sit down a little with me – we do not often have the chance to speak together.'

That is true; he spends so much time with his books, and the accounts for the land and properties; we do not converse often. He is an intelligent man, and extremely well-read.

I sit down in the high wicker chair by his side, but it is not easy to speak with him. My mind is so separate from his own; I have no knowledge of the thoughts and feelings that course through his brain – it is an unknown land to me. I would like to speak to him, but his countenance is so fixed and stern, it is hard to begin.

'Tell me what it is like in Africa, Thomas, you have been there and I have a great curiosity about the place.'

He smiled, surprised: 'You want to know of Africa — why, what possible interest could it be to a woman?'

'But Thomas, I am eager to learn anything, everything, I cannot fill up my mind with the piffling events of the day — meals, sheets and what the maids are about.'

He smiled gently down at me, and pushed back a stubborn black lock of my hair, which is for ever falling forward, and which he thinks he can train into place by a flick of his fingers.

'Catherine dear, you should have a child. There is not enough to keep you occupied here. A child will stop you brooding, will keep your mind busy in a womanly fashion.'

Alas, I felt a terrible rush of fear at these words. My heart contracted and I could not move for an instant. Then slowly I rose from the cane of the chair: 'I am going to walk in the orchard, Thomas, I will be back by luncheon.'

He nodded vaguely and picked up the *Saturday Review* once more. I walked, faster than was proper, up the garden, and round to the orchard at the rear of the house.

'Do not forget your bonnet, my dear,' I heard his voice call after me.

But I was gone, over the wall at the back of the garden, and into the sweet lush grass of the orchard; the leaves heavy and pale green like my dead father's eyes.

I am sitting now on the wooden bench under the old apple tree. The limbs are gnarled and misshapen; there is no smoothness on the branches and strange faces creep out of the wood.

I feel heavy and full of misgivings. O, what a mistake this marriage is! I should never have allowed Mamma to talk me into it; I was better before. At least then I only had myself to account to. I feel I am losing my Self in this union; it becomes buried under the rubble of dis-use. I will leave the orchard and get back to my writing; it is the only time I feel alive.

5

I must have been about nine years old. It was six o'clock on a bitterly cold November day. I had on a sturdy pair of Christopher's socks to keep my feet warm. Father and Mamma were sitting close to the fire; Christopher and I were making Guy Fawkes cards to send to one another.

Father was bored and restless; he kept getting up and pacing about the room, disturbing Mamma, who was busy with her needlework. Presently, he sat down and began to play with our dog. I observed him, cautiously, because Fido was my dog, and, being a dog of sound judgement, was not overly fond of Father.

Father picked up the dog, looked him closely in the eye, then hurled him backwards, so that Fido crashed on to the floor, getting the blow full on his back. He yelped, baring his teeth at Father. Father picked him up again, twisting the small dog about so as to avoid his fangs. I could see that Father was beginning to really savour this vicious sport. He lifted the dog high above his head. I could see his fingers melting into the animal's fur – then he hurled him to the ground once more. Mamma insisted he stop it for he would break the dog's back. Father laughed and continued with his game. Christopher's face grew waxy and pale, then it darkened over and his lips went ashen.

'Stop it . . .' he shrieked, his voice harsh and high. In the hush that followed this ejaculation, Father stood slowly up, the dog cringing between his hands. His mouth twitched, his eye flaps folded down, he looked hooded and evil. With extreme slowness, he raised the dog above his head, then crashed him down from this great height on to the floor again. The heavy thud of the dog's body contacting the floor, the severed yelp, the slow red staining from his mouth cut the cords of my voice. I turned away, feeling my stomach hit my throat.

I caught a brief look at Christopher. His physiognomy was fearful to behold – all pain, violence and hatred were held in that small oval. He flew at Father, tearing into his body with his hands. Father jeered, tossing him away like another puppy. But Christopher went back at him, kicking and slashing at him with all his might. Father then lost control and began to beat Christopher violently with his hands, finally knocking him a sideways blow across the face. It sent my brother to the floor, close to where the dog lay silent. I ran to Christopher, and crouching beside him, lifted his head from the floor. Mamma screamed at our father and he dealt her a vicious blow across the face. I saw the blood leak from the corner of her mouth.

'Detestable, odious ape; get out, get out, get out,' she cried; her voice beginning with a high screech and trailing off into a sob.

He did not go. He pushed me away from Christopher and dragged my brother's struggling form down the stairs to the cellar. I heard the door slam.

He came back into the room and surveyed us all with a kind of hatred. Edward said not one word. Mamma left the room.

'If you go anywhere near Christopher tonight I'll break your neck,' he snarled at me as he was leaving by the other door. 'No one is to speak to him, or feed him tonight.'

Then he walked back into the centre of the room, looked down at the dog for a moment, and kicked its dead body.

I sat down in a chair and began to weep. Edward

went away and the room was empty. My weeping continued until my eyes were swollen and red as though bitten by insects; my mouth dusty and dry.

Only then did I realize the futility of tears, the waste of energy and emotion that could so much better be expended in other directions. I washed my face with cold water and went down to the kitchen to find Lucy. She kept the keys to both the storehouse and the cellar.

'Give me the key to the cellar, Lucy,' I demanded.

'No, miss, no. The master says I'm not to let them out of my sight. He says there's been trouble and your brother's in there for punishment.'

'Give them to me, Lucy, or I'll break your fingers.'

She gasped with horror at my words: 'For shame, miss, what can you be thinking of, speaking to me like that?'

'Lucy,' I said, feeling my eyes and my facial bones steeling over: 'My father has just killed my dog in a fit of violent passion. I have the same blood in my veins and I will do the same to you if you do not release those keys.'

She ran off in a panic, and it was not until after dinner that I could extract them from her, after much wheedling and cant, and promises to return them forthwith.

I took them and left her sulking over the dirty dishes. I hurried down the stairs to the cellar, and very quietly unlocked the door. I could not see my brother, but after a while I could just make out his small form in the far corner of the room by a dusty window. He did not stir as I came in. I walked quietly up to him and kissed him on his swollen face.

He had not wept a single tear – his eyes had a strange glassy quality as if he'd spent too long staring at one object. I sat down close beside him and twined my arm around him. He did not speak, and I could find no words to comfort him.

We sat thus for a while. Then I left him and returned with cold water in a basin and a soft cloth. I wiped his face and eyes and dried them with as much gentleness as I could; I kissed his face all over and gathered him into my arms.

I see now, from this distance of years, that he was close to catalepsy at that moment. His state of shock was so severe, his body so rigid I could do little but be with him. And as always, what I felt was instantly transmitted to the inner organs of his body; my love filtered through the barriers and bones. He held tightly on to me, and took fright if I moved too swiftly. We lay together on the coverlet I had brought down and slept fitfully until dawn.

In that strange unreal hour, when the sky came up from hell and lit the cellar with a ghostly light, I could hear Father's footsteps on the stairway outside. I scuttled off to the far end of the room and hid behind some storage containers. Father walked slowly up to Christopher; he was reeling slightly, and peered down into his face. I cannot tell whether Christopher's eyes were shut or open, but I heard father gasp and stumble from the room in some distress.

The strange hard light in Christopher's eyes must have filled my father with the same pain as I had felt when first looking at my brother that night. He did not look like a mortal — more like a wild chained animal, a bad spirit, escaped from Hades. He did not look like my brother; he did not look like the weasel. And it filled me with a strange grief. For we had nothing to draw on but our ignorance, no one to turn to save each other. And for the first time, in that gloomy cellar, I had lost him; and the world never looked so bleak.

6

This brutal incident was never referred to in our household again. In some close way it was as if we had all been equally affected by it; we were all trying to block it from our minds – pretending it hadn't happened.

I buried the dog, with Lucy's help. We dug a deep hole in the far corner of the garden under a small pine. The burial mound was as small as I could make it; I covered the place over with leaves. I did not want Christopher to know where I had buried Fido. He never asked me, but he knew.

Although the incident was buried, it was a turning point for Christopher. After that cold, drear night in the cellar he emerged as a somewhat altered child. He must have made a decision down there in the lonely dark; for thereafter he was never quite the same.

The first years of his life had formed him into a shy, solitary person of a good and sweet nature; there was a constant gentleness in his expression. It left him. I did not notice the exact moment of passing, but it was close to the event I have here described; and I never saw that softness again. It was as though childhood was erased with one swift blow, and he had moved into the second stage of life prematurely.

Christopher grew painfully, from this age, when he was almost eleven, to the age of twelve. I think it was the most difficult time for him. The evolution from childhood to early manhood was too sudden, too sharp. It left strong scars.

Christopher was greatly tormented by Father. Father adopted a completely different attitude to my brother from that hateful night in November. It was the first time Father had experienced fierce, open resistance; perhaps also it was the first time he had seen the hatred. From that moment onward he was full of contempt, for all of us, but for Christopher in particular. He ceased for ever to try to encourage (by his own weird methods) any germ of creation in his son. If he caught a glimpse of something in that direction it became his pleasure to quash it.

On one occasion he discovered a small notebook which contained some short stories Christopher and I had been writing; stories about animals. Father found these. And, as was his wont, before he had had even a small chance of perusing them, he was jeering and dismissing them.

This fiendish and destructive behaviour continued and increased. He could not bear to think of any of us being able to construct anything of value. He had to humiliate and deride any venture we undertook. He mocked Christopher continually, trying always to make him appear foolish or small.

I do not know whether he believed we were indeed useless offspring, or whether it was his own bitterness oozing out on to our endeavours. It did not have an adverse effect on me; for, as I have said, I had no liking or respect for him; I had hardened my heart well by the age of eight. Christopher, however, did care; not because he cared for Father, but because he was acutely sensitive to any criticism. It defeated him utterly.

All this was interlaced with Father's increasing violence and anger. He was twisting slowly, on his own noose. And when he was about, there was no peace, just a growing madness in the air.

By the time Christopher was twelve, Father was dead;

had been dead almost a year in fact. We were deeply grateful for this kind assistance from Providence.

Christopher at twelve was a very formed individual. He had developed into a sullen, heavy-browed person, given often to melancholy and moodiness. He was constantly anxious, and very close to rages and passions a good deal of the time.

He had grown physically very rapidly. He ceased to be so small and skinny. His shoulders filled out and he began to get a dark down over his top lip. For some reason his mouth, which was not a big mouth, grew a little fuller and redder. He grew soft fluff on his body; but his stomach, which had always been exceedingly smooth and soft, remained that way – happily.

He seemed to grow more preoccupied with what he had between his legs all the time. I'd heard that boys played with their members. I asked Christopher if he did. He said he did a little. I asked him why, and he replied he did it because it felt good. It seemed a reasonable answer (it still does).

I was creeping up to the great age of eleven. My face had changed little – it still looked like another cast from the same mould as Christopher's. My body was straight and thin, I still had no budding breasts – alas! In fact, my body was almost a replica of Christopher's before he'd begun to fill out.

I continued to feel I was taking care of Christopher, and that his welfare was firmly in my hands. We had grown to know each other's bodies with a close intimacy. We had looked at the saucy pictures a few times, but not with great interest. I think Christopher had even sold one or two at his school.

We were exceedingly close; we seemed always to want to do the same things at the same time – there was no discord in our interests and desires. I understood the things that frightened him because they frightened me too. But I could not help much because

44

I was as ignorant as he was; and as time went by every-thing appeared to grow more difficult, and not easier as we'd expected.

Christopher read a great deal – anything that came his way. And he used to encourage me to read the books after him, so that we could discuss them, and explain our separate interpretations of various events. He loved Tennyson; and we struggled together to elucidate the genius of Milton.

He grew very demanding of me, and of my time. He required me always to be with him, when it was possible. Soon I began to realize, with some trepidation, that he needed more than love; it was as though he had a need to be worshipped. That way his very frail ego could survive. He wanted people to be humble. But he wasn't humble. And I wasn't humble. And I could not worship him because my nature was too independent. My own mind was developing fast; I wanted to be clever too; but I did not have the same need to be told.

We talked all the time, we never ran out of conversation; I never grew tired of his speech. I remember one particular conversation we often had. I remember it as though it were yesterday. The images that come to my mind are clear enough to be almost concrete and touchable.

'Catherine, when we've left school, we'll go away to the country, and read and write all the time. Life must be simpler and cleaner in the country. I cannot bear the constant crowd.'

'We'll find, won't we, a cottage made of stone, far away from the thoroughfares and towns? And it will be so quiet, so quiet. No noise like the clangour outside our bedroom window,' I said, filled with joy at the thought of so much quiescence. It never occurred to me (O, how foolish I was!) that we would not always be together. There seemed no need for anyone else –

45

he filled out my present and my future.

'Maybe I could write a book as fine as *Wuthering Heights*,' he said, and his black eyes shone, and his face lit up with an uncommon glow.

But Christopher alone with me was completely different from the way he was with other people. It was one of the reasons why I had such a desire to be alone with him – away somewhere where other people could not change him. When he had to be with the rest of our family or friends he changed radically. It horrified me – it was almost as if he were in fact two different people in the same body. He said he was; that he played one role for them, and the way he was with me was his real self. Sometimes, however, the two got confused and I could not be sure which was which; and which was real.

He was often very violent and very strange. He frightened the maids and he terrified Edward. He had no friends at school and he kept himself completely separate from old friends he used to have in the neighbourhood where we lived.

By the time he was twelve he had learned, slowly, some small control over his passions. But when they ceased to explode into physical bouts or vehement abuse, he began to withdraw; he crept into himself, and outwardly appeared more calm. Inwardly, a tempest was brewing. Living on his own resources, he was consuming himself.

He said my virtue was that I never changed, either in my regard for him, or in the manifestations of my own character. It was perhaps the only unchanging thing around him; his own character veered so violently from one extreme to the other.

We developed a cunning way of communicating without words. At meals, or when we were all sitting around the fire in the drawing room, we would both concentrate earnestly on each other. Lo and behold –

the message would reach under the table, or across the hearth – from one mind to the other. We soon developed this into a fine art; we were seldom wrong. Our blood link gave us an uncommon bond and affinity.

'What were you thinking tonight, Christopher? I know, I know, you were thinking about my eyes – the colour, I think. Am I right?'

'Yes. I was thinking what a strange colour they are today; almost colourless, like translucent orbs. I was also thinking how nice it is that Father is dead. He used to eat like a pig.'

7

I will write this chapter for Mamma. She is far from me now, but she is constantly in my thoughts; my thoughts of her are sweet.

Up to the age of ten I had not got on well with Mamma. She found me secretive and 'jumpy' and I was always getting under her feet. I was also a very tidy, neat child and it irked her that I was always tidying up after her – she was uncommonly feckless with things. She had a charming habit of beginning to drink some beverage or other and forgetting to finish it. She never finished anything – she always left something in her cup and something on her plate. When Father chided her for this, she always promptly replied that she was too eager – too busy – to get on with the next thing to bother finishing the last. Once it's been tasted, she would say, it is no longer of significance; it has become dull.

Mamma used to paint a little, and when I say a little that is in truth what I mean. She would commence with all enthusiasm, but before long she had abandoned it for something fresher: 'I cannot do justice to the perfection in my mind, I cannot put on paper the images in my head – O, it is indeed vexatious,' she would say. (And indeed I understand well what she meant, today.)

Father would grow fierce at this 'nincompoopery'; her whiffling nature frustrated him beyond measure, and was the cause of many a dispute. I think also, in all fairness, that he did recognize a certain ability in her sketches, and it irritated him that she would not do justice to them.

But let me tell a little of the way Mamma looked. She had a delicate oval face, with lustrous dark brown eyes and ebony hair. Her skin, however, was very pale; she had to pinch her cheeks and bite her lips to bring any colour to them. Her teeth had a small space between the two centre ones on the top row, and she had a curious habit of rubbing a finger along her bottom lip when she was thinking.

Mamma had lovely breasts, round and hard as apples. As children we were always pressing up to her. I remember especially the warm years when I snuggled up to her in her big feather bed. Her big breasts would engulf me in softness and comfort, and the feeling returned every time I hugged her.

Christopher looked more like Mamma than did the rest of us. It was the expression around their mouths that was the same; their chins were identical. I think Mamma loved Christopher best. She seemed to sense his fragility, and his need of protection from Father.

Mamma laughed a lot, and her nose turned up and the corners of her eyes crinkled. Her hair was always beautifully dressed, but when she undid it, it tumbled all the way down her back to her bottom – a nice motherly behind.

Mamma always gave Christopher the biggest helpings of nice things like treacle pudding and blackberry and apple pie. I didn't mind, because had I been her I'd have done the same. Edward resented it a bit. But Mamma was always careful to tell Edward how clever he was for doing well at school. It seemed to be her way of making up for the smaller portions of pudding. Mamma was rather insensitive, in that she was prone to dismiss Christopher's efforts at school work – which wounded him greatly. His eyebrows moved together, and a small muscle contracted at the left hand corner of his mouth. I'd want to kiss him.

About the time that I have arrived at in my story, that is to say, when I was eleven and Father dead well over a year, a new turn came about in our house.

It became very clear to us children that Mamma was up to something with the Frenchman.

The Frenchman's name was in fact Richard le Cordeur, but we always referred to him as the Frenchman. He lived in a big, well-appointed house not far from ours. He had the added distinction of having been an officer in the Franco-Prussian war; he had received a leg wound and retired from military duties; and had entered the family wine business. As far as I could tell (and doubt not I was always enquiring), he was now a wine merchant of some repute. Mamma insisted that he was a gentleman, and not a tradesman, since wine merchants were not considered to be in trade.

The Frenchman was unbearably thin; I used to think that if he stumbled and fell down he might fall to pieces, so brittle was his frame. He had a slightly yellow complexion, and thick, lank, jet hair. His face had a sneaky quality about it; and though I thought him physically revolting, he was in fact more appealing when I had got to know him a little. And his mode of speech was most pleasing – the soft caressing r's and the slow silky melody of his voice.

Mamma believed we knew nothing of the friendship that was kindling between her and the Frenchman. She obviously believed she was being very discreet about the matter, so we did not disillusion her. The Frenchman came to call some mornings at an appropriate hour, and left shortly after, swinging his cane in a jaunty fashion. But there were strange unaccountable happenings after we had all retired to bed. I could sometimes hear Mamma's sonorous laugh. I could not be sure whether the laughter issued from her bedroom, the front room on the second floor, or from the drawing room immediately below it on the first floor. In any event it was a strange noise to hear at that time of the night when no visitors were abroad.

Mamma loved frills and flounces. I have never again seen undergarments like hers. Her stays were beautiful objects, trimmed and trussed with Honiton lace, moulded from the finest silk with satin bindings. Her petticoats were floating ruffles, full, with much embroidery and fine workmanship. Mamma did not wear drawers; she told me when I asked her once that the reason for this was a matter of chastity. She declared: 'ladies who are overly concerned with draping their thighs with elaborate and costly coverings must indeed be "fast", for how can a chaste woman concern herself with this region when there is no opportunity for revealment?' I found this a little confusing in the light of Mamma's very fancy corsets and petticoats, which surely must come under the same category as being 'items not to be seen by anyone save the lady concerned, and the lady's maid'. Mamma also possessed a most beautiful crinoline. She tried it on from time to time – for my pleasure, she said. It swayed about her with a life of its own, rising and falling to display a small flash of ankle. Crinolines were not worn any more – 'too much damage to china and too great a temptation to gentlemen with improper inclinations,' she would say.

In spite of this, Mamma was at heart a straightforward person, she was honest and usually said what she felt. She did try to bring us up properly, although it was not easy for her; her flippant and gay nature tended to lead her towards extravagance and what was considered rather dangerous living.

Yet we all adored her, and would do much to spend time in her presence. This did not happen a great deal, because she was constantly out of the house, leading a life we knew nothing of. Sometimes, however, she would dispatch the cook from the kitchen and get out great bowls, and we would all help her concoct splendid puddings and cakes. I would be set to sifting flour; Edward to breaking and separating eggs, because of his careful nature; Christopher to stirring, which he did with great enthusiasm; while Mamma added spices and elegant touches to the performance.

Sometimes these good things would find their way down the Frenchman's gullet, which caused us some annoyance.

Now, I did not mind the Frenchman calling, but he was beginning to call rather more frequently than was proper. Edward thought it scandalous and that it would do Mamma no good. Indeed he insisted that he had heard talk about Mamma and that 'foreign person'. Christopher could not bear the sight of the Frenchman – 'a mouldy, worn out old stick with the face of an over-ripe lemon'. The Frenchman was well into his forties; his wife had died ten years ago and he had not remarried. We were fearful that he had marital designs on our Mamma. I did not relish the thought of calling him father, nor indeed of having another father. Edward, however, thought it would be a good thing if Mamma were to be married because it would stop the tongues clattering.

'I wish Mamma would sort out her affairs so I need not feel shameful with my friends,' he yelped truculently.

'You are indeed a prissy prick, Edward, and often I would like to punch my fist through your papery skull,' retorted Christopher, who could not abide the idea of Mamma re-marrying.

8

One sharp and blustery day, when I had no real inclination to step out of doors, Mamma summoned me to her side and bid me go to the Frenchman's house, for the purpose of delivering a letter. She said she could not trust the maid, for it was a personal matter. I reminded her that Lucy could scarce read a word. 'No matter,' she replied, 'I want you to take it.' I agreed without much gusto.

I went out, wrapping my shawl tight about me against the inclement weather; the trees were veering madly in the wind and rain clouds were hurrying across the sky. I felt a little put out; I did not think it was my place to take letters, and it was inconsiderate of Mamma to send me out on such an unfriendly afternoon.

I arrived at the Frenchman's abode in no time, and knocked loudly. Presently, a man opened the door.

'What do you want, little girl?' he asked, in that singularly offensive tone that servants sometimes apply to children.

'I have a letter for Mr le Cordeur,' I replied stiffly.

'Well, hand it to me then, pray.'

'Certainly not,' I said fiercely. Mamma had entrusted me to give it into his hands only, and I wasn't to be bullied by this person.

'The master is not too well today, I do not think he will be receiving visitors,' he stated emphatically.

'Tell your master Catherine is here and that I have an epistle from my Mamma for him.'

He gave me a scornful sniff and disappeared, leaving me out in the cold, jumping up and down once his back was turned.

The Frenchman then appeared at the door, hustling me in and using sharp language to his lackey. He escorted me into a large and splendid drawing room where a blazing fire lit up all the corners. I had not been there before, and I looked about with some curiosity. It was indeed a grand room, with a formidable marble fireplace housing the very generous fire. I noticed a lack of the many knick-knacks I usually came across in English houses; indeed the room was very uncluttered, very sparse of furniture or objects of any kind. There were a few uncomfortable-looking chairs and a chaise longue, which he then reclined on. I remained standing, till he gestured me to a chair close to the fireside. I sat down nervously, and then leapt up to present him with Mamma's letter. He read it, looked up at the end of the second page, then re-read it. Thereafter he put it down and seemed to lose interest in it altogether.

'Is there a reply, Sir?' I asked.

'No.'

'May I then go, Sir?'

'No.'

'I was somewhat taken aback at this brisk and unexpected reply and shuffled back to my fireside seat.

'How old are you, Catherine?' he demanded.

'Eleven years, Sir.'

'Umm – you are small, then, not much developed; still, there is something.'

I didn't care for his tone much, but could not ask him again so soon if I might leave. He was regarding me closely. I knew I was supposed to keep my eyes down in a modest fashion, but his clothes fascinated me. He had on a bold waistcoat, which contained many exotic colours, and seemed to have an Oriental flavour to it.

'So, you are a little magpie – you look at my waistcoat. Perhaps you like pretty things, like your Maman, eh?'

'Yes, Sir, some.'

He reached up and rang the bell; when his man entered he ordered tea to be brought; and from his dressing room, a large box, which he described in some detail to the man.

Presently the servant returned with the box, and placed it on a table close to the Frenchman. The maid arrived with tea and was ordered to place it in front of me. It was a good tea – bread, butter and jam, and some dainty small cakes. The Frenchman ordered me to pour him a cup of tea; my hand shook a little and some spilled into the saucer; he frowned his disapproval. He drank his tea, but ate nothing. I ate three pieces of bread and jam and two of the small cakes. He smiled sardonically at my hunger.

After tea had been cleared away, and much to my relief, he opened the box. Inside was a wreath of tissue paper, scarlet in colour. He lifted from the paper a most beautiful emerald corset: construed of soft satin, interlaid with embroidered pink rosebuds around the bosom, and flounced with pale green lace.

'Ladies do not wear these in England. It is very French. Here they have less of the laces, more of the whalebone. I see you like it, try it on.'

I was amazed at his boldness, and though I desired to try on the lovely thing, I flushed and turned away.

'You are shy; very well, try it on top of your robe – probably it will fit better that way.'

I did not move for a moment, and then slowly began to approach the tantalizing greenery he had laid flippantly on the floor. I picked it up, and walked with it back to the fireside, looking at it closely, counting the lace holes. He said nothing at all, and in a short while I had forgotten him, so greatly was I engrossed with the lovely undergarment. I held it against me and, after some time, put it around my slight frame. It was much too large, the holes for the laces overlapped with a generous margin; still it was beautiful and I was happy to have it against me. I approached the long and heavy gilt mirror to my right and looked at myself in its shiny depths. I felt my small breasts with my hands, and felt relieved that they were beginning to bud at last; small and hard swellings like under-ripe apples. My hips too were emerging, less slowly than the breasts, and I had a waist at last.

Suddenly, and with some alarm and guilt, I remembered the Frenchman. He was observing me with a strange look upon his face, a look I had discerned sometimes in my brother. It worried and excited me, for I knew well what it meant.

'You are looking very lovely. Come and sit by me, child,' he said in a strained voice. I began removing the corset with all speed and took it back to him. I retreated again. He handed me a pair of white silk stockings, saying they were a present. Mamma had always impressed upon us the rule never to accept presents; but at this moment I was stung by the realization that this green corset was very like one of hers! I took the silk stockings, sat down on the floor and removed my socks and shoes, forgetting the Frenchman for an instant. I rolled the fine stockings up my legs; they reached to the very top of my thighs, and I had to fold over the extra length a few times. I spread my limbs out ahead of me and giggled quietly to myself, feeling very grand and grown-up.

'You had better go,' he said brusquely.

I started and made a move to remove the silk stockings.

'No, take them and be gone,' he muttered savagely,

turning aside. I looked closely at him, and was moved to see elements of suffering and pain. I did not comprehend the reasons, but my own small experience in the suffering of my family made me feel a sharp compassion for the man. Indeed, it has always been a fault in my nature to be drawn to wayward and frail personalities; I sense in them some common bond with the restless stirrings of my own perplexing nature.

I left the Frenchman, with thanks for the tea and stockings – feeling a little despondent.

My spirits soon lifted on the way home with the thought that I could now tell Christopher of my experience, and show him the beautiful stockings. I felt sure he would like them.

'Well,' Mamma said as I entered the drawing room, 'where is the reply?'

'Indeed, there was none, Mamma.'

'O,' she replied crossly, and vacated the room.

Christopher was not in the drawing room, so I went to seek him in our bedroom. Edward had gone for his music lesson.

I closed the door to our chamber with a bang, Christopher looked up startled; he was reading *The Old Curiosity Shop*.

'What on earth are you doing in those things?' he demanded, spotting my silk stockings at once.

'The Frenchman gave them to me. I wanted the green corset,' I blurted out in some confusion, beginning to sniff a little (a sign of distress).

'You don't have any drawers on.'

'No, Mamma says it is more modest.'

'What?' he shrieked, his laugh reaching shrill proportions.

I plumped down on the bed, a little distressed by his mirth; he came and sat down beside me and enclosed me in his arms. There was about him a tenseness that day, an impatience; I felt I might have angered him in some way. Perhaps by not being with him that afternoon.

'Christopher, I do have a big love for you.'

'Yes. I was cross with you for going off and spending so much time with that horrible fellow; but we shall be friends now.'

'Is Mamma in her room?' I asked.

'Yes, she was a little disappointed that there was no reply to her letter.'

My pen falters at this point, and I hesitate whether I should speak of the intimacies between my brother and me. I would rather not, but I did resolve at the beginning to put down all the important events with honesty and frankness; it will be done, though it is grievous hard to do.

That day a new experience came upon me. I believe now, on looking back, that it was a very early happening, perhaps something that occurs late, or never, to the majority of women.

Indeed that is what I have been led to believe from the literature I have read. Women are not creatures of passion and sensual energy; it is a duty, a burden for them. Why is it then, I ask, that I am not made like other women; why do I seek pleasure where they do not; what was it about me at the tender age of eleven that made me behave the way I did? I did not find it sinful; the closeness between my brother and me was a true joy; it sustained me in my darkest moments, and indeed still does to this day, though tempered with much sorrow now.

Our gentle larking on the bed developed into a formidable passion. We rolled into one another's bodies with open and unabashed haste. In the midst of it, I felt a new and pleasurable sensation down the slopes of my cunny; a sensation soft, almost ticklish; heightening slowly towards a strange intensity. I heard my voice call from a far distance. It was as though the vast ocean washed over my small frame; drowning my ability to think with my head. My body took over all my senses, physical and spiritual. The waters cymballed, my legs clenched, my tears fell hotly. I held fast; the shuddering subsided as gently as the wind does after a storm.

We lay very still, washed up on a solitary, peaceful shore. I kissed his shoulder with gentleness; slowly he escaped from my body. O, what desolation of feeling! He clasped my hand firmly as a means of comfort.

'It felt different today, Christopher.'

He dispatched me one of his most weaselish smiles.

'You have grown up, little creature.'

'But what did it mean?' I prompted, full of ignorance and curiosity.

'It means what you felt. It means that you are now able to have a baby. Though you will not, because my seed is not seasoned enough.'

I pondered where he might have acquired this extraordinary knowledge. I see now that he must have been perusing some ill-informed document; (there are many in existence, usually the product of some ignorant apothecary – a creed of creature I much despise).

In the quiet I pondered over his words, and was much delighted at the thought that I might now have a child. How this actually happened, I had no idea, but if it was connected with the pleasurable sensations I had felt just then there was nothing to fear. I had often heard Mamma speak of the horrors of childbirth, and the delirium of child-bed fever. Mamma had suffered greatly with puerperal fever after my birth; she had been close to death, and had only been saved by her prompt removal from the lying-in hospital, a den of certain death to all would-be mothers who entered therein.

Christopher suddenly interrupted my thoughts,

'You could have done it with the Frenchman, Cathy.'

I thought about this for a short while. It had not entered my mind during my stay with the Frenchman. I thought now that possibly he might have liked to; but for myself I did not care for the idea.

'No. I should not have wished to, and I am sure, Christopher, you would not have liked me to. I know that your face would have fallen down, and you would have looked sad around the eyes.'

'I just wanted to know,' he said with some seriousness.

Christopher took the beautiful silk stockings back to the Frenchman, though I was not altogether agreeable in this matter. He informed me that he had returned them to the Frenchman personally. He had said grandly: 'My sister Catherine has no need of these.'

That night as we lay in bed, we chanced to look out of the window. The moon was fair racing across the troubled sky; clouds like moss banks piled up in verges. We watched spell-bound, wondering how the moon could travel so swiftly; its great golden disc hurling off into infinity. The clouds collided, and the rain gushed forth in all heaviness. I saw a dark figure cross the grass below and scurry furtively through the side entrance. The rain danced with heavy feet upon the roof, filling us both with much excitement.

'At night sometimes I think I might be a ghost, a creature of liquids who can seep through small gaps in the walls, sidle through the cracks in window panes — and terrify!' Christopher hissed passionately.

'O, yes indeed, and maybe you could creep up on Father and startle him the way he was always startling us.'

'Cathy, listen to the wind, how troubled it is, full of sighing. Could it be looking for lost souls wandering the night?'

'Do people who are dead go around seeking their old bodies? Do they look under the ground, or in their old beds to seek some sign of their old existence?' I asked in trepidation.

'I think maybe they forget that they lived. I'd like to think Father has forgotten us. I do not care to think of him wandering about seeking us; he might do us some mischief.'

These words filled me with some misgivings, but when the wind sobbed again I had a great desire to be out there; to let it toss me about as it willed.

'Come, Christopher, let's go out for a walk; it is cold, but if we wrap very warmly we will come to no harm.'

We struggled into our clothes, and crept out of the side door – the one we had seen the mysterious figure approaching a little earlier.

The cold hit us full in the face, the wind tossed us restlessly. A branch in the old plane tree was swinging wildly, the thin gaunt limb lurching up and down. We laughed for joy and hugged each other for warmth. We ran down to the bottom of the garden, and crossed over into our secret garden. How strange was the hue of the sky: grey-blue instead of black. We ran to keep warm; down through the coarsened grass to the beech trees wailing.

'Oh, how I love the winter, Christopher, it is my favourite season. I like the trees without clothes, and the screech of the wind.'

We did not linger long out in the cold. We raced back: hair flying, hearts beating, hands clenched together. Creeping up the back stairs, past the front bedroom on the second floor, I heard the distinctive sound of the Frenchman's voice in Mamma's room. He was speaking quietly – indeed he always did. Mamma appeared to be having difficulty understanding his meaning, because I could detect a note of impatience in her voice.

'I am not sure what you are trying to tell me. Are you implying that you do not have physical passions like other men?'

'No, indeed not, I do, and they vex me horribly; it is always my earnest prayer that my passions do not run out of check. But they are not passions as other men have, they run in strange directions where they should not. I am afraid of them; I must and will keep them in check.'

Mamma remained silent after this speech, which suggested she did not understand its implications or was out of her depth, because their conversation was not resumed. We wished it might, so we might scurry past under cover of their words. We waited till the silence passed – and the Frenchman indicated that he would leave. We fled past very speedily then, up the stairs and into our chamber.

9

One wintery day, when Mamma had retired to her chamber with the stirrings of a cold, the Frenchman called, to invite the whole family to tea. Mamma said she could not move from the warm, but that we should go if we so desired. Edward did not care for the idea, and Christopher refused to have anything to do with it. I was bored with being in the house all day; the amusements Christopher and I had contrived to while the hours away were losing their appeal. I said I should like to go, because the Frenchman was promising a walk in the park and then French pastries. I saw Christopher's pale face cloud over and his brows knit together, forming a black heavy line of discontent. I did not want to upset him, so I enquired whether he would mind if I were to go.

'Indeed not, Catherine, you must do as you please, as you always do.'

'Very well, I shall go then, and we can begin the story of the swimming cat when we return.'

He turned away in a surly fashion, and I felt perplexed and uncertain whether I should go. However, the Frenchman was calling impatiently from the hallway below and I had to make haste. I put on my bonnet and cloak and hurried off.

At the bottom of the stairs I looked up and spied Christopher watching me from above. His face looked pained, and I rushed up once more and landed a kiss upon his cheek.

We walked briskly down the road, the Frenchman

and I, not speaking much. We took a stroll in the snowy park, his tracks large and broad, mine small with tiny spaces between the imprints. He took my hand in his, and I was glad of the added warmth from his deep-furred gloves.

'Perhaps you had children once, Sir, and they died?' I suggested with my usual morbid curiosity.

'No, indeed, Catherine,' (he said my name strangely, the 'th' becoming closer to a 't') 'I have never had children.'

'But Mamma says you were married once and your wife died.'

'Yes, that is so, but we had no children. Ever since a very young man I have never had a desire for children, especially not girls. I had a sister as a young boy, but she died when I was thirteen.'

'How old was she, Sir?'

'She was eleven, the same age as you now, but she was very fair, not sombre-featured as you are. She had long golden braids and delicate features. We were very close; I loved her most dearly. I believe I have never recovered from her death, though it is more than thirty years ago.'

'O, do tell me about it, Sir, I am much interested in death; it will not give me bad dreams.'

He smiled and continued in silence for some time. Then: 'She died of the plague, there was much about at that time in France; we lived in a small country community and once the outbreak started there was little to stop its fiery spread. As soon as my sister began to ail, I was sent further north, where the disease had not reached. Before I went I had time to observe the ravaging effects on my sister's sweet face and form. She swiftly took on the appearance of an old woman: her skin eaten away, and a blackness in her face. It was torture to watch her lying there, a mere shadow; and though my father had much money there was naught he could do to save her. As I said, I departed. I remember her sobs as I was taken from her room for the last time. I had no desire to leave her, I would willingly have remained, but my father insisted I go. She died that same night.'

The Frenchman ceased to speak after he had ended this sad tale. I cast looks in his direction from the corner of my eye, and observed that he was much moved by the narration. I thought to myself that perhaps he had had the same close relationship with his sister as I had with Christopher. It occurred to me that this might be the reason why he had adopted a fondness for me.

'My brother and I, Sir, we are very close too.'

'Indeed?' he replied, a strange smile playing about his mouth. 'But, my dear Catherine, there are many forms of attachment in this life, and some are not well regarded by the mass of people.'

We walked in silence to his mansion. Tea was waiting in the drawing room, carefully laid out on a large mahogany table. The fire crackled in the hearth, and I placed myself on the small velvet stool he had dispatched me to on my last visit. I sat quietly, waiting for him to start the conversation; stretching out my buttoned boots towards the fire so that my toes might unfreeze. 'Take your boots off, my dear.'

I did, gladly, and wriggled my toes in the glow of the firelight.

'I think I understand why your brother returned the silk stockings to me,' he said gravely.

'I trust, Sir, you were not offended. I would have liked to have kept them, but my brother said I should not take gifts from people outside the family.'

'It was my fault for giving them,' he said moodily, looking into the flames and remaining silent until the maid came in with the silver tea-pot.

'Will you take tea, or would you prefer a little hot negus?'

I had only once taken negus before, and had not cared for it greatly; but the Frenchman's negus was quite delightful: the proportion of wine to water was much in favour of the wine, the lemon and spices were generously administered. My body began to thaw out from the inside, and a general feeling of well-being came upon me.

'Come and sit upon my knee, Catherine, it would please me greatly.'

'Certainly I will, Sir,' I replied, bounding over and placing myself upon his left knee. By this time I had lost some of my reserve towards the Frenchman, and his story had made me feel a trifle sorry for him. He seemed in need of kindness, and it cost me nothing to acquiesce.

Once firmly saddled upon his knee, tasting the ambrosial negus at regular intervals, and nibbling upon his delicious pastries, I felt completely content. At the root of my mind was a small nagging fretfulness concerning my brother, but it did not linger.

The Frenchman let his hand alight upon my knee, and from there it began to wander restlessly over the upper parts of my limbs.

'I am very fond of little girls, Catherine, very,' he said, smoothing my skin the while. His hand was reaching the conjunction of limb to trunk when I grew a little uneasy. He appeared to sense this, and stopped his hand in its wanderings.

'I would like to make some sketchings of you, child,' he said with strained ease. 'Your face has a singular peacefulness about it, the bone structure is good, the hazel eyes distracting.'

'I think Sir, my eyes are brown, are they not?' I questioned, not wishing an error to be made in so important a matter.

'But certainly not!' he expostulated, 'they are full of golden lights and feline flashes. No, not brown, decidedly not.'

Naturally I did not wish to question his judgement again, so I let the matter rest.

The warmth from the great fire, and the effect of the negus, put me in a soothed state of mind. I began to wilt upon the Frenchman's knee.

'You would like to take a small nap, perhaps?' he asked quietly.

'No, no, I must be returning,' I replied, rallying. I wanted to be home with Christopher, to tell him about the delightful negus and the pastries.

He was in our bedroom, half in a slumber upon the bed. I crept up on him and kissed him all over his face, half enclosed by the coverlet. He woke with a start and pulled me down on to the bed, enquiring what it was that he smelt upon my breath.

I told him all about my visit to the Frenchman, and mentioned that he had been friendly and nice, and I had sat upon his knee.

'What else were you about, Catherine?' he asked suspiciously.

'O, nothing, the Frenchman wishes to make sketches of me, but I am sure Mamma will not be in agreement with that. He insists that my eyes are hazel.'

'He must be half-blind,' he snapped, an unpleasantness coming into his mien.

'You must not be unkind, Christopher, he is not so bad.' I did not wish to say any more because my brother was not in a good humour, and I thought the best thing would be to snuggle down under the coverlet with him until his crossness had passed.

The Frenchman often came to call. He was always civil and kind to me, but he was happier if there were other people in the room; he could not abide to be left alone with me. He became nervous and cross, and invariably found some pretext to leave the room.

Life continued in much the same way: with the round of school and happy close afternoons with my brother. Nothing seemed to change in any great way; Mamma did not appear to be thinking of marriage with the Frenchman – indeed she was often quite aloof with him.

I was happy for the lack of change, always being a child most settled if events kept to their usual course. However, by the end of that particular winter an event of great import came about, and the effects of it were indeed far-reaching.

I shall write of them presently. First I have a few tedious duties to perform; I must set the maids to spring-cleaning the house. The air is fresh and brisk today and the house could do with a closer association with the elements.

I am now able to get back to my writing, and to where I left my story.

It was in the last days of my twelfth winter that I caught pneumonia. I was extremely ill for a long time, and to this day I suffer the effects of that terrible ailment.

The weather that winter was extremely harsh; the bitterness increased as the days and the year shortened. It was on a particularly cold day that Christopher and I decided to take a walk in the large and ill-kept cemetery near our house. We often took such excursions, indeed it was one of my favourite haunts. We had been forced to remain indoors for many a day due to the inclement weather and heavy snowstorms; thus we were anxious to be out and about again.

We set off. I buttoned my long grey coat right up to the very top of the collar, put on boots and hat while Christopher wound his woollen scarf round and round his neck.

The snow was thick, crunchy and hard and sullied round the edges and in the centre of the road, where the carriages had made black inroads.

We walked through the black iron gates of the cemetery and entered the white world of graves. The snow was as it had fallen, few footprints spoiled its virgin slopes. We climbed up the steps leading to the main part of the cemetery; behind the dead and desolate trees lay the silent graves and tombs. We saw no one; and the silence seemed to descend and wrap us in its eerie spell. The leaves cracked under the crunch of my booted feet; the snow clung to everything – to every dead branch, to every stone – obliterating every name and prayer.

Christopher held my hand and whispered: 'I can hear the voices of the dead ones talking; see their smoky breath on the air. I fear to find their pallid faces amongst the dark yew branches.'

'O, do not speak so,' I shuddered, mortal fear getting me by the scruff of the neck.

We walked swiftly to begin with, and then a trifle slower as the numbness wore off in our limbs. We began to shift the snow off the gravestones to read the sad messages. We saw many graves broken into and desecrated; the skeletons smiled up at us.

'When do you think the grave-robbers do their work, Cathy? Is it when the body is still fresh, or do they wait for the flesh to fall?'

'Well, the ones tampered with are mostly old graves; I suppose they just look for the grand ones where jewels might be stowed,' I suggested.

'Yes,' he said thoughtfully, 'but many ordinary ones are looked into as well, so perhaps they just enjoy rooting about amongst the dead – it might be interesting.'

'Will we look at Father's grave today, Christopher?'

'Might as well.'

After a time a sadness came upon us. It happened to us both at the same time; the gloom of the place crept into our bones and we ceased to speak, each wrapped in our own thoughts; we did not have to discuss them, we both knew what the other felt.

Christopher took my hand and tucked it into his arm. I began to wish we had not come.

'Cathy,' he said, knocking a snowflake off my nose, and placing a kiss there instead: 'I almost wish we had not come today. There is an evil in the day. Last time we came it was summer. The whole place was green and overgrown with ivy and creepers and weeds. It was a lovely, healthy tangle. It looked so different then. Like a huge forest, and we had to tear away the growth of creeper to make our way through.'

'Yes, I remember, I thought I knew a lot of the graves, but I am lost today, and sad.'

'We can go away if you'd rather.'

'No, let us look at Father's grave.'

Father's grave looked very new. We approached it slowly, half-fearful, the way we had always approached him in life. Christopher brushed the snow off cursorily. We stood there looking at the name, reading it over and over; thinking of him being inside it. Suddenly, Christopher spat vehemently at the grave; I looked at him, feeling slightly alarmed, cut off from him and his feelings at that moment. In a rage, he kicked at the grave, his features black, his mouth a frozen line. My stomach lifted, my hands rushed to my face. 'No,' I cried, full of dismay, 'O, please, let it be.'

'Jesus, bloody Christ, I hate, I hate, I hate!' he screamed, and fled. I followed him slowly, not rightly knowing what to say and do. Father had never brought out passions of any kind in me. My mind began to wander around his body inside the grave; I wondered whether all the flesh had fallen off by this time. I imagined his bones growing into the wood of the coffin, and the trees growing into his skull, the roots twisting around his rotting limbs.

Christopher was crying. I put my arms around him and held him fiercely to me. He just stood completely still. I rubbed the snow off an old log and sat him down upon it, sitting down close beside him.

'Tell me Christopher, I do not understand, what is it?'

'Nothing.'

'Tell me why you're crying.'

He said nothing; I curled up beside him, and

nuzzled my head against his neck. I kissed his neck, pulling the scarf away with my sharp chin. He rubbed his hand roughly across his eyes.

'I feel,' he said slowly, carefully culling out the words, 'as though I let him down, I hate him for that.' There was no gentleness, and no sorrow in his face now, only that stern, vicious look he wore so often.

'I don't think that's true,' I said firmly. 'I think he let *you* down, let us all down. He should have stayed with us and been a better father. He was a coward.'

'You must not say that, Cathy. He wasn't a coward, though he was a pig. I think it's brave to decide to end your life and actually go through with it.'

'Well, I don't think it is. It's easier than living if living is difficult. He found it difficult to live, so he killed himself because it was easier.'

I remember that day so clearly. I sit here in the warm and shiver to think of it. I thought that day that if I was not careful he might go the same way as father. Suicides, I thought, ran in families; and if I ever let him get that low in life he might do the same. I felt it was up to me to take care of him. I presumed I would always be where he was.

We were much fatigued; we decided to go home. We were heading for the side entrance when I spied a lovely pond, big and deep with two tall and stately stone figures, one on either side. The stone ladies intrigued me, they were facing each other across the iced pond so I could not see their features from where I stood. I got up on to the edge of the pool, and carefully placed my boot on the ice to test its strength before venturing further. My foot slid, I lost my balance, slipped and fell on to the ice. It was thin around the edge, it cracked with the sound of gun shot, broke beneath me and I was plunged into the icy water. It was not too deep, but the cold knocked the breath from my lung box, and my big grey coat weighed me down – I could not right myself for fear and cold for a few seconds. I saw Christopher's arms reaching out to me through hazy eyes, I saw his face a ghastly colour.

He pulled me out. I stood on the ground, and almost swooned. He pulled my coat and cardigan off me as fast as his shaking hands could move. Then he took off his coat and put it around me, doing up all the buttons. My teeth chattered, and I began to cry. We ran to the gates; my hair began to grow hard, shaping itself into winter twigs.

Mamma was home; when she caught sight of me she began to scream furiously at Christopher, blaming him for his lack of care, reminding him of my careless nature. She bundled me in front of the fire, stripping off my clothing and ordering blankets from Lucy; all the while yelling abuse at Christopher until I was forced to tell her to stop. Christopher looked quite ill.

A fire was made quickly in our bedroom and I was put to bed with many blankets and hot drinks. Christopher sat at the end of my bed like a small white ghost, not speaking to me, just looking at me, his face full of worry.

'Do not fret so, it was entirely my fault,' I whispered between chattering teeth (because nothing could seem to make me feel warm again). I felt as though my inner organs were freezing up; I could not prevent the shudders of my body though I dearly wanted to – to make the sad look leave my brother's sweet face.

II

I thought that the night would never end; and I must surely die.

I was consumed with a shaking chill, and a sharp stabbing pain in my side.

'Christopher,' I screamed, for he was not in my bed that night, but on an old chaise in the corner of the room: 'I cannot breathe, the shaking will not pass.'

Christopher came to me, and rushed to get Mamma. Mamma came and told Christopher to get dressed and go down the road with all speed for Mr MacDonald. Mamma sat by my bed and held my hand, but O, how I wanted Christopher, how impatiently I waited for his return!

He came back within twenty minutes with the apothecary. He was surly to be disturbed from his slumber, his Scottish bad humour in full flight:

'Are ye not a foolish wee girl to be falling into the water at your age.' He had a horrible way of slurring roundly and slowly over the 'r's' which I found vexing. He looked at me closely, with a scowl upon his lined and ugly face. 'Ah well, you've no' got a fever, just a bad cold, a water bottle is all you'll need tonight,' he said briskly, clicking his black bag together with satisfaction and making for the door with all speed.

Mamma showed him out, I vaguely heard their voices descending the stairs. I reached for Christopher in a panic and held fast on to his cold hand.

'I'm sure I am going to die,' I said. He said nothing, but tucked me in warmly. Mamma came back and told me to try to sleep. Christopher sat beside me, watching me for an hour. I could not sleep for the cold that flowed through me. It was about dawn when Christopher took off his nightgown and climbed into the bed with me, wrapping his warm body around my now naked and chilled one. Slowly, slowly I thawed a little.

I slept fitfully, feeling the warmth rise in me, holding fast on to Christopher, my head cradled against his chest.

I awoke in a fever. I could not keep still and the sweat was pouring from my body. My head was bursting with pain and I felt an odd fear of not being able to rise. I was alone. I shrieked for Christopher. He came rushing in with Mamma and Edward. It was like a horrible nightmare. I could not find Christopher's face. Everyone appeared to be moving all the time. Mamma kept fretting and asking questions. I heard Edward say that the apothecary must be called again. He left to this end. I could just make out Christopher's face bending over me, full of suffering. Mr MacDonald arrived and took my pulse. All about me was commotion. Every time I took a breath the stabbing sensation in my side became more acute. I began to cough.

I slept a little in the morning. My rest was full of blackness. When I awoke I heard hollow voices round about me. When my eyes closed it was as if a huge blanket had been thrown over my head and was about to suffocate me. If I slept awhile, my dreams were full of devils with red eyes, and burning hell fires. Sheets of redness kept falling about me. My faculties were much confused by fever and terror; my predominant wish was only to have my brother by me. In my more quiet moments his presence was the only ease to my wretchedness. When I opened my eyes he was always sitting quietly beside me, wiping my face with cold towels or holding my hands.

I felt if he did not stay by my side, watching and guarding me, I would certainly die. I knew he could catch me back any time the black terror was about to claim me. My fear of death was so strong I did not altogether trust my eyes to close; it was not safe to sleep in case death crept up on me.

The fever would not leave me. But nor did my brother. My cough was grievous harsh, with bloody brownish expectoration. He held my head patiently and his eyes never shut in his vigil. Often his eyes were swollen and rimmed with red with the fatigue of it, but he did not sleep, unless I slept. The fever grew. I recall unclearly the Frenchman coming with his physician; I heard him say our apothecary was all that was needed, because good care and nursing was all I required.

So Mr MacDonald continued to care for me. His low, harsh voice was often in my ears, admonishing me for my evil ways, telling Mamma that all sickness was a punishment from the good Lord.

'Indeed, good madam,' I heard him say to Mamma once when I was sufficiently awake to take in the conversation: 'It is my firm belief that disease comes upon those who have entertained bad ideas and associations – such has always been my experience. For myself I am very rarely ill; the common cold has been my worst affliction.'

He applied leeches to my body, which I found detestable. Though I could feel little, I could sense their suckers draining away my blood and strength. They were a torment to me; I thought they must surely be dirty, evil creatures to live off human blood. I cried bitterly on every occasion and was left in a weak and prostrate condition. The nausea I felt increased on every application, until I began to vomit violently. I became delirious. A vision flew in the window and settled itself on my bed-head. I knew it to be a visitor from the other world come to herald my death and fly off with me. Its wings stirred gently with a noise of rushing wind. I was sore afraid, and tried to escape from my bed and flee the room. I felt oppressed and suffocated, I sprang for the door and wrestled with the lock. I collapsed; kind hands lifted me and bore me back to my bed. I rested my head upon my brother's arm and let the blackness come over me. My fever was then profound; the vomiting frequent. I was trussed up in a tight-fitting jacket and my chest was severely strapped, which slightly reduced the pain in my lungs. My fingernails and skin turned blue in colour, and my breathing was shallow, almost a grunting. I could not sleep; there seemed no breath left in my exhausted lungs.

I could see Christopher's gaunt face by my side; I saw my death in his eyes. We were cocooned in a little world of terror and blackness. I became aware of nothing but his face; it floated before me, swaying gently in front of my eyes; even when my eyes closed his face did not leave me. Then a blackness descended and even he left me. I was in a deep, timeless pit with no small spark of light, my mind went out like a lamp. The last sound I heard was a low soft sobbing.

When I came round, I was perspiring freely, my sheets were saturated and water plashed off my face and body. I felt cold, and my breathing was sluggish.

I slept.

I slept for a whole day. Nothing disturbed me. I could breathe, the fever had left me, my gasping dwindled. When the morning came I was very relieved. I felt it was safe then to close my eyes. It felt like winter again, the summer had gone out of my body. I was weak and sad. My fever had lasted seven days.

Then I began to get well; but I was left with an

inexpressible sadness. But the worst was the wretched-ness of mind: it kept drawing from me large silent tears; they fell down my cheeks constantly for no reason, and there was nothing I could do to stop their flow.

How long that cough lingered! It lasted me the entire winter; and not all the honey and lemon in the world could send it away.

The day the fever left me, Christopher brought me my mirror and I tried to comb my hair. My face in the glass shocked me greatly. My dark eyes had sunk deeply into their sockets and were surrounded by heavy black markings. My hair was wild and tangled; my face was devoid of colour, like old parchment, and there was no feeling in it at all – only a weariness. I put the mirror away dejectedly. Christopher brushed my hair gently.

I looked at his face for the first time properly for many days – indeed it seemed like months. He was thin and tired, his eyes red, the skin blackened around about. Terror had taken root in him: it loomed out of his eyes and in the drawn line of his mouth.

We looked at one another in silence, each regarding the other with sorrow, but much love.

I think now that Christopher and I half-died together in that terrible week, and afterwards, when the terror has passed, we were never quite the children we had been before.

12

I was obliged to remain in bed for many weeks; my cough had weakened me considerably; the snow kept on falling. How bitter and unkind the winter looked outside my window. No trace of green was visible, no relief from the bleak, black branches under their white veils of snow. My ennui increased with the days; spent mostly in solitude. Mamma came and sat with me sometimes, but not for any length of time, for her impatience would soon divert her to some more pleasing occupation.

Christopher was back at school, and Mamma would not allow him to stay away on my account. At luncheon breaks, however, he would race home with speed, bringing with him a book or some humorous tale to cheer me up.

When he was at home, he remained at my side; he used to tell me stories. They were stories about a dormouse; the way he lived and the things he did. After a short while the dormouse had become a real person, and gradually he evolved into a Christopher person, at least the kind of person Christopher would have liked to have been. Because the dormouse, far from being shy and retiring, was at all times a very witty and fine person; full of industry and cleverness.

During this time of mending, and for the first time really, I begun to develop a keen dependence on my brother. My fiery, independent spirit had been somewhat consumed in the fires of fever, and I became very needful. I felt restless and unhappy when Christopher was not with me. Sometimes the lady next door, a kindly soul, called in to see me, but she was only an intrusion. The Frenchman called once or twice and brought me little posies of flowers, but I had lost my feeling for him and was silent and morose on these visits. I could not speak to other people. Only my brother seemed to sense how I felt and thought – he would not vex me with trifling matters or words of good chéer.

Mr MacDonald called frequently. He would take Mamma off to the corner of the room, presumably in an attempt to shut me out of their conversation.

'Madam,' he would whisper to Mamma, 'the child does not ameliorate; she is listless and full of bad health. In the circumstances, she is prey to all manner of infection.'

He was a constant source of pessimism, and indeed was more likely to make a person ill than to cure any malady. Having decided that the inherent evil in my nature had brought on the disease, he concluded that the reason for my slow recovery was the fault of 'feminine body functions'.

'Tell me,' he hissed in Mamma's ear, 'has the child been afflicted with the menses? This could indeed be the cause of the deterioration?'

'Indeed not,' Mamma replied with some irritation, 'she is but eleven.'

'Madam, that is neither here nor there; in particularly forward girls, or those with a tendency towards unclean habits or general dirtiness, these very girls are prematurely rewarded with the opening of the wound in the womb.'

'Mr MacDonald,' snapped Mamma, 'Catherine is no way a dirty child; the very reverse. She has suffered a severe illness and I do not find any surprise in the fact that she is slow of recuperating – she is not a strong child.' Mr MacDonald, however, was a firm believer in the inferiority of womankind:

'I would not be too quick to dismiss my suggestion, Madam,' he replied menacingly: 'in my experience it is the wayward who are bitten first by that sly serpent, the menses.'

I, for my part, had no idea of what disease they were referring to; indeed it seemed a most fearful one. Mamma would have no truck with it. Mr MacDonald left with instructions that I be given quinine or tonic bitter to stimulate my appetite, and that the windows should at all times be firmly latched.

The next time he came he insisted on giving me a thorough body examination. This was much to my embarrassment, and very much against my will. Mamma was told to leave the room, but I insisted that she stay.

Mr MacDonald felt all over my body with his cold scratchy hands, prodding at my stomach and the very small swellings that were the beginnings of breasts.

'The child is advanced, as I feared,' he hissed over his shoulder at Mamma, 'indeed I do not hold out much hope for her.'

I complained of the cold and drew the covers up around me again.

'Littte girls, Madam,' he said, a pious smile upon his mushroomy visage: 'are the scourge of the earth. They have no future, but to grow into that unhealthy state of womanhood, with its unclean festerings and grotesque swellings of the abdomen. I would that little girls could stay always the pure young things they are before the age of eight. It is too late for your daughter; she has almost reached the awful state.'

Mamma looked at him with some incomprehension, and after this outburst he did not come so often. The next occasion I had to see him was when he called round with a bottle of spring tonic – a most odious concoction, mulberry in hue and disgusting in taste. It fell to the floor soon after its arrival.

The last time he called I was much better. He had just come from another child's deathbed, and the experience had moved him greatly. 'O, what joy there is,' he expounded, 'in the saving of a wee girl from the dangers of this life. She has gone to a purer place where none can touch her.' I shuddered at his words, and the unhinged look on his face. Fortunate indeed I felt that I had been spared his ultimate remedy.

Time passed, gradually I grew stronger, and I felt relieved to note that an impatience was creeping in on me to be up and about. Then one day, suddenly, the weakness and melancholy left me and I felt like the old Catherine once more. I remember the day most clearly:

The door slammed downstairs and I heard my sweet brother's footsteps thumping up the stairs. My door opened and his dark face popped around it, bright and hearty from the outside cold. I lifted my arms towards him and felt so glad he was back from school. He hugged me slowly, infinitely gently, as if he was afraid to break my bones. I hugged him very hard, and he told me what had gone on at school that day. I had been alone all day. Mamma had only come in for a few minutes in the morning. So it was a relief for me to speak at last.

'The snow stopped today. I got up and watched Mrs Brady taking the washing down the road. The gap in the top of the window is a lot better now that you have secured the cord. I feel so cold and alone when you are not here. I feel as the snow feels: it falls on the ground, but the ground does not take it up. Why, when it's winter, does it seem that the spring will never come?'

And he said: 'The spring will come when it's ready. And everything will change again. You'll be well, and

I'll take you for long walks in the country. Your hair will shine in the sunshine and crackle when I brush it. The birds will soon be back, and we will pick flowers in the park; and you can sleep in my little bed again.'

I began to think of the essence of change. And suddenly I was afraid of change. It seemed menacing. I realized that the sadness and bleakness of the winter really suited my nature best. It had made me feel more real; sadness now seemed more real than happiness, more permanent; and therefore easier to bear.

Time and the snow trickled away slowly. The icy winds took themselves off to blow elsewhere. As spring approached I became more hopeful. I was back at school at last. When I walked home through the park, small buds were poking their heads up through the soil. My cough had gone away, and my weariness was slowly being replaced by something akin to vitality. The bulbs Mamma had planted in the garden in a fit of energy, and a sudden whim to 'get my hands in the soil again', had raised their green snouts and were sniffing the air cautiously, seeking the sunlight.

I went back into our little white room with the blue curtains – I had been moved downstairs next to Mamma's room on the second floor during my illness. Mamma had thought this might be a good time for me to stop sleeping with Christopher; but I pleaded fear, and because of my weakened condition, she gave in.

It was strange to be back in bed with Christopher. The time away had seemed very protracted. It was a great comfort and joy to be back; we took off our nightclothes so we might be even closer to one another.

'Do you think you are well enough for us to do it?' he asked.

'I think so,' I said, because I was a little nervous. It seemed a long time – everything did.

It was different, as I recall. The sensations were just as pleasing as before, my body responded the same way, but in my heart I felt weepy and overcome. I clung to him, and I do not think he understood the reason for my tears, any more than I did. I was afraid, but I could not put a name to the fear.

From this time we were extremely close. In our heads and in our bodies, so much so that I felt that half of his body was mine and half of my body was his; and which way round did not signify. There was a new equality, a new cohesion in our intimacy. I no longer felt I was taking care of him, and I was well enough for him not to be taking care of me. We began, for the first time, really to take care of each other. And as we grew closer together we grew away from everyone else. Our life became a little cloister; and I never wanted to leave it. The idea of change haunted me, and I was in need of constant reassurance from my brother that things would remain the same.

Edward continued as before, a most secretive boy, and always most withdrawn from all the family. He lived inside his books and he had only one close friend. The fact that he was completely outside Christopher's and my company and activities seemed of no concern to him. Once I said to Christopher: 'I wonder what he does all day in his room up there; he only comes in to say good morning and good night.' Christopher said, 'I think he plays with his private parts when he's reading; if not, he must be planning a mass murder.'

Even today that remark does not seem particularly strange to me. There was something quirky and sinister about Edward; about his silence and his lack of curiosity about what went on between Mamma and the Frenchman, and indeed about what went on between Christopher and me.

13

I see, in the re-reading of this, that I have remembered much. At some points in my story it is true to say that my pen faltered, and I was obliged to force myself to continue. During this writing I have been subjected to grievous pains in my head and wicked cramps in my belly. O, the clouding behind my eyes and the hot weariness of my body! I feared I might have contracted some awful ailment, but common sense told me that perhaps the effect of this writing had rustled my mind and given rise to bodily manifestations of ill-health.

My dreams, too, have been troublous, and I have often woken, deeply disturbed by their content. I have had to keep this matter from Thomas, which is a trial, as often I awake with a half-formed cry upon my lips; any mention of this would naturally be deemed by him as the ravings of an hysteric.

These dreams have put me in mind of the childhood dreams I had after my illness. I think I understand their intensity now: the time of the illness and its aftermath was perhaps the end of all innocence. Death had been confronted and held off, and my brother and I emerged with an altered and matured view of one another.

After the return to our old room I had a number of fearful nightmares – so frightening was their content that I was thrown back into the weakened state of my former illness after each attack. The dreams brought about fits of screaming and wildness, and I could in no way control myself.

Dreams are deemed by some to be the workings of the devil, but I now know them to be a demonstration that a person is in bad mental health, close to madness. It may well be that I was in such a state after the illness. Certainly my brain held counsel with strange fears and notions, which must indicate weakened faculties. I was mortally fearful of things changing and I became convinced of my impending death. The attacks always came on after night-fall; quite suddenly the colours of my dreams became too vivid for me to bear, and I awoke screaming.

One night I dreamt I was out in a small vessel with my brother; I trailed my hand happily in the cool water. Swiftly, and with no warning, I was pulled out of the boat and drawn into the depths of the sea. I could not get back to my brother and this was my terror. My screams became the gurglings of brine, my lungs filled with salt. My lips continued to mouth my brother's name, but no sound issued forth. I could see him disappearing into the distance, his face shrinking away.

I woke from this particular dream calling Christopher's name. Mamma rushed in, white night-gown flowing behind her; Edward staggered in, a crossness in his face. Christopher endeavoured to calm my frantic screams and gyrations; yet I could not free myself from the awful panic of the dream.

Mr MacDonald was summoned. He glared fiercely at me, his appearance unkempt and agitated. He said in a low growl: 'The child is in a most fearful passion, such a wild and unnatural attachment to her brother.' Whereupon he left the room and returned with a bucket of water which he hurled over us. The icy water doused both Christopher and me, and split my voice in two. I stood there limply for a second or two and then swooned.

I woke to find myself in the old illness bed next to Mamma's room. Lonely, I went in search of my brother. We spoke for many hours that night; how well he understood the terror I had felt, and how gently he held me.

Christopher told me he had heard Mr MacDonald tell Mamma to be 'vigilantly on the watch for any sexual temperament' in me; any 'squirming in a chair or unnecessary interest in my vital organs'. He had urged the use of an opiate if my condition should return, after a generous application of cold water.

The dreams continued, but Christopher soon learned to control my fits of screaming: he would slap me firmly upon the face and this was sufficient to bring my distorted senses back to normal. Often I would merely wake in a fearful state, and after I had told him of the dream its terror would dissipate rapidly.

Now I realize how fortunate I was then to have someone to confide in; someone to speak to of the frightening inner turmoil of those long nights.

My dreams of late have been indeed strange; I try to unravel some explanation for them, but it is seldom that a solution presents itself. I dreamt that I was playing the piano in the drawing room of our childhood home; Christopher stood listening by the window. He called to me, saying a funeral was passing; I left my seat and went to watch the black carriage roll by. It stopped, however, at our door and I heard the man tell that he had come for the body of a certain Catherine Roach. And indeed, it was my funeral that I had been watching, and my body that was brought out and placed in the carriage.

I dream also of my wedding night, with butting clarity. I see myself by the window of my present bedroom, looking over the gardens; I am filled with an inexpressible sadness. My husband Thomas approaches me and leads me to the bridal bed. He removes my night apparel and then his own and I am transfixed with horror because he is without the male member – all that resides in the space between his thighs is a burnt-out stub – like the hacked branch of a tree deadened and blacked by many winters. Then my scream rises and fills my ears and I am turning, turning and finding no way out of this chamber of despair.

It is my duty to clarify this matter; it would be too unjust to leave the impression that my spouse was not a man. Since he is, I find it hard to understand the dream. The only conclusion I can give for this dream is the fact that I have been perusing a medical journal in the last few weeks, which contained a horrifying account of a number of young men who, it seems, mutilate their male organs for fear that they might be afflicted with some dread disease, or that they could not contain the restless urges and inclinations of their sex.

I will relate here the correct, undreamt version of my wedding night, and the events that led up to it.

I did not wish to be married with any passion, though I was fond of Thomas; but Mamma insisted that I was passing the marriageable age – I was close on twenty-nine – and it was possible that no further opportunities would present themselves.

Vanity compels me to mention here that over the years I had had many suitors; some pursued me with an intensity that I found remarkable, in the face of so little encouragement.

We were living in Oxfordshire at this time, and Mamma's new acquaintances after her marriage to Mr Charles Hatherley – a professor at the university – brought many a young buck to our house. I viewed none of them with any great interest, though indeed many were handsome and intelligent fellows. Sometimes we made friends and enjoyed long conversations; more often I was deemed cold and forbidding and their attentions waned speedily. This caused my Mamma much anxiety; it mattered little to me.

I was busy stocking my brain with the wealth of books and opinions open to me in a new and forward-thinking environment. I took no pleasure in the balls and outings, theatres and pic-nics. I was solitary; subject to spells of melancholy and idle day-dreaming. I was not, however, unhappy; there was much that I wanted to learn. I would gladly have taken some form of employment, but that was of course out of the question; so that the only other form of passing the time was in the pursuit of literature and the arts.

The slow pattern of free-thinking was coming to my attention, and marriage as an unquestioned institution was beginning to be reviewed. I was excited that the lot of women would gradually improve, but I could not speak of these matters within our household because it would not have been considered genteel. Mamma, since her marriage, had become meticulous about what was right and proper, and what common. It caused me much amusement, because I remembered well her antics of former days.

I felt shuttered living with Mamma and my new and rather dour step-father. I would have preferred to have gone off and lived my own life, as my brothers had done. I could not see why a man was permitted to make his way in the world of his own choosing, while a woman was obliged to stay at the hearth, trifling her days away. My need for self-expression grew. I began to write a number of poems and short articles for magazines, under a masculine pen-name; it gave me much pleasure to see my words bold and black upon the page.

It was after living in this close fashion for six years

that Thomas Spencer appeared on the horizon of my life. As I have said, I was impatient with the lot of women, but the alternatives offered me were not of my desiring, so I had settled into my studies and sought, despite Mamma's constant entertaining, to lead a quiet life.

One evening, Mr Spencer came to the house with other guests for dinner. Mamma insisted that I attend, and on this occasion I could not by any wiles or pretext persuade her to excuse me from the table.

Thomas Spencer impressed me immediately. There was about his person a gentleness which attracted me. He had almond-shaped grey eyes; pale hair; a long and high forehead and a most sensitive curved mouth – too ascetic, perhaps. He was more advanced in years than the other gentlemen present – I considered him to be approximately thirty-seven, perhaps even more.

We spoke little that night. I recall some small dialogue about the bizarre works of Ruskin – he had dismissed the man as a maniac. I knew very little of his works, as my step-father refused to have them in the house.

I did not see Thomas again until after the winter – he did not live in Oxfordshire. Then, one bright Spring day he called, wishing to see my step-father about some matter. He was shown into the drawing room where I sat reading, and Mamma was dabbling with a most intricate piece of embroidery. I caught his eyes upon me as he exchanged niceties with Mamma about the weather; he stayed and took tea with us. During tea he addressed many questions in my direction; and I felt that he sensed my unrest.

'Do you read a great deal, Miss Roach?' he asked kindly.

'Indeed yes, all her time is taken up with reading,' Mamma replied on my behalf. 'I declare it is bad for a young woman to be always in a book – damaging for the eyes – she does not get out and about enough – such a pallidness in the cheeks.' I blushed at this and wished Mamma would hold her tongue.

'I am sure it is a good thing for a woman to fill her mind with good books, Madam,' he replied quietly in my defence. 'There are a great many more foolish pursuits open to the young these days.'

He called often after that and a friendship developed between us. I found him pleasant to listen to and he never made any demands upon me. Mamma decided he was developing a passion for me, which she encouraged as much as was proper. I myself had had no clue as to his intentions and was more than prepared to see how things transpired; not wishing to have to make any decisions one way or the other.

14

One rainy afternoon as I watched the heavy, brooding cumuli deposit their wet offerings on to the garden, Mr Spencer was announced. He took my hand and we commiserated on the gloominess of the pluvial afternoon. He partook of a cup of tea, and since Mamma was not present, began a somewhat intimate conversation; 'Catherine, we have known each other a year now – I think we are friends, are we not?'

'Certainly we are,' I replied, unsure of what was to come next.

'It would be a great pleasure and joy to me, Catherine, if you would consent to be my wife,' he said firmly.

From Mamma's chatter I must confess that I was expecting something of the sort; but the forthright and cool manner of its presentation startled me somewhat. Noting my confusion, he continued thus:

'You are doubtless thinking of the difference in our ages Catherine. I am forty-three, you but twenty-five, your Mamma tells me.'

He would have continued, but for my interruption: 'I am twenty-nine next January,' I said firmly, not wishing him to be deceived by Mamma's coyness.

'Be it as it may,' he said, 'there is still a considerable difference – I, as you know, have been married before, and would be still, no doubt, but for God's intervention. But, I see no problem in this matter, you are a mature and sensible woman – advanced for your age in mind and thoughts, I perceive.'

'No, Thomas, the age does not worry me,' I blurted out awkwardly.

'Perhaps, then, you do not care for my appearance, or the fact that you would be obliged to reside with me in the country, away from the high life of Oxford?'

'O, no indeed, you are well aware that I do not care for the high life, and I would be much happier in the country, I imagine, although I have never lived in the countryside before.'

I was hastily gathering my shattered thoughts about me, so that I might answer him properly: 'It is simply,' I began slowly, 'that I have always felt that there should ideally be some love between a man and a woman before they embark on the perilous path of matrimony.'

'Ah, I perceive then, dear Catherine, that you do not love me as I love you,' he said sadly. 'For I have cared for you from first acquaintance with your mind and gentle nature.'

There was little I could say; and I felt grieved that I was unable to say that he was wrong, and that I did love him. I could not, however, and the slight contraction of the muscles around his mouth moved me greatly.

'Perhaps you will consider my offer?' he said. He came and sat beside me, and lifting my shifting hands, he trapped them both within one of his own and, looking at me carefully, he said:

'Catherine, I am not a young man, I am almost an old man, and I know my mind. My previous marriage was not a happy one and I have had time to consider the reasons why. You are young, I find you most agreeable in manner and appearance, and I believe I could live happily with you. You are gentle, reserved, without fire or passions and I think we would make an excellent partnership.'

O, how my heart and spirit rebelled at his words,

how I longed to say that I had more spirit and passion than he could dream of! But I held still, fighting back old memories, old longings, as he pressed my hand lightly to his lips and was gone.

I did consider his offer over the next months, and I decided that in all honesty of heart I could not entertain the idea of such a cold marriage. For my part I liked him well, respected his mind and education; and his gentle disposition. But I had no love for him, and the idea of living closely with a person I had no passion for filled me with misgivings.

Mamma, however, was overjoyed at the idea, and was constantly urging me to accept, and pronouncing all manner of warnings if I did not.

My life drifted on in an aimless fashion; I could not rid myself of the old and over-riding passion of my childhood. I decided eventually that no one would ever, could ever, be what my brother had been to me all those years ago; and that I must attempt to re-frame my life. The thought of physical intimacy alarmed me, however, more than all other, and I realized that I would perhaps have to force myself to overcome my fear.

In thinking back, and it is now only sixteen months since I was wed, I realize that I entered the marriage in a state of apathy; simply under-going it because of Mamma's pressure, and because there seemed no other real alternative apart from marriage open to me. I thought also that as a married woman I would find a certain measure of independence which I did not have with Mamma.

We were married in the winter of my thirtieth year; in the parish church of Lechlade in Gloucestershire. I was overtaken by a terrifying fit of nerves prior to the ceremony and Mamma had to administer some strong words and a little laudanum.

We were married on a brisk, but friendly December day: sunlight fell in honeyed patches through the dark trees.

It was not a large wedding: I insisted that this be the case, although Mamma had had other plans. I had wanted to wear a simple low white gown but Mamma demanded it be a high white gown. I pointed out to her that I was marrying a widower, so perhaps it would not be proper to wear a high gown, but to no avail. It was indeed a most beautiful dress: of heavy trailing silk covered with layers of Honiton lace, and encrusted at throat and wrists with seed pearls and orange blossom.

I walked down the aisle in a state of complete inertia, my senses muffled by the laudanum. I observed Thomas turn slightly as I approached, and a small smile flickered around his solemn face. I wished with all my heart that he could have been my brother.

I remember little of the service, apart from willing that there might be some dramatic interruption at the crucial point. I made my answers roundly, and smiled at Mamma as we walked down the aisle and into the cold sunlight.

The village children outside threw flowers along our path, and we then made our way in a grand carriage the short distance to my new home.

The wedding breakfast was a trial; Mamma had seen to all the details and was terrified she might do the wrong thing; however her books on bridal etiquette bore her in good stead. There was an abundance of soups, entrées, chicken, grouse, partridge, pheasant, duck and every conceivable jelly, cream, custard, champagne and wine. I could eat nothing.

I found myself a little sad-hearted on this day when I should be most content. Happily, Mamma took it for natural trepidation.

We left amongst a flurry of good wishes, to honeymoon in Cornwall – this was my special request. I had not been back there since the fateful holiday with my family and I thought often of it.

We spent the night in the Grand Hotel of Penzance – a superb old building, very ornate, with much red and gold in its fittings. I was most fatigued by the day and we retired to our chamber soon after ten. Thomas was kind and gentle and turned his back while I disrobed. I was glad of this consideration, but somehow it also made me smile because I could not help but recall the complete lack of coyness of my childhood. We got carefully in at opposite sides of the bed, me wearing my chemise and a nightgown and Thomas well attired in a nightshirt of voluminous proportions (how different again from the naked intimacy of days gone by!)

If I were writing as a typical novelist of today, I would of course draw a discreet curtain over the intimacies of the connubial bed; however, I am not a typical novelist, nor indeed a novelist at all, and this is written only for my, and perhaps my brother's benefit. I would like for my own part to be able to compare the events in black and white, as it were, with the descriptions I have suffered over previously in this tale.

I lay silent and passionless as a nun in the great bed, stretching my limbs out slowly till they were straight. My arms came across my body and my hands folded across the small mound between my thighs.

'I was thinking, Catherine dear, how lovely you looked in that pearl-grey outfit today, and how proud I felt of you,' Thomas said, reaching across for my hand.

I smiled in the darkness, for indeed I could see absolutely nothing, since Thomas had turned down the lamp. He seemed to me at that moment a creature of sweetness, and though my hand felt lifeless he squeezed it firmly. He moved over to me and wrapped one strong arm about my person. I felt my body stiffen with apprehension.

'Catherine, sweet child,' he whispered – for he had sensed my involuntary tautening, 'please do not be fearful of me, I would claim you with all love and gentleness, do not make me feel a burden to you.'

O, how greatly I wished I could feel some spontaneous answer in my heart, how I wished I could respond to his tender entreaty with some small passion; but alas, I felt unutterably cold, and very close to tears. My new husband rolled over my body and placed kisses lightly upon my face and shoulders, lifting the lace layers of my night apparel. I remained silent and tense throughout his attempts at gentle wooing and his entry of my body, though the pain was often fierce, and a foolish desire to scream rose in my throat. He seemed unaware of the intensity of my mental agony, and when his passion was spent he rolled slowly off my body, turned over in the bed and in a short while was fast asleep.

I lay quiet, after wiping the wetness fiercely off me with the sheet. My face, my body, seemed to set in a gel; I did not move; I did not weep; I felt nothing at all. My husband slept; I could not sleep; I lay waiting for the gentle dawn to creep through the curtains and ease my numbness.

In the fevered chambers of my brain I knew that things were greatly amiss, that it was unnatural for me to feel so immobilized of natural feelings. I told myself that time might alter things, that I could perhaps come to respond to my husband's love-making; but in my heart of hearts I knew I was deceiving myself. I knew myself to be doomed; locked for ever in an empty sea, washed over with madness, dreams of serpents and endless funerals.

15

I am no nearer to understanding my strange dream; I feel distressed because I hoped relating all these things might have helped me find a way of deciphering it. Perhaps, though, I should not be trying to find a direction through the mind's maze. I well know that my action in relating the dream and pondering over it, and the exposure of the events of my marriage night, would be the object of fierce vituperation and disgust.

It is abundantly clear that the unfortunate nature of my marriage consummation was in no way the fault of Thomas (so why then the severed member?). The blame and the misery all stemmed from me. He was dutious and tender and in every way considerate; I was totally unable to bring myself out of the numb and constricted state I found myself that night.

Thomas is not physically repulsive; indeed he is pleasing to look upon. It is obvious then that the problem lies within me, not within my body, but within my mind. It is my head and heart that separates me from Thomas — I cannot cross the divide and find myself caring for him. There is some old and gnarled block between us, and I know well that it resides in my mangled head. But without feeling I cannot give myself to him; and the feeling is not there, it was lost many years ago. Once given I cannot take it back unto myself and bestow it elsewhere.

Alas, the patterns within my head are so tangled and twisted — I suppose if I were a sensible creature I would just go off and make pudding (cooking is supposed to be the cure for woman's worrying – 'nothing like a little busyness to keep a woman out of evil thoughts and deeds' my grandfather used to say).

But all is not gloom; my initial and almost hysterical behaviour in the matter of physical intimacy has lessened somewhat; although I cannot say with honesty that I have come to respond to my husband. I try to console myself in remembering that I have been well-versed in the current school of thinking; that woman is merely expected to submit her body and nature to the bestial tendencies of her partner. Yet I *know* this not to be true inclination of my nature; I *know* there is passion and feeling within these veins. I wish I could but tap a small portion of the love I had for my brother and bring it into my present existence. Can it be true that a woman loves but once, and cannot thereafter give herself to another? O, but I was not a woman then, and it is so long, so long ago; yet it is all still within me. Nothing has changed in my heart.

So, it is clear then that it was wicked of me to enter this marriage. I was wrong to tie myself to a man for whom I can feel little. The strange thing is: Thomas seems uncommon content with his lot. He does not seem aware of my lack of feeling and interest. He is at all times gentle and well-pleased; he expects little, and by God, by my definition he gets little! This should then make me feel less wicked. Alas, his goodness only serves to heighten my contrition.

I do not think I am an evil woman. I never felt evil until my brother told me we had done wrong. What I am doing now is evil; it seems to me that to live in a way that is contrary to one's own nature, to live in a way that is false, that is the evil. The discontent grows like a cancer, eats away at the vitals and poisons the entire body and the air around about. It will surely come back on Thomas and cause him pain.

Yet, as I said when I began this narration, the first

year of our marriage was in many ways special and agreeable to me. I had escaped my Mamma; I was mistress of my own house and had a little more freedom.

I ponder about the strangeness of life: I was content because little was demanded or expected of me. Thomas never forced his attentions on me, and after the initial months of rapture (on his part) he retired more into himself. So I felt at peace and unburdened. And yet it irks me not to be able to wander about the country as I please and to have so little access to modern literature and ideas. There is no one about these parts with whom I could feel a real kinship; the country gentry are a stiff and pretentious lot, with the heavy unenlightened faces of farmers.

I move like a shadow in this house; the servants go about their business; my husband goes about his business; the seasons change and find me the same. Nothing touches me, nothing makes me laugh or weep, I have no real substance. I perform my small duties efficiently, speak to people when they call, and shut out my heart and brain from the motivations of my body.

I felt that this way of life would continue for ever, there seemed no way it could be interrupted. Then one April afternoon I persuaded Thomas to let me take out the governess cart. Previously he'd always insisted I take a carriage and be driven, but I pleaded the need for exercise and he acquiesced, advocating only that I take a maid at all costs. But I could not abide the thought of some silent, stupid wench imposing on my solitude, so I departed alone.

I travelled a great distance up and over the soft rolling hills, feeling the wind through my hair – having discarded the bonnet without much ado. It was a glorious sensation: I had not felt so free for many years.

It came to me that I might go on, and not turn back to my drear home. I felt much elated and brave. Over the next hill and away I drove, planning a new, free life beyond the horizon. I thought I might take work as a shop girl or even a servant; perhaps I could cross the seas. The daydream continued as I raced down unfamiliar roads. I had no idea whither I was going; the main thing was to keep going, not to turn back.

It began to grow dark, a chill crept into the air. I realized I had no idea where I was, and indeed I was right in the heart of the country, and had seen no village for some time. I continued more slowly, and then, with much reluctance, began to retrace my route. It was no easy matter; the fields looked much altered in that darkening hour and the horse was wearied. When I returned home it was very dark; the house loomed large and forbidding, and I felt like a small child who had attempted to run away from home, and been driven back by the fear of darkness, or the thought of dinner.

I entered the side door, hoping not to cause a scene, thinking ludicrously that my absence might not have been noticed. I tried to creep up the stairs, but as I passed the drawing room the door swung open and I beheld Thomas, looking extremely angry.

'And where, pray, have you been, Catherine?' he demanded most coldly. 'We have been greatly concerned about you. I thought you might have had an accident, you are so late.'

'Forgive me, Thomas, I drove much further than I intended, and the night came down most suddenly.'

'You did not take the maid with you. You know it was my express wish that you should.'

We were in the drawing room at this point, with the door closed. I felt like a naughty child being reprimanded, and the idea irritated me; Thomas's acidulent manner was one I had not experienced before and

I found myself saying sharply:

'Must you fuss so, Thomas? Really it is of no consequence and I am back and safe now.'

'O indeed, and you think that is the end of the matter. It does not occur to you that I have been most troubled about you; you do not stop to consider that it is not proper for you to be roaming all over the country – hatless – and without a maid – looking like a gypsy person.'

I began to get very angry, I felt my colour rising. I forced my mind to circle the beautiful events of the day: the spring freshness, the green shoots, the steel grey of the sky on my return. But Thomas had not finished.

'Catherine, I forbid you to leave this house again without a chaperon. John Littlestone informed me he caught sight of you fair racing down the road, hair blowing behind you in disorder and with a decided lack of propriety in your mien.'

I smiled inwardly, letting his wrath amass as it would. Anything I might say would certainly not help.

'You are silent, Catherine; can I take it that you will not disgrace me so again?'

'Disgrace?' Again the wrath rose, 'I can see no disgrace in a woman riding out alone on a spring afternoon. I am indeed sorry that you were fretting about me, but I fail to see how I have disgraced you.'

'I do not like to be told by my neighbours that my wife was observed careering about in a governess cart ... without a bonnet, moreover.'

'O for God's sake, why does the bonnet signify so?' I expostulated.

'Catherine, your language is quite disgraceful,' he muttered pompously, somewhat taken aback by my words. 'I think it would be best if you were to retire to your room and set your appearance and mind in order.'

I sniffed, and I observed Thomas wince at this small vulgarity. It surprised me that he had not witnessed this characteristic of mine before; but I recalled that I had not ever really been natural or my true self with him; having always to abide by the intolerable detail of proper behaviour.

I walked slowly to the door, Thomas took up a stern position by the fireplace. There was a hurt in his face but it did not touch me.

'I will get the maid to bring you some dinner presently,' he said. 'I dined as usual at half past seven.'

'Ah, so your anxiety did not prevent your usual appetite,' I retorted. There was no rejoinder.

My buoyant frame of mind could not be deflated. I leapt up the stairs two at a time, and closed the bedroom door noisily behind me.

The face that gazed back at me out of my mirror was one I had not seen for many a moon. My eyes gleamed and danced, my cheeks were rosy and my hair clustered dark and wild about my face. I felt alive for the first time in a very long while. I felt as I had felt as a child so long ago, and it was perhaps this one experience of freedom that opened up my heart and brain again and set me to writing this tale.

I could see why Thomas felt threatened by my new spirit. It was one he did not know, did not want to know, and certainly could not understand. The disorder of my hair and dress was a trial to him too, it was contrary to his image and expectation of me.

But I was wild and elated that night. I lay on the bed and travelled back in my mind. And then determined to put my feelings down on paper.

Today, still, I know the time of deadness is past. Often I sink back into the careful sham, but deep inside me some portion of my life is over and something new is about to commence. I am consumed with eagerness to try and express myself again. Whatever happens in the next months, I will not go back to the subterranean existence of the last year. I will write the past out of my head, and perhaps when that is done, my life can begin again in a more fruitful manner. I am full of optimism and fiery with impatience.

And yet, I fear the next portion will cause me grief and open old wounds; and a chill creeps around me. My new elation wavers, and I must not delay.

16

The summer Christopher had promised me came at last. I was altogether better, the dreams and phantoms had gone on to other minds and I was less tormented. It was almost time for the summer holidays; we did not usually go away for the holidays, but Mamma had decided to take us to the sea in Cornwall. She thought I was still frail and that Edward had been working too hard and needed a change of air.

The night before we departed for Cornwall Christopher and I found it quite impossible to sleep, so great was our excitement at the prospect of being close to sea and country and fields. We talked late into the night; Edward kept banging on our door telling us to be silent for our giggling kept him awake.

We were reminiscing about the last holiday we'd had – the only one I could remember; we had gone to Brighton when I was nine and Christopher eleven. Father had been with us then; indeed it was the only time he had been with us so regularly. We had taken some rooms in a very pretty house close to Brighton Bay for a fortnight. It was a deliciously hot summer, touched with strange events.

How clear are the details! We arrived hot and dusty one afternoon and were welcomed by a round and jolly person who was to take care of our holiday needs. She thought Christopher quite a darling in his shiny new sailor suit and black curls. He grimaced horribly as she ruffled his hair.

Christopher and I had a generous view of the sea from our bedroom on the third floor. There were two small beds in the room, but we only slept in the one by the window – which pleased the maid. I had my very own toilet table with a row of pretty silver-topped glass receptacles. There was a rosy pitcher and basin. One look round the room and we were in our bathing costumes and impatient to try the sea. We had some cold lemonade, and Mamma and Father accompanied us on this first occasion to test out the safety of the bathing. On the beach Mamma settled herself beneath a large striped shade and dabbed herself with cologne. She fanned herself gently and spread out her pale lavender voile dress with tiny roses between the stripes, adjusting the straw and flowered bonnet. Father strode off on a tour of inspection.

We raced to the waves, even Edward seemed in fine spirits. O, the joy of being knocked over by a white-lipped breaker, the swallows of brine and the stones between the toes. Edward could swim quite strongly, so he left us to our childish pranks. Christopher tried to coerce Mamma into trying the bathing machine, but she would have none of it.

We made no child friends on the beach, preferring to seek out the less crowded spots and escape the crowd. Indeed, the people were the only irritation; we could well have done without their presence.

However, we did make one good friend and he turned out to be a constant source of amusement and wonder to us.

One sweltering afternoon, as Christopher pursued my shrieking form up the beach, I tumbled over an old gentleman's legs. From my sprawled position at his feet I glanced up at his face to see what my fate might be for this clumsiness. I saw a smiling and gentle physiognomy that looked behind and beyond me.

'I am very sorry for disturbing you, Sir,' I said, rising

hastily. I then observed a white cane by his side, and I swallowed a second gulp of alarm, perceiving that he was blind. From this untidy start there emerged a singular friendship between the gentleman and my brother and me.

His fingers were the most sensitive antennae; they nosed along every object we handed him so he might accurately tell us their substance and precise form. He was given the name 'Sherlock', and he entered gladly into our games and banter.

'You'll never guess this one, never!' I challenged, handing him a tiny stone shaped like a shell.

In mere moments he rejoined: 'It is a rare and delicate stone, worn paper-thin by the waves, I believe it is of a pinkish hue.'

'O, indeed and you are right,' I cried delighted, running off for further finds along the errant shore-line. We walked for miles each day collecting shells and stones polished and rounded by the waves; Christopher made me a necklace of tiny shells of pink and blue. He carved statues from the sodden and swelled driftwood when it had dried in the sun.

Sherlock was a creature of wondrous skills: we brought him paper of every different colour, and merely by touching the texture of each he could tell us its exact colour. We never tired of finding him objects of different colours to place before the scrutiny of his sensitive fingertips. He began to teach us how to tell colour by touch, and within a few days I could pick out black and red and blue with no trouble at all.

'Everything you pick up, you must feel, feel,' he would insist. 'Do not rely always on the evidence of your orbs, there is much delight to be gained by the sensations of touch.'

Christopher was fascinated by this, and by the time a week had passed he was quite remarkable at picking out the colours, even the difficult ones like yellow, which I could never master.

This gift we kept over the years, and soon discovered that it would not leave unless the use of it was discontinued. For my part it is many years since I have thought on this, and therefore many years since I have tried it. I wonder today if my brother remembers, and whether the gift is still with him.

I recall those beautiful days so well: the white frilled children furrowing the beach, the carcasses of crabs, the big white steamer floating by on the haze of an afternoon. Tins rusting in rocks, old men panting away a last long summer, the sweet scent of cologne, the reds and blues of beach balls and shades, the straw hats whisked off by playful, salty winds...

Sometimes I took Sherlock out to the edge of the sea, when there were not too many noisy, hurtling children about. He would roll up the ends of his trousers very tightly and carefully; and hand in hand he and I would wade out into the water. It was a great pleasure to him. He had lived all his life on the south coast, and he remembered the days when Brighton was a very grand and exclusive summer retreat. 'Too many people of sundry character these days,' he would growl, 'the grand folk take themselves off abroad these days; don't know what's to happen, I'm sure, with all these new-fangled inventions and electrical gadgets – the quality of life is changing, my sweet child. Glad I can't see it.'

What a dear man was Sherlock, I loved him greatly. I would read him, slowly and not too well, passages of Jane Austen, whom he greatly admired, and after a few painful moments of this his head would sink on to his chest and he would snore gently in the afternoon's lull.

One night Father took Christopher and I out for a stroll to get some cockles from the fish stand. It was a lovely evening and father was in good spirits and telling us about the times he used to come to Brighton as a boy. We purchased the cockles and were setting off for home when I asked if we might take a promenade along the beach. The tide was out and we walked quite a way to see the little waves nuzzling the cool stones. I spotted a dark object over to our right and asked father if I might see what it was.

'It could be treasure, could it not?' I asked hopefully.

'More likely a body,' said the gory weasel.

The nearer we got to the brown lump in the failing light the more difficult it was to tell what it might be.

'It does look like clothes,' I said, confused. When we were close to it, I could see a pair of legs, the calves still in the water, the thighs and tattered drawers exposed. It was obviously a woman, her dress was flung over her trunk and head as if she had jumped down into the water and her skirts had risen and caught around her head.

Father turned away, but Christopher crouched down in the sand and lifted the dress away from her face. O, what savagery the cruel sea and gnawing fish had done to that face and eyes – it was a black and grisly sight.

'She's dead, there's nothing we can do,' Father said, his face an acid green and fear marking his eyes. 'Get away from that hideous thing, Christopher – we must go home.'

'I wonder,' Christopher pondered, 'if a body turns into manure if it's left to mould away and go down into the soil?' His detachment again startled me, as it had on many other occasions; he saw this tragedy with simple curiosity, noting the details, meticulously considering the end result; the horror did not touch him. For my part I was curious as to why this woman had come to such an ugly end, but the mass of rotting flesh filled me with sickness and fear. I did not want to think about it.

'Christ, you are callous, boy,' Father said, turning away and making for the stones again. I wondered wickedly where Christopher might have inherited this quality.

These were the things that Christopher and I thought about on that night prior to setting off for Cornwall. Finally, we fell asleep when our memories had run out, and no doubt dreamed of sea-sides and yellow ice-cream and of Sherlock who must be dead by now.

We woke early and packed all our treasures to take to the sea-side. I could not be parted from my brown bear and Christopher wanted his books and telescope. Mamma had had three new dresses made for me, one cream, one brown and one covered with green flowers and I packed them with a great deal of care and tissue paper.

We were to go to a little coastal cottage near Land's End, that belonged to some friends of the Frenchman. They retired there only in the spring, so he had arranged for us to have it for three weeks in the summer. Mamma assured me that there would be very little domestic help, only one maid, and that she would be doing most of the cooking herself. She said she wanted it to be a simple family holiday, just the four of us, and she was going to spend a lot of time with us for a change, and do things for us the way a mother should.

The station struck me as a sad place, with people waving goodbye, but exciting, too, with the steam puffing and snorting and the hiss and bustle, the ladies' tears and the children's shrieks.

Christopher and I could not be confined to the carriage. We hadn't been on a train for some time and we wanted to see everything. The nicest bits of the train were where the carriages joined and you could stand on the bumpy bit and look down through the crack at the track below. It gave one a wonderful precarious feeling.

Mamma insisted that we come and sit down quietly, which we did for a while; but after Mamma's hatbox had fallen down and missed my head by a mere fraction once or twice, the weasel and I left the carriage and went exploring once more. Very full the train was, too; mothers and fathers, and children sucking barley sticks, old ladies looking out of place and clucking crossly at the enthusiasm of the children who were rushing up and down disturbing their snoozes.

We looked in to make sure Mamma and Edward were faring well from time to time. Edward said that since we had paid for the seats we ought at least to sit on them occasionally; but Mamma just sighed and leaned back in her chair, dabbing her forehead delicately with a lace handkerchief.

There was an old man in our carriage; he smiled at us kindly and told us he was going to Land's End for the last time. His hair disappeared round the base of his skull, and freckles the colour of jaundice shone out of the crown of his head. He was very thin, with broad hands covered in freckles of the same strange hue, and he ate a lot of brown bread and butter cut neatly into soldiers.

Mamma had brought a big wicker basket full of good things to eat for our lunch. There were thick slices of ham and cold beef and tomatoes, fresh brown bread and even some ginger beer and cherries. I ate too much and fell asleep on Christopher's shoulder. When I awoke we were nearly at our destination. We arrived in Penzance after dark; the train shuddered to a steamy and exhausted stop. The night had caught up with me and I felt very tired and shaky. Christopher helped me down off the train and my feet stung on the platform.

It was too late to go further, so we took rooms in a station inn for the night. It smelt of straw and dust and we didn't care for it too much. We slept early, and woke with the sun streaming through the dirty windows and the day bright with expectations. A round and unjolly porter took our trunks from the inn and found us a pony and trap for the remainder of our journey. With much ado we clambered into the trap, Mamma covering her head and face well from the sun's rays. She fastened a bonnet firmly upon my head with threats of no swimming if I should remove it from its rightful place.

How hot the sun was! How we fussed and niggled, complaining every half hour for refreshment to revive us. As I reflect on that feverish day, it seems to me that the heat has gone out of the sun since those long, molten days of my childhood.

I fell asleep after the steady clip-clop rhythm had worn down my enthusiasm. I awoke as the driver called the horse to a halt. My face burned. Christopher helped Mamma to alight and I began to take note of my surroundings.

And there it was – our holiday house – all bright and beautiful in the noon glare of that August day. A small stone cottage, tall, very old, very solid in appearance. It was completely covered on one side by passion flower; curling cosily round the window on the other side bloomed a most productive purple clematis, her children scrambling up and down the walls. The front door was a deep green, which seemed most bold, and the neat front garden contained the scented blooms of yellow roses.

Christopher and I were through the front gate in no time, it whanged shut on Edward; we heard his angry yelp as we skirted round to the back of the cottage. The back garden was long and narrow with a high hedge hemming it in on either side. The grass was overgrown and there were a few scraggy flowers and shrubs struggling for life amongst the weedy terrain. It was wild and simple, and altogether different from the rather well ordered and pretty front of the house.

I was no longer tired, there was a singing behind my ears and it felt like the beginning of wonderful things.

We entered the house through the front door to see two neat maids standing side by side in the kitchen talking to Mamma. She was surprised to see them there, but it seemed that they were local girls who would come in every day to see to our needs. Mamma dispatched them to buy groceries while we unpacked. We had a picnic in the garden at the back of the house. Mamma laid all the delicacies out on a large white tablecloth and we had cold chicken and cheese, fruit and ginger pop. Mamma then retired to her room for a rest, and Edward settled himself in a wicker chair in the garden and began to read.

Christopher and I darted out of the back gate and down, down on a deeply declining path to the sharp cliffs around the sea. It was three o'clock and exceedingly sultry; we saw no one; heard nothing save the clamour of the gulls and the wind's wawl through the rough-blown trees. We stopped at the cliff's edge and looked down at the brutal surging sea. So angry it seemed! Ripping at the rocks, smacking the seashore; it was the roar and the imagined feeling of being on the edge of a volcano.

There was a narrow pathway down to a small beach, which we had been informed was for our exclusive use. Christopher started down this acclivity first, holding my hand as I followed. It was very rugged and difficult, and I was obliged to tie a knot in my dress to prevent it getting in my way and sending me headlong down to the sea. We stumbled a few times, and the puffing of our breath and the wind's whip round the cliff edges and our bodies made me want to dance and yell with excitement.

Closer to the end of the path the rocks were wet and slippery; dried seaweed smelt in the sun. The spray prickled us lightly all over, my hair had gone into tiny wisps as it did in the rain, and when I licked Christopher's chin it was salty. We leapt down into the sand and our feet disappeared. We plopped down and removed our shoes and stockings with all speed. O, the pure joy of the buttery sand between our toes; of rushing down to the sea and running back and forth as the waves chased us.

We saw then that we were in a deep, secluded cove with great high cliffs either side; the sand golden and good and free of the pebbles we'd had in Brighton; the sea dark green and heavy and the clouds coming down to the edge of the water.

We ran to where the rocks jutted out making a natural cave; it was darker here and cooler. A wonderful dwelling place for a hermit. We explored for a moment and then ran into the sea; the water was freezing; my petticoats kept trailing into the water and then slapping coldly against my warm legs. We splashed one another, and the sea crept higher and higher up our legs as we ventured further out.

Christopher grabbed me by the hand and we ran laughing back up the beach again and into the cave. He began to remove his clothes; shirt, trousers and all, and stood there naked, leaping up and down like Apollo. I laughed and threw sand at him. He helped me take off my dress and the petticoats and the chemise and drawers and then we ran laughing and naked back into the water. It was so cold, so cold. Ah, but the wild excitement of having nothing between the body and the sea — a wonderful freedom never tasted before. Presently I became a little nervous of the sea's swell and tumble and retired to the beach to dry in the sun. Christopher continued to lunge about in the water. I sat down in the sand to watch him, rubbing the sand off my body as the sun dried it. Christopher came out and lay beside me, then we ran off to the mouth of the cave. We looked at each other's tingling and sun-dried bodies and smiled; my lips were cold and my hair hung about me in seaweedy disorder.

He held me firmly by the shoulders and placed a hot kiss upon my mouth, and the look of the weasel came into his eyes. The sand was warm where the sun had kissed it earlier. We made a bed of sand that took the shape of my body, and the patterns of our passion; we left them there for the sea to carry away.

17

I have received a disconcerting letter from my brother Edward. This is an unusual event in itself as Edward and I do not correspond, and I have in fact barely seen him since the time of his marriage some five years ago. I attended the wedding with Mamma, and thereafter only saw him and his wife occasionally or at Christmas. He continued in his childhood habit of keeping himself very separate from the rest of the family, and we knew little of his life or activities, apart from the fact that he had had some success in the legal profession. I thought to myself that it must give him great pleasure to prosecute.

Now, he has requested that Thomas and I take ourselves to his home in Kent for the week-end. He gives no reason for this unaccustomed request, and I was immediately going to refuse. However, caution made me re-read the letter, and in so doing a certain uneasiness came over me. There was something in the letter that made me feel I could not refuse this request, something that seemed to suggest I dare not. I could not say precisely why I felt this, until I came to the phrase: 'I know that you will not refuse this request, as I have not let you down when I might.'

I knew to what he referred, and a warm flush of fear came over me. No, I cannot refuse; and I am fearful of what he plans for me. I must go. And it annoys me greatly, because the spirit moves well beneath my pen and I am mindful not to lose it. I do not know when next I shall be able to get back to this writing.

18

Thomas did not understand my reluctance to go to Kent, and being himself an only child, deemed that I was fortunate indeed to have brothers, and could not see why I did not see more of my family.

The journey was arduous and we were glad to be shown into a comfortable drawing room. Edward lives in a large manor house, very dark and heavily timbered. It is obvious that he has much more wealth at his disposal than Mamma ever imagined. I was thinking on this when Edward sauntered in. The sight of him quite took me aback. He did not walk in the shuffling, silent way of the Edward I knew. He was full of confidence and very gracious, and obviously felt he had the advantage over me in his position as master of the house. Gone were the furtive glances from below those heavy Irish eyebrows; the smirking smile.

'Ah, my dear Catherine, what a pleasure to see you, and to meet your husband. So sorry I could not make the happy event, I was in Europe, I regret. I would so have liked to have seen the little sister on her wedding day.'

All this was said with a charming smile as he ushered us to seats and as servants approached with refreshments. Yet I noted the insidiousness in his manner, and observed that a slight snicker still lingered in the corners of his well-trained mouth.

'Where is Helen, Edward?' I asked.

He addressed his answer at Thomas, and seemed a little ill at ease for the first time.

'She is, I regret, ill; indisposed; has been for some time ... not much to be done, you know.'

Thomas nodded politely as if he totally understood the whole matter.

'What is the trouble then, Edward?' I asked. He ignored my question, and addressed a remark at Thomas about the setbacks of the Boer War.

When we had rested and partaken of lunch, he announced that he was now going to take me to see his wife, and then he would show Thomas over the house and grounds.

As soon as Edward and I were alone together I began to speak to him directly, as I had always done; this approach had always caused him most discomfort.

'Edward, tell me what this is all in aid of. You have had no desire to see me for years; why now the strange request of a visit?'

He was alarmed by the forthright question, and began to mumble meaningless niceties. Noting my impatience, however, he soon turned into the old Edward I remembered so well.

'Well, if you must know,' (a slight petulance creeping in now) 'my wife is very ill, no, it is worse than that – the woman is mad, quite mad. It occurred to me that you would be the best person to deal with her – after all, you dealt with my brother, also mad, with much proficiency, did you not? O, how well you dealt with my dear brother Christopher, how you cared for and coddled him. Well, now you can do something for me.'

I tried to speak very calmly, but my mind was a torrent of strange feelings and fears. 'Edward, I do not know how you think I can help. Your wife is surely your responsibility, not mine.'

'I have decided to make her yours for this one weekend,' he replied coldly. 'I cannot bear to see her, you see, I cannot have anything to do with her. It was my intention to put her in an asylum; but she has used her wiles on the doctor, and persuaded him that she needs some feminine company to ease her mind. I could not refuse what seemed to be such a simple request. I could not, could I? And then it occurred to me that it was a wonderful opportunity to see a little more of you, and I knew you could not refuse me. She is just playing for time, of course, she knows what I am about to do, and she is trying to keep off the day with these tricks.'

The cool way he spoke of her plight and his cruel determination to have her put away frightened me. He was so utterly without feeling in the matter, I could not believe he was talking of his wife: a quiet, gentle person I had seen but a few times, but who seemed intelligent and sweet-natured. I had wondered at these times what she could possibly have seen in Edward. My curiosity aroused, I told Edward that I would now go and see her.

It was a singular meeting and I shall record it in some detail.

He left me at the door and disappeared immediately. I went in. A woman lay reclining on a high, heavily draped bed: the covers were magnolia, trimmed with thick cream lace. I approached the bed and she looked up, startled.

'Who are you?'

'O, did you not know I was coming?' I asked, confused. 'Edward has asked me, and my husband, to visit you for the week-end.'

'Ah, I remember something of the kind,' she said dully. She lifted her hand feebly in greeting. I learned later that she was my age, indeed younger: twenty-nine, but her appearance was much older. She seemed like a woman well over forty years. Her black hair hung lank and heavy about her face, and she kept tossing the strands on the left hand side over her shoulder.

Her eyes were close set and she did not look directly at one — she flashed quick suspicious glances from the corners of those wild orbs. She made me feel ill at ease. It was then that I caught sight of row upon row of neatly ranked dolls, dressed sumptuously in heavy silks and lace, with waxen, painted faces, set smiles and fixed and staring eyes. Everywhere one looked one met the dead gaze of a smiling doll. She saw me looking at them, and demanded one be brought to her. I passed her what was obviously a much-loved object: its clothes were slightly soiled, the taffeta dress drooped and the lace was coming away from the borders. She held it to her; and, keeping her darting eyes upon my countenance, she pushed the doll at the back, and a horrific shrill voice began to utter plaintively, over and over again: 'where is my Mamma? where is my Mamma?' ... A feeling close to nausea came over me.

'Will you take tea with us?' she asked of me; and I realized that 'us' was her and the dolls. She handed me a cup of tea, and some small, finely cut sandwiches. She ate nothing and drank nothing. I decided I must pull myself together and try to speak to this person.

'You collect dolls, obviously; where do you get them from? they are very fine.'

'They have always been mine, always. My papa gave them to me as a child. I had a mother, she died, he gave me dolls after she died.'

Her strange, twitching mouth and shifting, nervous eyes filled me with pity now; the apprehension was fading and curiosity began to take its place.

She sat staring at me, her mouth slightly ajar. 'You're pretty; how old are you?' she asked.

'I am thirty-one,' I replied.

'You have babies?' she asked, more anxiously.

'No,' I said, and as I said it I felt a quick stab of fear as I recollected that my body had not been functioning quite normally for the past two months, and that I discerned a heaviness in my breasts and belly.

'Please, go away now,' she said, turning her face from me suddenly and burrowing into the great pillows.

I left instantly, closing the door quietly behind me. I observed that a maid sat silently outside the door, and as I left she entered, casting a small sneer at me through the closing crack of the door.

Thomas was engaged in conversation with Edward when I returned to the drawing room, so I took a walk in the grounds which were indeed splendid: great long lawns and many gnarled oak trees. The rose garden was large and beautifully tended; the buds were well formed and about to break out of their green shells. I spent a few happy hours wandering the property, and then my maid helped me to dress for dinner.

Helen did not dine with us. Edward said she had not left her bed for the past year. I felt compelled to ask him a little of her story.

'What is it that ails your wife, Edward?' I enquired, slightly nervously, for indeed his manner was not one which inspired questions of any kind. Yet he seemed calmer than when I had spoken to him alone; and he obviously felt the necessity to put on a show for Thomas.

'It is hard to say,' he pondered. 'She has seen the best physicians and specialists and none can find any real cause or impediment. We feared for a long time that she might have consumption, but it is not the case. Now she malingers, grows weaker every month, complains of great pains in her belly and head and gives no one any peace.'

He brooded awhile, toying with his soup. Thomas frowned at me by way of discouragement, but I did wish to know more of the matter.

'Perhaps, then, there is some sadness in her that might explain the malady?'

'Yes, indeed that is part of the matter. She is unable to produce children, and this has caused her much distress and grief. For my part I was most disappointed to lose hope of an heir, but now, after the events that have happened under this roof, I believe there is a definite malfunction in her make-up; perhaps it is a blessing that we have no offspring ... and now, Catherine, I have no further wish to discuss the woman.'

I was obliged to be silent, but determined to speak more to Helen the next day. Later, in the privacy of our rooms, Thomas saw fit to caution me about her.

'You seem to have taken an interest in this person,' he began didactically, 'I can't see why, but it is in excess of normal dutious concern. She has been known to erupt into violence and savagery; she is constantly under surveillance and she does not ameliorate, nor respond to treatment of any kind. Let me make it clear to you that I will allow you to spend time with her only on condition that you are never alone in her presence ... by all accounts she is fiendish cunning.'

I made no reply because it was obvious that my brother had been whining and simpering about his marital problems, and Thomas had accepted it all without question.

The strange creature preyed on my mind the following day, I tried to dispel her from my thoughts by the reading of a new French novel, but to no avail.

At tea-time, when the house was quiet, and Thomas and Edward had set out to survey the pasture-land and sheep, I made my way to Helen's room once more. The sharp-faced maid let me in without a word; I heard her chair scrape back to its position in front of the door as I closed it behind me.

Helen's face lit up a mere fraction when she beheld me and I took a chair by the side of her bed.

'I thought you might like me to read to you,' I suggested carefully.

'No, I would not; I would like to talk, I am never allowed to talk to anyone...' then, she stooped towards me and hissed low, 'they think I am insane, but I *know* I am insane and I don't care a fig.'

I found this an interesting point of view, always having believed that the insane were the only ones who could not see their own sickness. It made me smile involuntarily, and she responded to the smile with a barking laugh. I was not sure how to continue, and upon what subject we could converse, but she soon solved the problem.

'I have just lost a child,' she said.

'I am indeed sorry to hear that,' I replied, watching her small vacant eyes as they scuttled about in her head.

'Yes,' she continued: 'my body swelled up, and I felt much nausea, my breasts expanded and I could feel the quickening within me; but' ... and here her voice began to rise and there was much agitation in her movements, 'nobody would believe me, I know they did not believe I was with child. O, they were kind and considerate but they would not buy clothing for the child, they would not get me a cot and blankets and a perambulator.'

I felt most disquieted and wondered how best to turn the conversation to less distressing matters; but then her voice came out, as though pressed through fine muslin; very still and clear and tight, she said: 'And then, one day, everything went away. I had been waiting, sitting quietly, not moving with haste; I was waiting for the baby. And when I thought it was about to come, suddenly my belly began to subside, the pains went, my breasts flattened, and the movement – there was nothing inside me. It had gone away, again.'

She lay very still, rubbing her hand occasionally across her mouth.

'I am so sorry, indeed I am,' I said gently. 'Was this

the first time you lost a child?'

'No,' she said, 'no, it has happened before, and now they think I will never have one, so they will not buy the clothes. But if he let them buy the clothes I am sure the child would come; it has nearly come. I know it has been inside me, I have felt it move, heard its heart, known it. And now I feel this terrible loss, this gaping wound inside me, bleeding and easing nothing. My hands are empty – I have nothing to hold.'

She wept bitterly, and her face, furrowed by tears, seemed a hundred years old. How bitterly I felt her grief, how strongly I sensed that she was wronged in this great old house. But I could see no hope for her: she was considered mad, her children were her illusions; they could not take them away from her but her spirit was truly broken.

I left the room much upset, and with an overwhelming sense of helplessness. The maid again slipped in after me, tossing the same sneer through the door as she slowly closed it.

My mind then began a strange journey; Helen had instilled some of her terror into me. A great fear came over me; a certainty that I was with child. I had not faced up to it before, but the facts could not be ignored any longer. I felt my body carefully, remembering the small cramps in my back and belly, the faintness when I rose in the morning.

These thoughts bore me down and by the time Thomas appeared in our chamber to dress for dinner I was awash with gloom. It did not escape him.

'What is it child, you are pale, what is it?'

I remained silent, averting my gaze. He continued with his questions: 'Have you been with Edward's wife? Has she done you any harm? Speak, pray...'

'I have been with her but she was quite calm. She tells me she has lost a child; it dis-spirited me, that is all.'

'O, indeed, she has phantom confinements all the time, it is nothing to concern yourself over; it is part of her malady, no doubt – hysterical nonsense.'

How speedily he dismissed her pain, how cruel was his intolerance; I had no further wish to speak to him.

After dinner Thomas and Edward seemed in high spirits. I left them together consuming a bottle of port with much relish; there was something about Edward's camaraderie that sickened me. I went quietly up to see Helen once more; the maid let me in without a word, and she did not bother to respond to my question as to whether Helen was awake or not. It amazed me that a person of such animosity and rudeness should be in sole care of my sister in-law.

Helen was glad to see me, and readily made a place for me to sit beside her on the large bed. She seemed calm and in good spirits, so I asked her the question which had been puzzling me for some time: 'Why did you marry my brother, Helen?'

I thought perhaps she might be offended, but she was not; she began to speak freely, but carefully, as though she wanted to be sure she was being quite honest.

'I married him, I think, because he seemed quite strong; he told me what to do, and took my decisions upon himself. I was at the time disinterested in my Fate, apathetic as to what became of me. I think he realized this, and in some way it made him feel he had a hold over me, or could have without too much opposition.'

'Yes, I can see how that might appeal to Edward,' I murmured.

'I never contradicted anything he said at first; I was in a strange frame of mind, much saddened by recent events ... it was only later in our marriage, when I had returned more to my normal self, that my intelligence began to assert itself. Things he said angered me, and I was wont to disagree with him, which he cannot bear,' she said, nervously beginning to pluck at the coverlet.

'Go on,' I said gently.

'Well, this caused conflicts between us, and one occasion comes to mind most vividly. A few business friends of his had dined with us, charming people, and I had actually dared to question a point of his. It was something trivial – to do with the penal system – but he was enraged. He turned towards me with real anger and then, just as abruptly, went silent for the rest of the evening.'

She halted again, but I felt sure there was more to the story, and that she wished to reveal it, yet something kept her back.

'And what transpired after that?' I asked.

'I should like to speak of it, and I do feel that you would understand and not misconstrue what I am about to say. Still, he is your brother, and it is a most intimate matter ...'

'Have no fear on that point, Edward and I have never been close, I have always found it impossible to have any real feelings for him.'

She looked thoughtful.

'I'm sorry,' I said, 'I interrupted your story, pray continue.'

'Well, when the people had left, he sat, I recall, looking very flushed and vexed, consuming large glasses of brandy. I felt some remorse that I was the cause of his misery and determined to make amends. I went upstairs and prepared for bed. In the midst of this Edward stormed into the room, glass in hand. He stood glaring at me. I went up to him, and did something unusual: I kissed him upon the mouth and said I was sorry. He recoiled a little. And then a most alarming thing ... I do not think I can speak of it ...'

'You will probably feel better if you bring it out

into the open,' I suggested; but in truth I was consumed with interest and more concerned with easing that than her conscience.

'For the disclosure to have any clarity, I must reveal to you that at this time Edward and I had been married almost a year, and' – here she leaned forward and said in a lowered voice: 'and our marriage had not been consummated.'

'You felt a – repugnance for him?' I suggested carefully.

'No; on the contrary, he appeared to have no desire for me. In fact I found his attitude very hurtful, and did not know what to do about it; any small advance on my part was quickly repulsed.'

She seemed upset by this, and her eyes began careering about in her head once more. I was about to let the matter drop when she began to speak again:

'On the evening I was referring to, after he had retreated from my kiss, he walked into his dressing room. I watched him walk and detected a slight uncertainty in his gait. He did not reappear for some time, so I got into bed, presuming he would spend the night in his dressing room, as he did quite frequently. I was falling off to sleep when he approached my side of the bed. He looked strange, agitated and obviously in some state of ebriety. He fell upon my person, and I noted a most vicious and determined look in his face, coupled strangely with a look of uncertainty, as though he were expecting me to reject him. I did very little, feeling it wisest to remain passive. He then leapt off me, stood up, and displayed to me, triumphantly his, his...' she faltered here, but soon continued '...I was greatly alarmed by this procedure but managed to say: "Edward, come to me." He began to laugh, horrifically, and fled the room.'

I was as deeply shocked by this disclosure as she was in making it. 'Did this ever happen again?'

'Yes, on one other occasion; when, I recall, I was trying to broach the subject of children. He reacted then in a similar way, perhaps even worse; yes, definitely worse. I was telling him how desperately I wished for a child. He immediately began to accuse me of trying to use him as a breeding animal, and of not caring for him. I denied this, but he insisted that I had no feelings for him, and moreover that no one had ever entertained any feelings for him. Then, he seemed to soften and acquiesce. He moved slowly over to me and started to caress me; he seemed to be trying to excite me to some passion, and having done so, he just as swiftly withdrew, left the bed and spent the remainder of the night in his dressing room.

'I lay stunned, unable to comprehend his extraordinary behaviour, and determined not to expose myself to such madness again. Perhaps, Catherine, you might be able to explain this to me; perhaps there is something in his past life that might account for it: such blatant malevolence. I have often suffered horrible mental cruelty from him, and I cannot see why. I do not think I have given him any real cause of complaint, though naturally incidents like the ones I have referred to have made me very wary of him now.'

How could I answer this wretched creature?

Slowly I said, 'I lived in the same house as Edward up to the time he was twenty-three, and indeed I often saw this acrimony, this deep resentment of which you speak ... but I cannot be sure whence it comes. I had hoped that marriage to you ... I think that the best thing I can do is to try and understand Edward a little better – for both our sakes.'

19

We were to leave Kent on Sunday, but before we went Thomas was anxious to take me down to the sea at Hastings. He had spent some happy holidays there in his youth and wanted me to see the place. I was pleased with the thought of seeing the sea once more.

At Hastings it was bright and sunny and a few urchins made castles in the sand and paddled up to their knees. How carefree they seemed: shoeless, sockless, holding their skirts up and jumping the blue waves. We walked along the esplanade; it was a long walk and Thomas was disheartened by the stalls and tea shops sprouting along the way.

I felt weak suddenly and requested to sit down. Thomas was concerned and would know the cause. I replied that the smell of the seaweed made me feel most nauseous. We sat a while and then returned to the carriage, and in due course, to Edward's house to take our leave.

I went in to say goodbye to Helen and to assure her that I would write to her, and hoped she would reciprocate. She seemed a little alarmed by my departure.

'I wish you might stay for a long time, Catherine. I thought you were my friend, and now you too desert me. No one speaks to me here; Edward never visits me and the maid has said he is attempting to have me put away.' She was holding her favourite doll and was a most piteous sight.

'I am sure we will meet again soon, Helen,' I said, some instinct telling me that Edward had not yet accomplished the design he had for me.

'No,' she said faintly, 'we will not meet again, I feel sure. I sense bad things stirring in this house. Since the baby, well, since my loss, Edward will not come near me; I think he finds me repulsive.'

'O, no, indeed not, you must not think such things; he has been perplexed with business matters.' But by her look I knew she was not fooled, and I had a sudden thought that perhaps it was the 'fools and madmen' who held the knowledge, and not we so-called sane ones.

'Will you do me the honour of taking this doll?' she asked.

'Oh, I could not; she is your favourite; if you like I would be happy to possess one of the others,' I replied.

'No, you must take Mathilda, I insist,' she said, thrusting the faded doll at me. I took it, and she pulled the cord at the back so that the child's wail issued forth once more. She smiled happily and I felt uneasy at her odd and altered condition.

'I too have a gift for you,' I said, lifting a square packet from the floor and handing it to her.

She opened it with the eager, expectant fingers of a child, ripping off the paper wrapping in excitement. Inside was a small vanity box I had found at Hastings, made of beech wood and covered with small glazed shells of many shades. She was greatly pleased with the gift. I left her then with some sadness, her blank eyes followed me to the door as the whey-faced maid took my place.

Before we left I contrived to spend a few moments alone with Edward in the drawing room.

'Well, Edward, I have been a good companion to your wife for this week-end, which was apparently your desire. I have come to feel affection for her, and some sympathy, sentiments you sadly do not seem to feel. She tells me you decline to go near her.'

'She disgusts me. I am in no way responsible for her madness. It is inherited; her mother was the same; it is nothing to do with me.'

'In any event, Edward, she is a very intelligent person, and could no doubt be helped with some kindness and understanding; you cannot put her in an asylum. I have heard fiendish things of such places.'

A rush of feverish words sprang to his lips: 'You do not understand,' he snapped. 'It is easy to feel sympathetic, spending a few days with Helen. She is mad, but at times she seems quite rational. The frightful thing about her malady is that she is exceedingly plausible, and she is well able to trick people – as she has obviously tricked you. I cannot continue to live in this whirlpool: it has purloined my peace of mind, my sanity. She tricks the maids; sets fire to her bedclothes; confuses me at times with her Papa and tries to entice me into her bed. She insists at all times on examinations of her internals by our doctor and demonstrates a most lubricious nature. She will surely drive me mad if I am not rid of her.'

'Yet, there must be *something* you can do to help, Edward. She craves your affection...'

Then with a vengeance he turned his attack on me: 'You have always been the same, you say it is my fault, our family have always done that. I had a chance with Helen, I thought, but she could not care for me either. But mark my words, I have not done with you, sister, I am going to make you pay – and I have the means ... I have not done with you!'

I walked out of the house immediately and got into the carriage. Thomas joined me after saying his goodbye to Edward. He could not understand why I was so pale and angry; I could not explain. I looked up at Helen's room as we drove slowly down the long drive; but there was no sign of her.

I was so glad to be going home. The day was balmy

and the carriage edged along at a restful pace. The fields were green and flowers budded and danced in the hedgerows; the smell of lilac floated in from time to time.

And how good it was to be driving up to our house; russet and restful it seemed after our time away. The staff greeted us joyfully and had prepared a fine dinner. Thomas, too, is happy to be home, never being one to enjoy other people's company for too long; he is glad to be back to his books and familiar fireside.

Now I am eager to get back to the cottage in Cornwall and continue with my story.

20

When we arrived back from our jaunt by the sea, Mamma was extremely vexed at the state of my hair and clothes, and set us to unpacking forthwith.

Christopher and I took a small room right at the top of the house; it was obviously a room for two maids but we were very happy with it. It was small, with cold, rough walls painted white, wooden scrubbed floorboards and floral curtains. The wall sloped steeply down from the ceiling on one side and another wall contained a neat round window that overlooked rough scrub land.

Edward's room was one floor down, as was Mamma's; then there was the drawing room and a tiny music room with an old piano on the first floor, and pantries, kitchen and dining room on the ground level. Everything was finished with great simplicity; the furniture was comfortable but sparse; the white walls clean, with a faint smell of fungus and damp. The drawing room had a fine collection of blue plates, which matched the deep pile of the rugs; there was a big hard chaise covered in the same fabric as the drapes – a lovely plummy colour. And very agreeable it all was.

We slept well that night, with the sweet husky voice of the sea humming in our ears – how far away it seemed. I woke the next morning with the sun shining through the round window, tickling my face with its warm fingers. I woke first, and the weasel sneezed and snuggled down into my shoulder once more.

'Get up, get up!' I urged. 'We can go down to the sea.' He was up in a flash, and into his clothes before I was. Mamma was having breakfast when we got downstairs, and the maids were rushing about with feather dusters and mops. We had scrambled eggs and scones and tea.

It was the beginning of August, as I have said, and extraordinarily warm. I made a resolution that I would encourage and help Christopher in all his pursuits, so that he might relax and forget about the things that tormented him so. Mamma obviously had made a resolution to spend time with us, and look after us in a way she had not done hitherto. She suggested we all go off with baskets to gather blackcurrants and raspberries down the lanes, so she could make a splendid pudding for us.

Mamma and I put on our hats; I wore a dark dress for fear of spilling the blood of the fruit all down myself. We set off in wonderful spirits; I was happy to observe that the set line around my brother's mouth eased a little. We took the path that eventually led to the sea, but branched off towards the farmland and found ourselves amid winding lanes, bordered with heavy bushes laden with berries. I was constantly caught putting the blackberries in my mouth and not the basket. Their little furry bodies stained our fingers and mouths and I wanted to rub their juice all over me. Mamma informed me it was a fine beauty treatment but she'd rather I did it when I was older and could clean myself afterwards. Even Edward was full of mirth, and he was not in the habit of laughing. I began to feel a trifle guilty that the weasel and I left him out of everything because of our closeness to each other. It had clearly left its mark, because he had become very solitary, and found it difficult to speak to people for very long without rushing off to the comfort of his books or his inner self. Yet at the same time he often wanted to annoy Christopher, to imitate him in a slightly cruel way; Christopher responded with annoyance and contrived to be rid of him on these occasions.

But on this day we all wanted to be friends. And Mamma encouraged it. She looked delicious in her summer outfit. Her hat sat neatly on top of her folded hair; with a ribbon tied in a soft knot beneath that definitive chin; her cheeks were rosy and her brown eyes sparkled. Away from the rush of everyday life she was happy to be with us, and determined that we should all get to know each other better and have a good time with her.

'I can smell the cows in the fields behind these bushes,' Christopher called to me from his position much higher up in the lane. I ran up to him and climbed on his back to see over the hedges; lovely fat black cows they were; we did not see cows often and their slow heavy gait amused us greatly. Mamma busied herself collecting the berries we could not reach, and her lovely white hands were scratched by the prickles, though strangely she seemed not to care.

When our baskets were full we took them home and chattered together and said how beautiful everything was; and how nice the air smelt and how good it was to be in the country. We had a glass of ginger pop at home while Mamma got the picnic things together so we might go down to the sea. We set off once more, with wicker basket and rug, and a large beach parasol so that Mamma should not be exposed to the sunshine and catch freckles.

When I could no longer content myself with the elegant pace of Mamma's promenade I set off, with great speed and hair flying, down to the sea. Christopher had some difficulty in catching up with me. We took a new and more treacherous way down; Mamma and Edward found a longer but simpler descent.

The flies buzzed round the seaweed; dead crabs were used to terrify Mamma. Edward disrobed in a discreet corner of the cave, and, attired in his long grey woollen bathing suit, he leapt into the sea with great gusto. We watched sceptically from the sand; saw him chopping away at the waves, ducking and fighting his way through until he had reached his own private rock and felt at peace.

There was not a soul around; not even the sound of another person in the distance. How it pleased us; I had often felt in Brighton that I would like to brush up all the bodies on the beach into a giant dustpan and put them at a generous distance from myself.

Mamma looked thoughtful; after she had pondered awhile she declared: 'Edward seems alarmed to find himself with all of us at the same time; he is quite content with me on my own, or even with you or Christopher, separately, but never together. I wonder why it is?' But then she began unwrapping linen parcels of bread and chicken and pies and forgot the matter.

We had a swim and then a fine picnic, and were forbidden to enter the water for at least two hours. Mamma settled herself happily in the shade and took out her sketching pad and pencils and began to draw the sea. We were both rather amused by this, because it was some time since Mamma had done any sketching; and we well recalled the scenes between her and Father in the past over this subject. She was a little hurt by our laughter and the weasel told me to be still. She became defensive.

'I'll have you know that as a girl my papa thought I had much talent. A gentleman was even hired to come in and give me artistic lessons, and I did extremely well.'

'But, why don't you ever finish them, Mamma?' enquired Christopher.

'I'll thank you not to come out with the comments of your late father,' she snapped. 'I do not have time to finish them. Before I met your father I used to go often to Kew Gardens and do sketches of all the exotic plants and flowers. I finished them then, but as I grew older I got more impatient with things, and more aware of my limited ability.'

We watched Mamma silently for a moment or two, and, once satisfied that she was fully absorbed in her art, we set off in search of the lighthouse far over to the left of the cliffs. The cliffs here were steeper and sharper; and I had to stop myself from looking down, because the great depth and the shouting sea below made me dizzy.

The lighthouse was not as far away as it had seemed. And it was not in the sea as I had expected. It was set on quite high land, and as we neared it, it began to look less like a lighthouse altogether. It had a neatly kept path leading up to the door, with flower beds on either side; and the door had a bright and shiny brass knocker on it.

When we reached the door we were not sure how to proceed. 'Shall we knock and ask the lighthouse keeper if we may look around?' I suggested.

Christopher was looking through a window and I did the same. There was much disorder in the way of old ropes, old steel crowbars, buckets, rusted tins and a mound of newspapers. The place took on rather a sinister note, particularly when a large black cat jumped on the window-sill from the inside and sneered at me through the glass.

'I am not sure that I like the look of this lighthouse, Christopher,' I said nervously.

But he pushed open the door with no hindrance from a lock, and I was obliged to follow. Inside it smelt damp and we began to whisper, for no reason other than the gloom of the place and the fear that we might be trespassing. But it did not seem possible that anyone could live here. My brother, extraordinarily brave for once, was climbing the staircase as though propelled by some unseen being from behind.

The iron stairs led to another room – it had the vague appearance of a kitchen: there was a bunch of withered carrots on a long wooden table. The cat had followed us up and was observing us suspiciously from one corner of the table. Up the stairs again. This time a door barred the opening at the head of the stairs. We looked at each other a moment. Christopher knocked quietly; there was no reply, so he slowly turned the knob. The cat waited.

It was dark inside; the only light came from the very small window on the far side of the room. We stood by the door for a moment and looked around. It was a drawing room, with heavy old chairs of pale blue, and a small mahogany table. The walls were cluttered with pale faces in heavy gilt frames: demure, damask damsels smiled listlessly from velvet surrounds. On a stand there was a glass dome containing a stuffed bird surrounded by a mounting of shells and painted twigs.

Then I saw her. Her presence fitted so well into her surroundings that the shock of someone being there was not so great. At first sight she might have been an evil grimalkin, so fierce was the stare from those cold porcelain eyes. She did not stir at our intrusion, did not appear even to blink, or breathe. No one spoke. I remember wondering why she wore a shawl over her shoulders on such a warm day. I sensed that she was waiting for me to speak. Her skin was almost transparent, it was so fine and fair; I could detect small blue veins around eyes that did not blink; I considered for a moment whether she might be dead.

'I'm sorry Ma'am, we did not think anyone lived here,' I said.

Still she said nothing, but she appeared to be willing

us to come nearer. We stood in front of her and now she seemed very old and frail and in no way evil. My brother began rubbing his nose – a sure sign of discomfort.

After what seemed a great age, she said flatly: 'I live here, this is my house, and you have no right to intrude. What do you want?'

We attempted to explain that we had been under the impression that lighthouses directed ships, and we had had no idea that people made houses out of them.

'People don't. I do.'

By her tone I knew that we'd offended her, and it hurt me to have done so. I did not feel frightened of her any more. I noticed that her hair was very thick and white and that the porcelain eyes slanted upwards at each end most delicately. Her eyebrows were too heavy for her elfin face, and her mouth was faintly blue. Her hands lay folded, thin and translucent, upon her lap and her entire carriage was perfectly erect – no part of her back actually touched the chair. I found her magnificent.

'My name is Catherine, and Christopher is my brother. We are staying just over the cliffs in a coastal cottage for three weeks with our Mamma.'

She smiled, and the eyes tilted further upwards; it was a sad, reminiscent smile and she took it back quickly. She gestured that we should sit down.

'How long have you lived here?' Christopher asked politely.

'Since my marriage, forty-seven years ago. My husband was in charge of this lighthouse – of course it was a proper lighthouse then, though fewer ships came this way in those days. Now they are threatening to pull it down, and put up a modern steel lighthouse.'

We did not ask her about her husband; we just knew that he was dead. We all slipped into a silence and then she said abruptly: 'They'll tell you soon enough if you stay around these parts a while ... the people around here ... they'll tell you I pushed him from the top window. It is impossible – the windows are too small. But nobody visits me because of it. His body was found on the rocks below; they accuse me because his boat was never found. Yet I am not troubled by the absence of other people. People are only a trial, when you have lived closely with a man who made others unnecessary.'

We felt sad for her; she would have hated that, I felt sure. We moved to go, but she prevented us by asking our ages. She seemed surprised when we gave them.

'Remarkable. No wonder I have always felt intimidated by children. They seem so wise. And you two – you watch me with patience and tolerance, as though you comprehend the nature of what I am saying.'

'Do you have no children?' I asked.

'There was a little girl once, she died when she was but four months old – her heart just stopped.'

'Do you go out of here at all?' Christopher asked, because she looked as though she had grown into the wood of her chair, and could not possibly move.

'No, never in the day. Sometimes, when it is growing dark, I venture outside for a moment. Perhaps you noticed the flowers outside the front of the lighthouse? A gentleman does them for me. I hardly ever see them, but he leaves me milk and eggs and sometimes a fresh fish or chicken.'

'Who is he?' I asked, curiosity prevailing as always.

'He is a man I knew as a girl,' she smiled wanly, straightening her hair. Then she rose stiffly from her chair and walked slowly out through the door behind her.

We looked at one another and then left; down the dingy, resounding stairway and out into the well-kept garden with the flowers kept so lovingly by the gentleman. We walked back slowly to the beach, not speaking.

Mamma had finished a few pastel sketches, we told her they were lovely, as indeed they were. Edward, who was fairer in complexion than either Christopher or I, had got burnt in the sun and Mamma was plastering him with calamine; only his two dark eyes peered out from the white mask.

We told Mamma a little about the lady of the lighthouse. She was rather perturbed, and remarked it would be wiser not to return. But we had other plans. I had taken to the old lady and felt she might have wonderful stories to tell.

We went home then; it took much longer than we'd anticipated. Mamma simply could not resist stopping every time she spied a bush laden with raspberries or blackberries; and she was not content to move on until she had stripped the bushes of their luscious bounty. She sang while she was picking, and snapped every time we pushed an insensitive hand into the midst of her berries to stuff into our mouths.

That night she cooked us a most remarkable pudding. I watched her cooking up the raspberries and blackberries with lots of sugar, stirring them under her warm gaze. Then she made some sponge mixture and poured it all over the top of the fruit.

Into the oven it went, all golden; and when it was done the sides of the pudding had risen to high proportions on every side, and the middle had sunk away – leaving a perfectly round, perfectly pink hole in the centre. Mamma was a trifle distressed by this culinary failure, but it was the best pudding we had ever had. And though we asked her many times to repeat it, it simply never went wrong in the same lovely way again, however hard she tried.

21

After a day or two spent in this gentle fashion, Mamma became restless once more and determined that we should all take an excursion to St Ives. She told us loquaciously of its unspoilt character, and promised that we might see the little fishing girls busy at their work and watch the fishermen tending their boats and nets. I did not particularly wish to go; I feared there might be many people there. Mamma said there would be a nice watering-place, but I favoured the seclusion of our own little cove. However, not wishing to spoil Mamma's happy frame of mind, and somewhat fearful of one of her combustions should I refuse, I agreed that it was a fine plan.

We set off very early in a hired trap, and reached St Ives in under an hour. It was indeed a comely place, with many stalls selling sea wares and shells. Mamma found it all delightful. We travelled a little further along to find a watering-place, and without much ado we were in the water, while Mamma took for once to the bathing machine and spent a happy half-hour completely obscured from our view. Then she returned to sit quietly on the beach beneath her parasol while her flannel swimming apparel dried in a discreet spot on the rocks.

Christopher and I felt ill at ease amongst the other people on the beach, and were eager to return. Happily, Mamma was impatient to be moving on to fresh subjects so we vacated the place in the early afternoon and headed for home. It was an uncomfortably hot ride and we arrived home tired and petulant and had to be revived with much cold lemonade.

The next time Mamma decided to take us off for an expedition of the countryside, we begged to stay at home; and remembering well our ungracious complaints from the visit to St Ives, she was happy to leave us behind and set off to Truro with Edward for companion and guide.

They left very early. Mamma forbade us to go down to the sea in her absence, and we acquiesced readily. The day began in a cloudy fashion, and Christopher set to cutting the grass with an old scythe he found in a shed at the bottom of the garden. By the time he had completed this task the sun was shining fiercely and the clouds had floated off into infinity. He was very hot and we lay in the grass for an hour or so, talking, until the sun made me dozy and I dropped off to sleep while he read in the shade.

When I awoke the maids had left, leaving mushroom pie and lettuce for our lunch. I was a little burnt by the sun, so we had lunch in the shade of the house, sitting on Christopher's freshly cut grass. The weasel found a big brown bottle of cider and we drank rather more of this than we should. We had not had cider before and my head began to float slightly from the unaccustomed intoxication. We lay side by side in the tangy scent of severed grass, and soporifia began to set in. I felt I could not possibly move even though a hurricane rolled over me; Christopher was talking quietly about a big yellow butterfly that had alighted on one of our partly-consumed apples and was sucking away the last of its sweetness. There was a buzzing sound close by from the insects, and the buzzing penetrated my head and refused to go away. The heat had gone through to the deep tunnels of my brain; I felt prickly all over and sluggish. I went indoors and put my head under the tap, letting the cold water douse me thoroughly; it ran down my hot back and front and I felt exhilarated and refreshed instantly. Christopher came in to find me and I threw water all over him; I was a little uncertain on my feet from the cider and he laughed unkindly.

'Come and lie here, Catherine,' he said, lying down himself and closing his eyes.

I went to shut out the sun by closing the white shutters of the kitchen, then returned to look down at him for a second before I lay beside him on the cold slates of the floor. I kissed his nose, which was sun-red, and his black eyes. They fluttered open and I could see my face tiny in his eyes; he smiled, but not the usual sad smile. I moved my hands almost clumsily, and certainly shakily, because of my inebriated state, down the length of his body. I looked at his member which reminded me of a cherry. The weasel then woke from his drowsiness of the floor, and looked a trifle embarrassed. He moved my dampened hair, and straightened it with care, looking closely at me the while. He sat up and put his arms about me and we lay back on the floor again. His fingers touched me gently for a minute and then he was inside and safe and the security came through to me too. And, as it always was, so it was that day: simple, uncomplicated, totally tender and bodily and good. There seemed no question why it should not always continue in this way, and no reason why our bodies or our minds should change or suddenly not fit.

We lay quietly together for a while, and then set off for the sea, knowing Mamma could not return for some time. We talked about many things that day: of the places we would go to and the things we could do when we were grown up.

The sea that afternoon was quite different. It was rough and the waves high; and the sound of its speech was shrill and angry. We thought a storm might be approaching, for suddenly the sky came down and a darkness hovered over the waves. We did not want to go home, so we set off in search of our lady of the lighthouse. The winds fair whipped us along, and we kept a safe distance from the cliffs, for indeed there was menace in the sea that day and I felt she was willing us down into her deep waters.

The darkness descended, and rain began to fall lightly. We ran with great velocity towards the lighthouse, and up the clunking stairs till we reached her door. I knocked, loudly, because the rain was coming down heavily now and it was difficult to hear. She did not answer, so we went inside, to find her seated in the same chair, but looking out of the window this time, and not towards us. We approached her back; she did not turn around; so we were obliged to walk round to the front of her. Her face was so beautiful: so contained and controlled – it was not a face without passion, but a face where the passion was muted and held firmly in check.

'We were out on the cliffs when the storm began, so we came to you,' I said. She smiled.

'I'm glad you came, I think we are going to have a wonderful storm. The breakers are fierce and high, and I can hear much displeasure in the voice of the ocean.'

'May we go up to the top of the lighthouse to get a better view?' I asked. She nodded, and we leapt up a long flight to the very skull of the lighthouse. My main purpose for coming up here was to satisfy myself as to the size of the windows, and I was much delighted to see that they were indeed much too small for a man to be propelled through. We had a most magnificent view of the sea: like a giant cauldron it was churning and spitting, the waves frothing at the mouth.

When we returned she asked me abruptly: 'Was I

not right about the window, Catherine?'

'Yes, indeed, they are much too small, as you said.' She smiled at my lack of guile, and I felt that we understood one another well.

We sat beside her in the darkening hour, until the shadows swallowed the sea and we could detect nothing of the water apart from the white manes of the breakers. It was late, and I feared Mamma might be back and fretting about our whereabouts; so reluctantly we determined to set out through the darkness. The rain was not so heavy, and if we waited any longer the last faltering traces of light would disappear before we had time to get home.

'We will come back and see you again, if you do not mind,' Christopher said to the old lady.

'I should be very glad,' she replied graciously. She told us the simplest way to return, and let us go with stern admonitions that we take best care to keep to the path.

Out among the elements we were tossed about like paper in the wind; we clung together and ran back across the track which led us away from the cliffs and the sea's siren, and inland towards our cottage. Happily, Mamma had not returned, and in fact we became fearful for her safety; but it gave us time to change out of our drenched clothing and put on dry things before we heard the carriage approaching. By this time, we were sitting cosily in the kitchen looking as though we had never moved from this position.

'Your hair is wet, Catherine, you have not been out in the storm have you?' was Mamma's first remark.

'O, no, indeed not Mamma, I merely stepped outside for a moment to see if you and Edward might be coming,' I replied.

22

The days thereafter were sleepy and good and gentle. We busied ourselves with swimming and walking and exploring. We went nearly every day to the lady of the lighthouse and she was always happy to see us. She said very little, and in fact never told us the exciting stories I had expected, but she was a wonderful source of peace; and I felt drawn towards her containment and gentleness. The quick smiles she would throw at us, and then rapidly take back; the formal way she sat in her chair and the quiet repose of her hands and demeanour were a great joy to me. I hoped I might be the same as an old lady; the turbulent urges and impulses within me subsided in her presence, and after leaving her the felicity remained with me for hours.

When the evenings came we were so tired we went to bed immediately after supper. Christopher would read to me; sometimes we would write stories or tell each other imaginary tales or relate our dreams. Often we would sit silent and gaze spellbound at the moon's cleanliness, and wish we might visit her in a great air balloon.

The simple pattern was about to end, however; and Mamma's dedication to care for her children was all spent before the first week was over. She announced in a rushed way one morning that the Frenchman would be coming down to stay with us. No one spoke; Christopher looked gloomy (I'd always suspected he hated Mamma taking a lover); Edward pretended not to have heard and continued with his dissection of a butterfly; I sniffed, and Mamma beamed, unaware of our displeasure.

From that moment on, our private family life of pic-nics and puddings and Mamma's undivided and devoted attentions swiftly came to an end. She began to busy herself in plans to please him. I asked her saucily where he might be sleeping, suggesting he might be given the attic room (which was very stuffy, and could be made suffocating if we blocked up the small sky-light and door). We deeply resented the fact that he was coming down to ruin our holiday; and even I, who had hitherto been quite defensive about him, felt most distressed by the news. Mamma replied that he would be sleeping in the room next door to hers – where else was there for him to sleep?

She began to prepare for his arrival. The maids were set to dusting every nook and cranny, all the furniture was polished and the house was scrubbed from one end to the other; the gentle disorder we had been living in, with books strewn over the floor, and maps tossed on to tables and chairs, ceased from that morning. Mamma, as I have said before, was not a tidy or disciplined person; she further annoyed us because we saw that she was altering her basic personality to please the Frenchman, and that seemed to bode evil.

She began cooking tarts and French pastries and pâtés and all manner of delicacies in his honour. She became impatient with us, and decided she could no longer accompany us down to the sea, because her skin had darkened somewhat since she had been in the country and she must try to restore her former pale and bleached complexion.

It is possible that Mamma felt that the Frenchman was growing tired of her, for she went to elaborate pains to make herself beautiful for him. She made a wonderful concoction of rose-water, oatmeal, cucumber and lemon juice, stirred it well, and then spread it thickly all over her face, and left it to set. It set into a stiff, white mask which prevented her from smiling or even talking. If she moved her face the mask cracked and caused her pain. This sent Christopher into a fit of laughter, and I, as a more sober observer, banished him from the rest of the proceedings.

Mamma then removed this fearful death mask, and applied coatings of honey and fresh cream. I remember her placing me upon a high chair that she might scrub my freckles away with lemon juice. It was a painful business and she was obliged not to continue due to my noisy objections.

'Catherine, you are growing into a young lady, and it will not do to keep shrieking – the sun blemishes must be removed before they sink too far into the skin and remain there always.'

'But, Mamma, I have no objection to them and the lemon juice is stinging,' I answered with another yell of pain.

'It will be quite apparent to everyone that you have not been wearing your bonnet; one look at your face and your disobedience is betrayed. Besides, I will not have it said that my daughter looks like an urchin. Hold still, I am nearly done.'

Then I was obliged to help her wash all four feet of her dark hair, once with soap; once with lemon juice. The maids were scurrying about like worker bees with buckets and towels. After these ablutions, she curled her hair with tongs and a most unpleasant smell of singeing filled the room. She took to the tub then, and, to my great relief, I was dispatched from the room. Mamma then retired to her bed to lie in total darkness for two hours so that her potions might take effect.

Exactly two hours later, she descended the stairs and walked very carefully into the drawing room; surrounded by that magical aura which we knew to mean she felt there was a transformation about her person. I looked very diligently for some change in her face or form, but she looked exactly the same.

'Well, and how do I look?' she asked imperiously.

We all replied with one voice that she looked absolutely beautiful, and with that she seemed well content.

The Frenchman was due the next day and we went to bed heavy-hearted. I was dis-spirited to observe that Christopher, who had been in fine spirits since the beginning of the holiday, was retreating into his old melancholy. He had been so content: the sunshine had filled him with a new buoyancy, and the old scowl had gone from his face. Now, he was sad again, and full of his usual pessimism, insisting that the Frenchman's arrival would bring about a big change in all directions. He impressed upon me his strong feeling of incipient doom, and though I insisted it would make no real difference to the two of us, he could not be comforted, and I felt again the tautness in his body as he refused to be eased.

In the morning Mamma did not accompany us to the sea: she was making final preparations and was tense and fretful. Edward, Christopher and I walked down the path together, in silence. Edward was morose, Christopher downcast and sullen, and irritated because Mamma was insisting I go down with her to collect the Frenchman from the station that afternoon.

Christopher's prophesy of the night before had depressed me. I settled myself away from him and Edward, and they began to break open mussel shells with large rocks. I could hear the sharp clunk of the rocks smiting the shells; and soon I detected that Edward was at his old game of trying to arouse Christopher to a state of anger. He had not done this for some time – the last time he had so angered Christopher that he'd been punched savagely in the mouth, and had kept his distance since that time.

Today, perhaps because it was sultry and we were

all cross and anxious and unhappy about the French-man's arrival, he began again to taunt Christopher with small unpleasantnesses. Christopher kept his passion in check; but I could feel his slow-burning displeasure rising. Edward continued to badger him; I could not hear the remarks but I knew he was picking on known frailties. Christopher's face grew heavy and ugly, he lifted the rock in his hand. In a flash Edward had hurled Christopher on to his back in the sand, Christopher struggled like a butterfly on a pin under Edward's greater bulk and strength.

'And what are your intentions now, little favourite?' Edward mocked, sitting firmly astride Christopher's legs.

Christopher said nothing, it was always his way with Edward; but it only heightened Edward's cowardly infuriation.

Edward picked up a handful of sand and let it trickle very slowly into Christopher's eyes; even by closing them he could not prevent some of the coarse particles from flying into his eyes. He cursed volubly.

'Edward,' I screamed, rushing over and grasping him by the hair with all my might, 'let him go!'

'Oh, no,' he smiled satanically. 'I've had enough of the pair of you.'

Edward then dealt a vicious blow at Christopher's head and I flew at him, beating him about the head and face with all my strength.

Christopher was then able to escape Edward's clutches, but his eyes were blinded, so he could do little. Edward pushed me away, and, holding fast to a rock, he began to back off slowly.

'Get back, both of you, or I'll mash your brains, don't move or I'll surely throw it.' He was trembling all over and his face had a grey, sunken look about it. He retreated further, and escaped up the rocks and on to the path.

Christopher and I remained stunned for a moment: for Edward to behave in such a way was quite beyond our experience of him. To be sure, he had always taunted and vexed Christopher, but in the past he had known when to stop. This was the first time he had actually struck a blow. I was most alarmed.

The weasel and I walked slowly back into the shade; he would tolerate no comfort; turning from me he muttered savagely: 'It has been a long time. He has hated me quietly ever since I punched him, and long before, in all probability. And I never knew it. He has kept all that hatred inside him all this while. Well, I know it now, and I shall watch him closely. He will not get me again.'

So his prophesy appeared to be coming true: things were indeed changing, and the underground tension between my two brothers had emerged like a sinister green shoot above the soil.

The day was heavy with evil. We went home and there was a nasty and silent tension between Christopher and Edward: as one entered the room, the other left. Mamma did not appear to notice. She made me put on my cream linen dress and my good bonnet to accompany her to the station.

I looked for Christopher before Mamma whisked me into the waiting carriage, but he was nowhere to be found, and I left with a strong sensation of unease.

23

Mamma and I rode in silence — I knew and she knew that my presence was simply to lend a small air of propriety to the proceedings.

We waited for the train to come in; it was late and Mamma's anxiety increased every moment. When it arrived she strained her eyes up and down its great length for a glimpse of him; I spotted him quite quickly, his sallow, slightly sneaky face above the smart, dark-suited body. Mamma waved her lace handkerchief and moved in his direction. I stayed where I was. She had such a lovely walk; she seemed almost to float along, and yet if you studied her walk carefully it became apparent that she moved her body, particularly her hips, quite strongly. The overall impression however was of an effortless glide, full of grace and dignity; I felt she could go on walking for hours without losing the grace or becoming fatigued.

He descended the steps carefully, and kissed Mamma's hand; as she turned to walk back to me I could see her face, warm and excited, smiling at him with her dimples.

He stood in front of me very formally, lifted my hand briefly to his lips which gave me an uncommon sensation. 'Catherine,' (again the strange 't') 'how well you are looking.'

We settled ourselves in the carriage once more, Mamma sitting beside the Frenchman and myself opposite.

'How has the weather been?' he asked of Mamma.

'O, exceedingly warm and sultry.'

'And are you pleased with the accommodation? I feared it might be a little cramped and uncivilized for you.'

'No, indeed it is perfect, we are well content with everything. It was kind of you to arrange it for us,' Mamma said pointedly, giving me a sharp stare, so that I felt obliged to reiterate her gratitude.

'The beach is very good,' I stammered awkwardly, 'and nobody comes there save us; we have had much fine bathing.' He smiled kindly.

'Perhaps you will let me come bathing with you. It is a sport I very much enjoy.'

'Yes, if you wish, but the waves are very rough and strong at times.'

Mamma and he continued to make polite conversation in this way for the rest of the journey home; he sat very straight and prim resting upon a thin cane; I felt that I was making him ill at ease as usual, and busied myself studying the speeding countryside on either side. After a while Mamma stopped fidgeting and began to chatter quite amiably; I had a strong feeling that she was hardly able to keep her hands from touching him, and this thought interested me much. I began to conjecture as to their intimate relationship; there was definitely much passion in Mamma's nature, I had no doubt, but the Frenchman was so formal and mindful of correctitudes with her I could not be sure of his part. And yet, here he was coming down to live under our roof, with Mamma unchaperoned, so to speak, apart from three children. As Edward had said, it would cause a great scandal were it not for the fact that we were buried in a remote part of Cornwall, away from all society. I had further observed that Mamma had given the maids leave for the next few days. These things did not greatly trouble me, as they did Edward; but I was most curious as to their relationship, and decided to observe them closely in the next few days. Christopher had no doubt that the Frenchman's charm lay in his talent as a lover – he assured me the French were notorious for this; and I noted the fact with some interest.

When we arrived home, Mamma busied herself making the Frenchman feel at home, and offering refreshments. I disappeared down to the sea in search of Christopher. I found him on the cliff, and plonked myself down beside him.

'The Frenchman is at the house now, but there's no need to worry – he's very formal and trying to be pleasant.'

'You found him agreeable then?' he replied tensely.

'No, not really, it just occurred to me that he might realize he is not particularly welcome here, and try to make amends.'

'I went to see her at the lighthouse, she says we may call her Violet,' he said quickly.

'O, you went without me.'

'Well, you were not here. She was very kind and we had a long conversation together, I told her about the Frenchman, and also about Father a little.'

I was a trifle hurt that he had gone without me, and more so because he had obviously been confiding in her in a way that he had only done with me in the past. I felt a little distance spreading itself between us, and I fell silent.

'Today I feel like a stick, or perhaps like a china cup,' he said.

'I know that feeling,' I said, 'it is as if one is going to break in half, or crack – it's a feeling of not being complete.'

'Yes, it is also like the feeling I get sometimes of being a ghost, not having substance really.'

He kissed me on the cheek, and the smile I gave him was not altogether happy. We sat awhile in silence and then slowly made our way home.

That night we all ate solemnly together; Mamma drank too much wine and laughed a great deal. We three sat in comparative silence, watching them, watching each other. The Frenchman was indeed trying to be pleasant: he had brought me a doll, and books for Christopher and Edward. I felt too old for the doll, but she was very small and delicate, and dressed in cream French silk, trimmed with gold cord – more of an ornament than a plaything, I assured myself.

The following morning we all went down to the sea; Mamma did not linger to pick berries, and Christopher and I raced on as was our custom. Edward took another route and kept away from everyone.

We had disrobed and were about to plunge into the water as Mamma and the Frenchman ambled into the shade with an assortment of parasols, hampers and books. Edward swam off to his solitary perch on the rock, and Mamma and the Frenchman settled themselves closely in a shaded corner.

Christopher was a little distant from me and enveloped in his own thoughts; for once the direct line of communication between us suffered an impediment; we were both aware of it and it caused a small tension between us.

The Frenchman entered the water, fashionably attired in brown and gold swimming apparel. His body was so gaunt that the bones around his shoulders and neck prodded the skin almost to piercing point; he was not very agreeable to behold. For all his slight stature, however, he swam strongly out into the sea; I watched his dark head moving rhythmically from side to side. He swam back to me and suggested I go out with him; I protested fear and said I preferred the shallow water. Christopher was observing us very closely and I noted his displeasure and decided that it would be best to humour him. I was confused by his apparent suspicion and coolness towards me; I determined to be very gentle and loving, but to no avail; I could not penetrate his defensive barrier.

The atmosphere was not good and it continued so throughout the day. By the evening Christopher's depression was becoming severe, he was not speaking to anyone and had retired totally into himself. I was greatly grieved because he had not been in this state of mind since Father's death. I could not believe that the bout with Edward had been the cause of it, even taken with the Frenchman's arrival; the feeling persisted that in some way it was my fault.

There was, I think now, some foolish desire in me to take his pain as my own; I could not bear to be separated or distinct from any condition of his; it had to be related to me.

At breakfast the following morning I noticed an interesting behaviour in the Frenchman: it concerned the eating of his boiled egg. He severed the top of it with one clean stroke and ate the contents without making the smallest disorder on the plate: his spoon never touched the plate, no salt, no pepper, nothing; and when he had finished the egg he placed the top very carefully inside the egg-cup, and turned the egg over so that it looked whole and untouched. Now, if this had happened but once, it should not have interested me so, but it happened every morning, and there he was left with what appeared to be a virgin egg on a virgin plate.

'Why do you eat your egg that way?' Christopher snapped. I was amazed once more at the extraordinary communion between our minds: I was about to ask the same question.

The Frenchman looked ill at ease and Mamma said crossly: 'Kindly keep your attention on your manners, Christopher, and do not cross-examine people at breakfast.'

The Frenchman however, after a ponder, declared: 'Well, I have not thought of it, to tell you the truth, I have always eaten an egg in that fashion. There is something, perhaps, tragic about the destruction of an egg – it is such a pure, perfect creation – perhaps I like to restore it as much as I can.' He shrugged; I thought it a plausible explanation and felt satisfied; Christopher left the table abruptly.

He remained indoors for the rest of the day. I left him alone and made a collection of stones which I put into a heavy glass jar and filled with water, and watched the colours fuse and complement each other.

At six o'clock in the evening Mamma told me to take the Frenchman to the farm where the maids collected the draught cider. I did not wish to go because I knew it would anger Christopher and might enlarge the rift between us; but Mamma would tolerate no excuses, she was hot and flustered with cooking and she wanted the Frenchman out of the house.

We walked slowly; his gait was metrical, and it took me some time to discover that his left limb dragged slightly. The evening was so peaceful; fluffy pink clouds raced each other across the sky, and a warm breeze stirred the leaves. Very soon I forgot him; I felt as though I had never properly observed things before, and I was absorbed in trying to find images that fitted the objects around me; I was beginning to struggle with words and meanings.

We reached the farmhouse in due course. A small child chased in the chickens, and the farmer sat quietly outside his house watching the sun set; his weathered face looked relaxed and well content. I reflected that it was a good life that he led. I would have liked to have spoken of these things – as I would have done with my brother. But I had difficulty conversing with other people. It seemed to me that grown-up people talked in a small way, avoiding deep or thoughtful matters. Mamma's main topics with the Frenchman appeared to be the price of property, ladies' fashions and other such trivia.

The Frenchman bought the cider and we began the journey home; he offered a little conversation but I resisted this intrusion into my thoughts. However, he did try very hard to please and I softened a little towards him.

We sat down for a short rest in a field, as we had walked some way and my pace had slowed considerably. I was also somewhat concerned about his injured limb. The sun was sinking fast and the gentle dusk was about us. I wished my brother could have seen it; I thought of him sitting moodily in our room. I lay back in the grass; the Frenchman settled himself quietly beside me; his hand was rather close to my own so I moved mine. His face wore that strange, tight mask: he looked tormented, like an animal in a snare. He bent swiftly and kissed me upon the mouth. Strangely, I was not altogether surprised and therefore I did nothing, until I caught sight of his sharp, rat-like features. Then I felt sickened and pushed him away. He noticed the disgust in my face; it caused him pain and he rose quickly and left me.

I rubbed my hand fiercely back and forth across my mouth, trying to erase the hard imprint of his lips. He was walking away very swiftly now, gone was the disciplined stride; he was in confusion and would be rid of me.

I watched him go; feeling an odd mixture of wretchedness and pity.

I slammed the kitchen door behind me; Mamma was not there, only Christopher. He looked up from stirring the sugar round in the sugar bowl – his gaze was intense. I was nervous; he had a fine nose for sniffing trouble or discomfort. He suggested we take a walk down to the shore.

A reluctance to be alone with him washed over me; and a small sense of guilt was creeping about in my stomach. I decided things would be better after I'd told him what had happened, but I was nervous to confess; in his present state of mind he might react in so many ways.

We walked quietly to the sea and sat down in the little cove; he covered my hand with small rivers of sand. I felt dumb and cold. Finally, the words came, and at their conclusion there was a silence between us. Not our usual silence; this was a heavy, unkind silence and neither of us could break it.

Finally he uttered: 'I think you must have encouraged him in some way or he wouldn't have tried anything.' 'I did not.' But, then I stopped and reflected that perhaps I had by lying in the grass. I decided in my first really dishonest moment with him that if this were the case and I had encouraged the Frenchman, even if only to reject him in the end, I would not admit it.

'Did you enjoy him kissing you?' A profound question which I was too innocent to answer cleverly at that time.

'No,' I blurted out too vehemently and too fast, as I recalled that it had not been unpleasant until I had caught sight of his features which had never been anything but repugnant to me.

The silence returned; and I watched the pain spreading slowly across his clever, sensitive eyes and down to his mouth where it settled in a pool. I felt vexed with myself for trying to deceive him, because he knew everything anyway – he understood perfectly the workings of my mind. The injury lay in the lack of trust. The silence grew deep and unbearably painful. I could find nothing to say to him; I was hurt that he did not comprehend that the incident was totally unimportant to me. Yet I could not say that it was.

So the silence returned home with us, and with it a pain that settled deep somewhere in both our bodies. From that time onwards there was a definite gap between us. It closed from time to time, but there was a quality of things being not quite the same again, and a small sadness which settled on everything that we did.

When I woke in the morning Christopher was no longer beside me; his shoes were gone from under the chair. I panicked, and raced downstairs; he was not there. Mamma said she had not seen him; she had breakfast waiting, so I ate something and helped her to clear the things away before heading for the beach.

I felt sure that he would be sitting on our perch near the cove. I walked eagerly in that direction but as I got nearer I noticed I was walking slower and slower — almost dragging my feet. It was most curious; I was actually reluctant to face him. He had not really gone off without me like this before, and I felt it was a deliberate desire to avoid me. It hurt greatly, and brought about the old fear. A fear of things changing; of his face looking at me in an unfamiliar way; of our world altering and growing cold about me.

He smiled when he saw me; the pain was still in his face but it had made its way down to his hands too. They twisted and would not lie still. I sat down beside him and picked up his hands; they were nice hands, but that day they appeared bumpy, as though cold, and the day was not cold.

'I'll go away if you'd rather.'

'No. I'm glad you came; at first I wanted to be by myself but I missed you — I don't know what I want, really.'

'Why do you look so sad?'

'I suppose I'm being silly. The Frenchman, what you

did with the Frenchman, it *has* changed things; I feel very strange...'

'But I am not changed, and you know it is of no significance.'

As I reflect on this, I am made aware of a certain devilry in my nature. Could it be that I fashioned the whole thing in order to centre his pain on me? Did I in fact *have* to tell him about it at all, since it was not important? I think I wanted to grieve him, I wanted to test his love because his behaviour had made me feel insecure and I had to reassure myself, even at his cost. I wish now I had been above that, but I was not.

His sadness was the thing that bound him to me, his complexities, his split nature; the ragged form of his personality affected me in a way that conformity never could.

That day I wanted him to touch me, desperately I wanted him to touch me. But he did not, and I felt bewildered and pained, and could not say so. I could have told him of my pain before, spread it out in front of him like a map which he would look at and read correctly; never misunderstanding a single symbol. I couldn't then, we were too close and too distant, and I could not speak of the new pain.

I wanted, O, how much I wanted to take him in my arms and hold him until the pain went. To make everything better as before; to stop the hands twisting and the tight feeling in my throat from spreading all over.

We walked back together. I stopped and turned towards him and kissed him on the mouth; his mouth was still – it contained no rejection, it was just perfectly still, without feeling – it was like a dead mouth.

24

The Frenchman left, taking with him some of the tension, but leaving a great deal. The silent battle between my brothers continued: they had not spoken to one another since the incident in the sand. The days went by, hot and dry.

One day soon after the Frenchman's departure, a girl in a pony trap called to visit us, and informed us that her Mamma had sent her to invite us all to tea the following day. She had come from a farm just two miles away, and it appeared that her family were close friends of the owners of the cottage.

Mamma decided we would call. Edward would not come, declaring he 'had no wish to associate with farming people'. Christopher and I accompanied Mamma. We clattered up a long, tree-lined drive to a fine old farmhouse and were welcomed by the lady of the house and her daughter, the girl of the day before. Some chickens had escaped from their quarters and were clucking about in disorder in front of the house. The heavy, real smell of it all offended our delicate Mamma and she kept her lace handkerchief firmly to her nostrils.

For our part we were intrigued, never having been so close to a farm before. After we had partaken of a formal tea in a very imposing room filled with comfortable sofas and heavy leather chairs, we left the two Mammas to converse together, and set off with Nancy for an exploration of the property.

She was older than us; I thought she must be near

sixteen – Edward's age. She took us on a grand tour, and seemed amused by all our questions; we were intimidated by her superior knowledge and age.

When she had showed us everything to her satisfaction she took us to a big unused barn strewn with none too clean hay, and offered us some cider which she dragged up from under the hay in one corner. She was watching the weasel with much interest, more than I cared to see, so I kept my eyes firmly upon her.

She had thick, tangled hair that fell about her face in abundance. It was a corn colour, but streaked here and there by the sun, so that some parts were gold, some rusty and some pale blond. She was obviously not in the habit of applying a brush to it too often, because it stood out in a great bush around her face; which was quite pretty. She had strong full lips and she bit the bottom one a great deal (Mamma had once told me that was how to make your lips more exciting to a man). Her eyes sat close together, they were a faded blue colour, and her nose was a pox of freckles which Mamma had noticed with disapproval. Freckles, in Mamma's opinion, were 'the scars of peasants, things that young ladies simply did not have if they kept their hats well down in front and knew what was expected of them'.

Nancy did not know what was expected of her – or perhaps she did. For she sat in the hay with her legs spread out most indecently and her scruffy petticoats flung about in tempting disorder. I noticed Christopher watching her, and in particular the upper parts of her limbs, which sometimes were very much in evidence. The fabric of the dress she was wearing was silky and clung closely to either side of her spread thighs – when the petticoats no longer served as a chaste buffer. My small pure nature was rather disgusted by this – but at the same time I was fascinated and could not keep my eyes off her. She had a big body, long strong legs, golden arms and big breasts. And her hips – she made me feel I had no hips at all! Hers swelled out roundly from her waist on either side, her back arched formidably and soared right out again to set off a melon-shaped bottom.

It became abundantly clear to me that she was lusting after my brother. At first he had regarded her with shy and curious attention, but the longer we sat there drinking the warm cider the more alarmed I became. Presently she became a little more obvious in her desires. She stood up, drank heartily out of the bottle with her head thrown up and her throat and breasts tilted back; then she plonked herself down again, this time in close proximity to Christopher, and smiled sleepily at him. My eyes at this point would have excelled a hawk's. Slowly, the look of the weasel came over Christopher's face; slowly it dawned on me that he too was becoming intoxicated, with the liquor and with her. I understood this a little – how could I not – and yet I felt greatly threatened by it.

I found myself becoming incensed; particularly when my brother uttered something foolish or trite which was out of character, and which I knew to be said only for her amusement or benefit. The animal currents between them continued until we were summoned indoors because Mamma wished to leave. How thankful I was this time for her impatient nature.

We left; I well recall Nancy standing by the door, one hand placed licentiously upon her hip. Her mother slapped it down firmly and she pouted her annoyance; I experienced a small triumph.

Christopher said nothing to me of the girl, and I was too exalted to broach the subject myself, much as I wanted to. Yet he seemed a little happier, and possibly felt that the incident with the girl made us quits. For my part I was uneasy, simply because we had not talked about it, and I felt therefore that the implications were sinister. I did not know what he was thinking, and the distance between us had not been bridged. I had strong and bad intuitions about our future and the tension was a great trial to me.

25

It is strange how often Fate intervenes at a timely moment. I have been steeling myself to write the account of the final part of our holidays; it has been constantly in my mind, and I have remembered and made notes of all I can recall. Unfortunately, I recall too well, and it causes me great pain; how distant it all is and yet how present to my memory. O Christopher, you were able to destroy the beauty, but not the memory of the beauty.

Now, however, circumstance prevents me for a while, in the sad shape of Helen. She has been writing me mammoth epistles since our visit and I have responded as best I can. She constantly urges me to return. Thomas has been much against the idea, and I have had to decline. However, just the morning, I received an urgent request from Edward that I come to his wife: she is grievous ill and he fears for her life. It seems she begs constantly for my presence, and he now feels obliged to ask me to comply. It is a strange matter, for I know he would feel relieved by her death, yet there is a note of panic and supplication in his letter which I must respond to. Thomas is much against it for an assortment of reasons, but in particular, he insists, because it is unthinkable for me to travel such a distance in my condition.

This last month has been a great trial for me. I suspected some time ago that I was with child, and did all that I could to hide the matter from Thomas. I began by attempting all the foolish remedies of past generations of crazed women: hot baths, gin (which I cannot abide), leaping down the stairs three at a time, and wishful thinking. All to no avail. My body continued to change according to its own will, nothing could shift the determined embryo within me. It has been a kind of terror; after I accepted my condition I became desperate to hide it from Thomas, in the hope that I might be able to alter God's will. Then began the tight lacing. My maid was aware of the facts and did all she could to help me. Every morning I would brace myself as she wrenched my body into the tightest confines I could bear. This worked for some time, but two weeks ago it became impossible to continue: the tight lacing made me ill, or caused me to faint.

My belly has now grown into a well-rounded hill; indeed by my calculations I must be five months into my confinement. I was obliged to confess to Thomas, who had had his hopes for some time, he informed me. He was truly delighted, and to see him for once in a state of natural excitation was an unusual and welcome sight. Yet, my forebodings are not eased; I see I cannot alter my Fate; and the physician has now confirmed my calculated dates.

I cannot bear the thought of this thing growing within me, living off my blood, forcing its life upon me. I feel it grow and move within me. O, I am not ready, I cannot mother a thing I do not want. I move like a shadow amongst their smiles and concern; I feel nothing but doom, and a great fear if this shall finally come to pass. It cannot be good.

Thomas is full of anxiety that I might lose the child. He urges me to sit quietly, to rest and wait for the event to take me over.

Now, since the letter this morning, a new problem has arisen, and Thomas and I cannot agree.

'Catherine, it is not possible for you to undertake such a journey, I will not allow it.'

'But, Thomas, I cannot refuse, she is ill, possibly dying. I cannot see that the journey will do me any harm.'

'But there is no need to undertake it. If we explain to Edward, he will not think of your setting forth.'

'Thomas, think a little, Edward cannot possibly tell her the true reasons for my inability to come, so he will have to resort to saying I am merely ill, which she will see as an excuse and be much grieved. I must go, there is no question about it.'

'Catherine, as you know, I would not impose my will upon you, but it is my child that you carry, and it is precious to me. I am not so young, and it is just possible you might not conceive again – I am loth to take a risk for a mad woman.'

I understood well his concern, and felt a pang of remorse. Yet, I knew I had to go; possibly in the secret hope that his fears might be realized.

The matter has now been solved. I am to go, but I may not stay more than a few days. Thomas has reluctantly complied with my wishes, in the belief that I had a duty which I could not shirk. His sense of duty is highly developed, and it was the expedient approach in this difficulty.

I set forth the next day, in the early morning. Thomas issued strict instruction for the driver to take the greatest possible care, and to make the journey slowly. His face came round the window of the carriage to proffer further admonitions.

'Catherine, I trust you will take the greatest care. The driver will break the journey at an inn – he has explicit instructions, and I wish them to be carried out. I hope also that when you get there you will use all caution when dealing with this person, and let Edward know of my concern. I will be writing shortly.'

'Yes, Thomas, but please do not be concerned; I am

sure I will see a sick and weak woman who can do me no possible harm.'

'Write to me, my dear, upon your arrival, I will expect you back next week.'

The carriage drove off and I could discern the worry in his face.

I felt fretful on the journey. I worried how I might conceal my condition from Helen. Indeed, I did not look enlarged, for I had taken care to select robes that would conceal my shape without looking obviously like maternity garments. I knew, however, that she was no fool, and that her intuition was acute. I began to feel that if she knew I was in the condition she longed for more than all else, it might be disastrous. I determined that she would get no clue from me, nor from my appearance or attitude in the way of confirmation – if she should suspect.

I arrived most fatigued; having taken no pleasure in the lovely Kent countryside as I had before. I begged that I might rest before seeing Helen, feeling I needed all my strength for the encounter.

'Certainly, I will show you to your room immediately,' Edward said, escorting me out of the drawing room. But he wished for some conversation in the hallway.

'Tell me, what are Thomas' views on the wretched Boer War – I hear we are suffering fearful casualties and set-backs under that fool Buller...'

My heart fell and a great fear wrapped round my heart. I replied snappily, because he knew, as I knew, that our brother was somewhere in South Africa. It was a jibe at me, and I did not care for it.

'I did not come here, Edward, to talk about the Boer War. And I want you to know that I did not come here on your account, but on Helen's. You seem to think you have a hold over me in some way, and I would like to set you right on that score...'

'O, indeed,' he snickered, his face turning rather florid, 'but I do have something on you, don't I Cathy? I was the only person who witnessed what I did. You were well over the excuse of childhood then. It would be interesting to know what your nice husband might think of such goings-on.'

O, I well understood the fury and exasperation Christopher had so often felt with Edward as a child! I would dearly have loved to have 'torn him into little pieces', as Christopher once said in a rage. Yet he had disquietened me as well; he was playing on a memory: a memory I blanched at, and one that I have to share with Edward due to a cruel perversity and callousness on his part.

I tried to rest in my room, but I was plagued with the thought of the war. The Boers, according to reports now coming in, are a tenacious and savage lot, most accurate with their guns. It is rumoured that the outcome will be very bloody. The disaster at Ladysmith has shaken even the Queen's confidence; though of course there is no question of defeat.

Within the hour Edward was knocking at my door, and requesting that I visit Helen, as she was giving her maid no peace.

'I must warn you that she has been most savage. She even went so far as to attack her maid; fortunately the woman was loyal to me and agreed to remain.'

I said tersely: 'I have observed the woman you speak of; she is a most unwholesome person; and treats your wife like her prisoner. I am not altogether surprised Helen lost patience with her.' He took me to her door in silence, and disappeared promptly. I braced myself and entered.

How her countenance alarmed me! She was like a small, wizened old lady. Her hair was matted and sprawled across the pillow like a black stain. Her face was yellowed vellum, dark and sunken around the eyes and cheekbones. The smile she gave me split her face in two, and I observed that there was a black hole where a tooth was missing.

As I placed myself carefully on a chair by the side of her bed, I noticed that her bottom lip had a small black crusted wound on one side, and her whole mouth seemed faintly blue. Death, or madness, was oozing out of the corners of her mouth and eyes in great trickles. The spring daffodils that stood erect and potent in the vase beside her made a pitiful contrast.

'I am so glad you came,' she said, in a tone of infinite sweetness, placing a crone's hand upon my own.

'And for my part, I am sorry you are not well; but you will get better, will you not, Helen?'

She smiled, and moved her hand slightly, so that I caught sight of a thick violet welt across her wrist.

'How beautiful you look, dear Catherine,' she said with the same dulcet tone; 'your eyes shine so, and your face is full of health, and a certain quiescence too I detect, which I did not find before. Has anything occurred?'

'O, no, nothing of significance.'

There was a small silence during which we surveyed one another.

'What is it that ails you, Helen, or is it that you feel oppressed? I am very often downcast myself, and I have noticed that it often caused me to be ill, or have great pains in the head. Though you are of course much more seriously ill, the root cause might be the same.'

'Assuredly, my grief and my madness have weakened my body; I feel now that there is no point in continuing. I can see nothing ahead of me but blackness. I know now that I am mad; there might come a time in the future when I do not know it, when my actions are incomprehensible to me. By that time the demon will have me, and I will sink lower and lower until I become an animal, without reason, with not even my own intellect to guide me out of the gloom and help me understand my feverish actions and desires.'

I was greatly humbled by her self-knowledge; by her courage in the face of such overwhelming difficulties.

'How has this all come about, Helen? Could some experience in your childhood account for it?'

'Perhaps,' she replied thoughtfully.

'Will you tell me a little of your history, Helen? I would be most interested.'

'Yes, it would be a great relief to speak of it. I am calm today and happily in control of my faculties; your presence has greatly calmed me ...'

'I was an only child; as I told you before, my mother died at an early age – I was eight at the time. I remember little of her, except that she was of a nervous disposition, and often ill. Upon her death my father became my whole world to me; he spent a great deal of time in my company. We lived close to the sea, not far from here, and he would run up and down the sands with me, teaching me about the sea creatures and the tides. I am closer to the sea than I am to any living thing – it fills my mind and my dreams, and when I think of it I always think of him. Our life was quiet and peaceful, and as I grew older, he would teach me about religion and philosophy – he was a great admirer of Thomas Aquinas.

'Then, when I grew towards womanhood, his attitude towards me changed: he became disciplining and harsh; resentful if I wished to pursue activities of my own choosing. He began to mock and deride any new friendships I made – particularly if they were with gentlemen. Yet, I respected and admired him greatly, and more often than not I was willing to be persuaded by his judgements – though I see now they were selfish and only disguised as being for my own good. The matter came to a head over a certain gentleman with whom I was much enamoured. My father forbade the marriage, and shortly afterwards the young man went away and I never saw him again.

'My love for my father slowly turned to hate; and so painful was my existence with him that as soon as the next opportunity arose, I seized it. The next opportunity was Edward.

'What more can I say? There are many parallels in our times, and the times before ours. The wise Miss Brontë managed to rid herself of an over-riding father by turning him into the half-helpless, blind, child/husband of Rochester. I have read, too, that she also accepted a less than satisfactory marriage.'

Helen was growing agitated and tired, and though I wanted to know what happened to her father, and whether he was in fact still alive, I could see that to continue the conversation was taxing her greatly.

'Helen, dear, you must rest now. I shall come and see you in the morning, with some of the hyacinths from the garden.'

I left her; and felt most bitter that such an intelligent creature should be cloistered and driven to madness by the inability of anyone to help her. Tragic ill-health or madness was her only solution, married as she was to a man who so complacently felt himself to be her superior, and could in no way understand her desperate cries for help. As I thought of these matters Elizabeth Barrett Browning's words came to mind: 'We are sepulchred alive in this close world, and want more room.'

26

The Helen of the next morning was not the same person; gone was the mellifluous voice and the calm and rational words of yesterday.

She lay ugly and twisted upon her bed, her face black and wild, her eyes darting across their sockets, the hands twitching madly.

'Helen, how can I help you?' I asked, deeply grieved by her appearance.

She clutched my hand fiercely and hissed: 'I dreamed you died last night – in childbirth; I saw you, bleeding, bleeding, but the blood was my blood, and the child was mine and you had stolen it.'

Her fingers bit into my flesh, and when I withdrew I could see the livid nail etchings she had left.

'But, Helen, it was merely a dream, you cannot be angry with me for a dream.'

'Sometimes dreams are more real than reality, or they tell us of the future. Joseph's dream of the seven poor ears of corn devouring the seven good ears was a forecast of the famine. My dream might be warning me about your intentions towards me,' she said with a sinister grimace.

'Please, Helen,' I said carefully, 'I would not take your child. I do not desire a child of my own, let alone anyone else's.'

She sat up in a huddled fashion, wrapping her arms tightly across her stomach and watching me carefully. I was curious about the dream and wondered whether there was more to it, but caution told me to tread no further on this dangerous path.

'Helen dear, let me adjust your pillows and make you more comfortable, and then perhaps we can talk as we did yesterday.'

As I rose to do this she pushed me back with an abrupt gesture. We sat in silence. I looked out of the window – the sun shone brightly, lighting up everything in the room with cruel clarity.

She lay very quiet, her face drained of all colour. I sat and waited, a heavy feeling of unquiet growing with the silence. Each time I cast a surreptitious glance in her direction she appeared to grow weaker: the face seemed to sink, the colour became a milky grey.

Suddenly I caught sight of a red stain crawling across the coverings of her body. Hypnotized I watched it spread; slowly soaking the magnolia satin. Her head dropped; and woke me out of my stupor. I tried to speak to her, but she had fainted. I rushed for the door and as I did so her voice, sluggish and low: 'No, don't go, it's too late.' I took no heed and told the maid to go for Edward and to call a physician with all speed. Her cold sneer chilled me once more; then she turned and slowly descended the stairs. 'With all speed,' I called fiercely after her, and went back to Helen.

She was lying back on her cushions with her eyes closed; she opened them slightly for an instant as I stood by her bed. The red seep had grown into a huge red wound, it seemed alive and growing and I felt a panic rising in me. I knew she must be haemorrhaging and resolved to turn back those bloody covers and try to arrest the bleeding. Very carefully I began to draw back the sodden cloth. She did not prevent me.

My stomach smashed against my heart, and I cried out. Her abdomen was cut open from bowels to breasts, the blood gushed down each slope of her body, making pools where it fell. Her insides were writhing and thrusting to escape her body like grey worms in a furnace.

I began to weep, the sobs shaking my body convulsively. I covered her up gently. Her small blank eyes quietly surveyed my face; she reached for my hand and said: 'I had to make sure there was nothing inside me.' Then her eyes closed and her face was instantly calm and sweet.

I looked down at my first dead face in awe, my tears ceased to fall, and a great numbness filtered through my heart. I stood there for some time, with my hand still clutched in Helen's, until the door burst open and Edward rushed up to me.

'What has she done now?' he asked, looking at me and not at her.

'She is dead.'

His gaze flew from my face to hers, and then to the gory bedclothes.

'O, my God,' he whispered, sinking into the chair he never sat in. 'Has she severed her wrists again?' He would not look, he would not be involved; and I was full of bitter hatred and wrath for him.

Very slowly and calmly I heard my voice say, 'She took a small silver knife with an ivory handle, and she sliced her body open from top to bottom.'

I *would* have him see. I could not allow him to detach himself from the event; from her piteous death which he was so responsible for ... I unwrapped her and he was forced to look at her naked death. I wondered whether he had ever seen her naked.

The detachment, the inscrutable coldness fell from him: the jaws fell, the eyes flared in horror; his hands flew to the protection of his face: and he lurched from the room.

My sobs broke forth once more; I covered her up; her face was gentle and sweet in the sunlight, with no trace of the horror that had lurked behind it such a short time ago.

27

I remained in my room for some hours; I heard the physician being taken to Helen's room, and then an awful hush descended upon the house. I hid in my pain, and questions raced round and round my skull. Why had Edward insisted that I come into his house and life? Was it just to show me that he blamed me for the disastrous mess he had construed out of his marriage? was it revenge on Christopher and me? Even more sinister, did he feel he had a power to control me? Such power had always delighted Edward; I was sure it was the reason he had chosen the legal profession.

I was at a loss. He had forced Helen on to me because he could not abide to have any part of her, and then he had used my affection for her to avoid any direct responsibility. Clearly though, he had not expected her to kill herself, though the evidence of the past should have warned him. That he was deeply shocked to see her thus was totally genuine; but then, who would not be shocked, faced with such a macabre spectacle? I could make but muffled sense out of all this; it was not enough. There must be more to it. I determined to have it out with my brother before leaving his house for the last time. Now he had no excuse to exploit my guilt.

I put my things hastily together, and with some trepidation descended the stairs to seek out Edward.

He was in the library, seated in a large chair in a darkened corner. He rose and came towards me with slow, paced steps. He was wearing his old persona and smiling tightly, but the edges were ragged and it did not sit too well; around the eyes his fear and guilt were sprouting.

'I have come to take my leave of you, Edward, but before I do I demand to know what your purpose was in involving me in all this.'

He did not answer the question, did not even seem to hear it. Twisting his hands helplessly, he mumbled: 'Perhaps, perhaps I did kill her. I have often wished her dead – most often, of late – and see, now it has come to pass.'

'Edward,' I said sharply, 'what has been your intention in bringing me into your life at this stage?'

'I knew you would like her,' he said dreamily. He was becoming very abrasive on my nerves. I sat down. Suddenly he seemed to come to his senses.

'Ah, yes, you wanted to know what my plans were for you, didn't you?'

I nodded.

'Well, I wanted to see you,' he said with a little smile.

I held my tongue with great difficulty.

'And while you were here,' he continued slowly, 'I saw how I could be rid of her without suffering the comment that might be aroused by my committing her to an institution. I decided that *you* should have her.'

This was much worse than I had imagined. 'And how did you think you could force me to take over your responsibility for your wife?' I asked carefully.

'O, Catherine dear, do not be so simple-minded. You know how I could force you ...'

I recoiled, strong cold waves of emotion buffeting my clarity of thought.

'But what of my husband? how had you solved that problem?'

'O, that was no problem. It was quite obvious that

the man ate out of your hand; and I had gone to some pains to make myself agreeable to him.'

'Edward, I think you are demented! It is not possible for a man to discard his wife and foist her on to relations while he is alive and present, and well able to take care of her himself.'

He said coldly and very deliberately: 'It would have worked without a doubt. I could have forced you into it: you cannot afford to lose the security you have found in your marriage.'

'There is a word for all this, Edward,' I said, 'you must have come across it often: it is blackmail.'

'Assuredly,' he smiled, 'and very effective it is, too, as I have often learned in my dealings with the criminal class. In any event, I had a further reason for leaving her in your capable hands: I was resolved to take myself to South Africa and have a pot-shot at those damnable Boers; might even have had a pot-shot at the well-loved brother, eh?' He laughed. 'O, you would have been proud of me, Cath. I really convinced old Thomas that I had a passionate feeling about the war; he would have admired me greatly had I gone.' He laughed again, and then abruptly stopped, as if remembering something painful.

'Well, everything has changed now; there is no need for me to sacrifice myself. I made a mistake, I think,' he pondered, almost to himself – 'I should not have told her that you were going to have a child...'

'You told her that!'

'Well, I wrote her a note. To the effect that you were having a child, I was going to South Africa and she was going to stay with you. It obviously turned her head.'

'Edward, you disgust me; how could you do such a thing?'

He tossed me a low, sad smile: 'O, how well you taught me, Cath, all those years ago. Helen, too, she could not love me and I was not going to spend my life looking after a lunatic. I thought it was the least you could do. It was not too much to ask, was it, Cath?'

How our childhood had snarled each one of our lives. I left him sitting in the dark.

The slow journey back was precisely what I required to piece together my shattered composure. I sat very quiet in the carriage and let my mind fully explore all the things I knew of Helen, and all the untold stories which I suspected; attempting to saturate my head with her to be rid of her unquiet presence. She was probably doomed from childhood; perhaps from the day her mother died, and her father took over the organization of her life; possibly, even, from her birth, with the seed in her of the writhing, up-rooting plant of later life. And she had chosen Edward, unwittingly, or even almost consciously, to complete her destruction.

Thomas was much surprised to see me back so soon, and bustled me into the house.

'You are so pale and wan, Catherine,' he said, full of concern and gentleness, which only served to open the flood gates of my tears once more.

He was deeply distressed by this unaccustomed sight. 'Catherine, what is it? Have you lost the child?'

'No.'

'Well, tell me, pray; I cannot bear to see you so overcome.'

I tried to tell him as best I could without mentioning the awful details, for, I confess, I did not wish to think further on them. But he would not let it rest.

'You mean she took her own life?'

I nodded.

'But how?'

'With a knife.'

'O, my God!' he cried, and then regaining his composure, 'I trust you did not witness any of the horror of it.'

'I did Thomas; I was sitting beside her as she bled to death.'

He looked at me strangely then, not understanding the experience; being unable to relate the grisliness of it to me, or to my telling of it.

'You must not think of it any more,' he said firmly, after a silence. 'The woman was mad, she had no possibilities. I suppose it is not so strange, though I did not expect anything of this order; how anyone could so mutilate themselves is quite beyond me.'

How simply he explained it all away. I had done the same thing with him as I had with Edward; I had tried to make them both see the blood. But neither of them wanted to see it. And yet, Helen's tragedy is the direct result of the terrible masculine pomposity that rules over countless women's lives; leading them to desperate measures or intolerable existences.

'Catherine, you must go to bed now and rest awhile. We will not speak of this again.'

28

I have been unable to write all this month. Helen's death brought about a numbness, a frightful inertia of mind and will. I have remained in my room and tried to sit quietly. I sew small stitches, moving slow through the muslin; taking small steps when I walk, trying to be contained, to keep the inner void from spreading like the red seep upon her bedclothes. My mind is fragmented, split between Helen and my brother and this unborn thing growing inside me. The sniffs of childhood return to put me in mind of old anxieties.

It is late June, and the days are warm and oppressive. I am full of heaviness; a great barge swimming sluggish through thick waters. How my size amazes me! I cannot escape from it. My skin so firm and taut – stretched like the waistcoat of a corpulent gentleman. And the sea motion within me; stirring; growing into the corners of my body, attaching itself to me, putting out roots.

It is more than a month since Mafeking Night. Buller was forgiven his blunders and all of London ran mad for two days: great rockets and illuminations, flags and buntings lit up the streets thronged with humanity, all cheering and singing. But it is not over. We are good at hiding our sorrows beneath a grand British show of exuberance; perhaps the Queen has showed us how, moving proudly through happy streets with a heart full of grief as her children fall away; and her Empire devours the weak and helpless.

I see in *The Times* that casualties are reaching monstrous proportions, disease is spreading throughout the camps and Botha is full of resolution and cunning.

I wish I had word of my brother; it is a torture not to know what has become of him. I do not feel that he is dead; I know that if he were, at the exact moment of his passing I would feel it, throughout my body and brain. But uncertainty is hard to deal with; it eats away slowly at the soft cores of hope.

These thoughts have burdened me; but slowly now the numbness begins to wear off. I take my meals downstairs again – one cannot survive too long on a diet of shadows.

I no longer sleep with Thomas. I have moved across the hallway to a smaller suite of rooms. I can see the orchard from my window and beyond it the soft hills and a lovely emerald cluster of elm. It is peaceful here; Thomas does not disturb me much, only to bid me good night and good morning and to ask after my health. I sleep badly and toss constantly, but my condition enabled me to grasp a little more privacy and solitude. Thomas was a trifle distressed that I should want to quit his bed, but he saw the sense of the arrangements, and no doubt he sleeps better now.

He is so proud of my bulk; I can see his eyes on me as I walk. He came once and asked if he might feel my belly with his hands, and was much amazed by the stirrings and hardness of it. He is full of pleasure and sweetness, and there is a new peacefulness in him. I wish that I might feel it too. I feel only this fear: of being swamped, and losing myself in the creation of another; I think it would kill me by its borning; or I it.

The servants are full of care for me: they cook me good and nourishing things and send me large glasses of milk. I cannot drink milk, the sweet lactic taste has always stuck in my throat. All eyes are upon me, as upon a sick person or a great event. I move quietly in their concern and am touched by it, but cannot be part of it.

I go for long walks now in the garden, and sit sometimes under the old oak and read the hours away. It is a great pleasure to read. But the garden is so alive that it is menacing. It is so full of health and activity. How ripe and full the flowers and fruit are: the strawberries are plump to satiety; the tomatoes are splitting their skins; and the sun, how fiercely it draws out life.

Today, then, I went to the bottom of the pleasure gardens, and on descending the old stone steps I tripped, and my body crashed down to the bottom. I lay perfectly still, waiting for the pains to bite, the blood to flow, but nothing happened; the inner fortress remained intact. Only a long strip of skin was pared off by the stone, leaving bloodied marks along my thigh, and destroying my underclothes, which I will now have to hide.

I came upstairs to change discreetly and wipe the dust and marks off my apparel, so the maid will not ask questions. I have opened the windows wide to let in the small wind that struggles with the heat of the day, so I may write again.

I feel a strong urge to escape all this abundance; to slip back into the old blue pinafore and childhood slippers of my thirteen-year-old summer in Cornwall.

29

With the Frenchman back in London, life at the cottage became homely once more; the maids returned and Mamma was less harassed by daily chores and cooking. She determined, once more, to keep us happy and amused and close to her. She came on pic-nics with us again and made our favourite puddings. But we did not feel quite as moved by these endeavours as we had at first, remembering how quickly she had been distracted by the Frenchman.

Mamma was going to take us to Land's End for the day. The journey was extremely hazardous; the trap was old and rickety, and certainly not road-worthy; she was not too efficient at keeping the horse in order and she would not allow Edward or Christopher to take the reins. So we jogged precariously down narrow green lanes, crossing our fingers at corners, watching the road anxiously for boulders or pot-holes. Mamma was having a wonderful time, urging on the steed, leading our laughter in a most un-genteel fashion. Occasionally we would pass a farmer, and once the local vicar, and it was splendid to observe her adjust her face accordingly and put on a gracious mien.

We reached our destination safely, and walked right down to the tip of Land's End. It made me feel very solemn; for out there across the seas was France and beyond that the whole of Europe, and I wondered whether one day the weasel and I would set forth from England and see all the places we'd learnt about in school.

We found a nice green meadow not far away and had a pic-nic in the sunshine. Mamma unwrapped tongue and lettuce sandwiches and apricot juice and cherry cakes. We ate everything, and then Mamma read to us from *Jane Eyre*.

Slowly the sky darkened, and soon the whole of the blue was covered by great black and purple bruises. The rain leaked slowly through the sky at first, and then descended with a vengeance and speed that were quite alarming. It was as if a great mirror in the sky had shattered and all the tiny fragments were descending. Never have I seen such rain! Christopher thought it most splendid and leaped up and down, catching the great drops upon his tongue. Mamma became increasingly impatient, for nobody would help her load the trap and she was fretting that I might become ill again. The horse did not care for the weather and it was difficult to coerce him into moving at all; finally we stopped for shelter under a generous tree, with Edward boding evil with his constant chat of thunder. It stopped raining as speedily as it had started, and the sun emerged to smile at our mangy condition. Mamma was not so cheery on the way back.

That night we had hot soup made from carrots and potatoes, and brown bread and butter. After dinner Edward disappeared to his room to read; while I was dispatched off to bed to safeguard my health. I felt cold and lonely by myself, and I could hear Mamma humming and talking to Christopher in the kitchen as she kneaded a new batch of bread. Christopher did not come, so I fell asleep.

I woke at about midnight; the sky was violet and the house was perfectly still and dark. The rain tapped gently on the window, and there was the low growl of thunder, far away. Christopher was sitting up by the circular window, his arms wrapped round his knees, looking out at the night. His breath had fogged up the pane and he was drawing circles on the frosted glass. I could see his face in the occasional flashes of lightning. His eyebrows were close together, and now and again he rubbed his nose; I watched him silently for a while, smiling to myself in the dark.

I felt warm and good towards him. I got out of bed and went up to him, putting my arms about him as I had done since my baby days. He swung his legs down and looked at me.

'Did I wake you up, thing?'

'No, I'm not sure what woke me – the thunder perhaps. Why aren't you in bed?'

'I'm thinking.'

'You think too much.'

'Maybe.'

There was a small silence and precious, because it was not uneasy, and the peace spread from me to him without any impediment.

'Come to bed,' I whispered.

'Cath,' he blurted out; 'I don't know – I've been thinking – I don't think we should do it any more.'

A light went out in my head, and a lonely silence followed, because now I did not know what to say, and my head was rushing away, taking me down all manner of perilous paths and finding no way back.

'Why not?' my voice asked very, very carefully.

'Well, I've only been thinking about it like this for a while. But for the first time I'm not sure. I don't think it's right for us to do it – being brother and sister. I mean I've always known – or rather, always felt more than known – that it wasn't right.'

'Who says it isn't?'

'I don't know. But it cannot be right. It worries me now, it didn't before. I think before I did not really want to think about it ... but I have always known. Haven't you, Cath?'

'No. And I don't know what you're talking about. It

is *better* because we are brother and sister, because we really know each other; we are the same. I cannot see that it is bad.'

'Yes, but that's the whole problem, Cath. It's because we are the same. We shouldn't because we have the same blood.'

He looked most distressed, and after he had thought for a while he said: 'I think I was always attracted to that book on mythology because there were so many brothers and sisters who loved each other the way we do. I used to console myself that it was acceptable because of that. I have always known that what we have is singular and strange, and I'm not sure that, having said that, we can go on with it.'

My head was full of confusion, and a nasty green thought was growing slowly inside. Perhaps it was just an excuse, because he did not want to do it with me any more. Perhaps it was because he wanted someone else instead; that girl from the farm with the big body.

I spoke, feeling the pain in my throat, 'I don't know if I do understand, Christopher. We have never felt bad before. It just happened and there was no harm in it. I see no harm in it now – I cannot feel suddenly that it is wrong.'

'Cath, you're younger than I and you are easily swept along by events; we *must* think about this, and decide.'

I said hotly: 'Well, I think you have decided already. But, even if it is bad – and I don't see how anything that has always seemed good can suddenly be bad – but even if it is, why does it signify? Nobody knows.'

'Yes, but why does nobody know? It must be because we have deliberately tried to hide it.'

'Mamma tries to hide things too.'

He took my hands gently and spoke with much

urgency. 'Catherine, listen to me, you're young, you're a girl...'

'O, hell it!'

'Look, please listen, one day when you're older you'll get married and what we have done might hurt and upset you ... I don't want that. I must decide for both of us.'

'But Christopher, I cannot think of things that are in the future. We are here now, you and I, we are real. Other people in the future are not real, I cannot think of them.'

The feeling that he didn't want me was growing stronger. It caused pain in my stomach and a smarting behind my eyes.

'Perhaps you'd just rather have the girl from the farm? You might at least tell the truth.'

'I see. You think I don't want to do it with you now, that I need an excuse. That is stupid of you, Cath. I am closer to you than to anyone in the world; you know what I think, you know that isn't true. We have never spoken of this before because we didn't *want* to.'

'No, that is not so. There never seemed anything to talk about before. It just was; I never questioned it, I didn't think you did.'

'Well, perhaps we aren't so close, then, after all. I have always avoided talking about it because I didn't want it to stop. I thought you knew that. You've always known everything about me – there is no one like you, Cath.'

'You talk as though I'm going away.'

There was no answer. I left him and went to lie down on the bed with my face to the covers. The pain palpitated, my head throbbed.

O, he was clever because he knew I knew he was right. But I just didn't want it to be that way; I could not bear to think of anything changing. I wanted it to stay the same dear way it had always been; ever since I could remember.

I wanted to say great things to him, to make it all better; but it was not possible. Once he had spoken, the spell was broken; we could not pretend any more. We had to stop being children.

'Please. Once more.'

I had said it before I knew I'd said it. Yet it was precious and vital, and I thought in that second's silence before he replied that if he refused I should die.

He walked slowly from the window to our bed; stood at the far end and looked down at me; his face was painted with dark colours. He took off his clothes and walked around to where I lay. I sat up and pulled my nightdress up over my head and out of my arms. He sat down on the bed and held me very tight, his bones cut into my flesh. I began to shake; I had the strongest desire to weep, yet I could not because he would hate that. My throat was tight, so was his. The blood rushed to my head, and to his. It flowed behind my eyes so that my vision became blurred.

I dared not look at his eyes so I concentrated on his mouth: there is a small black mark like a pencil dot on the bottom lip. It becomes darker when he is in pain. The tears began to fall, but silently; they ran into our mouths.

It was like doing it for the first time and knowing for the first time that you should not be doing it. Because suddenly it was wrong.

He entered me very slowly; the whole of my stomach grew warm. He moved slowly, slightly. My legs stiffened, my stomach muscles grew taut. The wind was behind my ears and a great stirring of life moved my veins. I was overwhelmed. He did not stop, his hands caught in my hair, pulling my head down, bruising my mouth. My limbs grew weak as his movements became violent. He began to shake, very slightly all over. I could hear his breathing: the breath seemed to come from my own lungs. He shuddered and cried out; his eyes were wet as my body. My hand moved slowly and took his; we were complete and at peace. There was no sound save the patter of small kisses.

30

Dear God, this writing has left me weak and bereft. How the deep and hidden side of one's nature suddenly re-asserts itself and must be heard.

This quiet person wearing the neat everyday smile could no more have written that last chapter than could the Virgin Mary. Yet I did write it, and worse — I lived it. What wild forces swim in the subterranean strata of my soul; I thought I was free of them.

And yet, and yet, looking back over these events, still I cannot rue my actions or my thoughts or my deeds of those days. For then I knew who I was, and I was what I was. Now I see myself, a useless, wasting sham drifting in an empty sea.

I thought today that perhaps I should leave here. Yet it is too beautiful. I took a walk to the highest hill and looked down over the lovely watered valleys and the gentle rises. The green and grey of Gloucestershire fills me with a peace I have felt in no other place. The streams are swollen with trout, the trees and grasses are alive and singing. Their health touches me.

It is a far cry from the wild, fierce beauty of Cornwall. This pale tranquillity is a vivid contrast to my own surging thoughts of those last days spent by the sea.

There were two days left. Christopher and I could not bear to be together. I became very withdrawn and the more I thought about Christopher and myself the more complex the matter became. Mamma noticed my quietness and attributed it to the fact that I was growing up and having private thoughts.

I told her I did not want to sleep in Christopher's room any more and that I wanted a room of my own. She looked at me strangely and I was much affeared that she could see through my calm exterior to the searing pain inside. I took the room next to hers – the room the Frenchman had used. The first night alone was the worst.

A bed has never been the same since. As in the olden days when whole families slept together in one huge bed and gave warmth and comfort to each other, so my sleeping with Christopher had been. I felt very small and alone, shaking around in my own bed that first night. I lay looking up at the window. I thought he might come to me; after an hour or so I began to pray he would come, but God wasn't listening. He has a way of not listening when you most need Him.

If I could have felt then, and now, that there was some evil in what we did, then I could have borne it. But I could find no evil in it.

The shattering of our intimacy was as sharp as a knife that new night, alone and comfortless. Until the age of three I had slept in my mother's warmth, and ever afterwards in Christopher's. Nothing could comfort me. I felt his pain and his solitude mingle with my own, but I could make no move towards him, for I had decided that it was his rejection of me that had brought about this separation.

I traced the events that led up to it: my dealings with the Frenchman, his dalliance with Nancy. They seemed paltry in comparison to what we had had. How soon it had been deprecated; how simple and speedy is the destruction of a flower.

I struggled with myself all night, and in the morning I knew I could not accept it. There had to be some solution.

Feeling better, I left the cottage and went down to the sea. The air smelt delicious and my gloom had lifted. I was wearing my pink linen dress with the two frilled petticoats, and I felt beautiful.

Christopher was not by the sea. I took off my shoes and stockings and the petticoats, lifted my dress above my knees and walked out into the green. Happiness came over me; I felt as though everything was new and polished and clean. I knew Christopher and I could not be separated by his foolish guilt. Even if it could not be as tender and sweet as before, we could surely grow closer together in all the other ways. I could not believe he could look at me and not feel the same stirrings; he could not look at me and be unmoved. It was no more possible for him than it would be for me.

I sat in the sand until the sun had dried my feet; put on stockings and shoes and set off in search of Christopher. My need for him was great, I had to speak to him, to tell him that everything would be all right.

He was nowhere along the cliffs, so I walked off down the blackberry lanes towards the fields. I walked slowly at first, and then more swiftly. I was getting desperate: I had walked a long way, and tears of annoyance were welling up behind my eyes.

I had reached a small cluster of trees; there was about it some air of menace, but something made me enter its green depths. Just at that moment I saw them, my brother and the girl from the farm, sitting close together in the grass. Christopher was twisting a long strand of grass nervously; I could not see his face, only his dark head.

I knew what was going to happen, but I could not move away; nothing could persuade me to leave that spot – my feet were growing into the earth, my body turned to stone. She tossed an arm about him and kissed him hard upon the mouth. My stomach rolled over; she pushed him down. I could tell she was wiser than he and she probably thought he was a virgin. I watched her hand move up his leg and touch him, then she bounced up and stood emblazoned before him.

She lifted her skirts up high and yanked off her petticoat and drawers. Then she undid her skirt down the side and let it drop to the ground. She kicked it away and stood there naked from the waist down, a small bush of golden hair between her browned thighs. She turned her back to him for a moment and I saw her face, flushed and full of laughter.

My brother was just watching her; he did not move. She undid all the buttons of her blouse, and then unlaced the bodice she wore beneath it. She flopped down naked in a happy heap, and began to remove Christopher's clothing. They did not speak, the only sounds were her joyful shrieks, and the occasional smack as she landed loud kisses upon my brother's stoic face.

I could not breathe; my head urged me to be gone, my heart would not let me.

Then the weasel seemed to awaken from his inactivity. He moved across to her in the long grass and took over the proceedings. A strangled gasp rose in my throat and I became aware of my tears. They and the grass obscured my vision. I saw Christopher move above her and I could hear their thrashing; her moaning.

Then I picked up my skirts, turned and ran as fast as I could; through the trees and into the clear land beyond. I ran and plunged until my lungs felt stretched to splitting. I fell into the grass; my breath was coming out in long painful sounds, my tears rained and my teeth tore at the flesh of my hand.

I felt totally betrayed. I could not understand all

the subtle reasons why he had behaved the way he had. All I understood then was that he had gone off and done it with someone else. This had to be the reason why he had said he would not do it with me again. Everything he had said seemed meaningless and tawdry; a ring of lies. I hated him most fully. I imagined myself rushing in and tearing them apart, but in these visions I could hear her saying ... 'so that's how it is, how disgusting'.

With startling clarity I realized that I had come, at last, to see that it was evil. Coming after his betrayal of me and the ending of our physical intimacy, it was too much to bear.

I found myself walking towards the lighthouse; my feet clunked up the old stairs and stopped outside her door. I knocked and then walked slowly in. She did not turn as I entered and I was obliged to walk round to the front of her.

I felt a hundred years old, and a little dirty. My eyes were very red; my heart and head ached. My tears had stopped and I felt very dry, inside and out. I did not hate Christopher any more, I was incapable of hating or feeling anything; the numbness spread slowly all through me.

The pale eyes looked at me, she took my bitten hand in hers. I collapsed in a heap at her feet and the tears burst forth in another torrent.

'What is it, what is it?' her lovely undulating voice, full of concern, floated over my head.

My whole body was on fire now, huge tremors shook me; I could not control the gasping and heaving in my throat, my belly, my limbs. She waited very patiently for the storm to subside.

Slowly it dawned on me that I could not tell her what distressed me. How could I tell her? Before I could have told her, but not now, not with my newly acquired wisdom. It was evil and dirty and I could not tell her; her with her gentle peace and simplicity; how could I tell her of the miasmal emanations of my body and mind.

Finally I struggled up and left; I tried to smile for her but I could say nothing for fear of breaking in half. I turned when I reached the door, she was looking back towards me.

I wanted to say: 'We are going home tomorrow, I will probably not be able to come and see you before we go. This is the last time I shall ever see your lovely straight back that never touches the chair, and your eyes that slant up at the corners and your hair combed back so bravely.'

But I said nothing; I closed the door behind me softly and walked past the flowers and along to the cliffs; and slowly, O, so slowly back home.

31

The wind led me along the cliffs; the sea snarled and hissed below – a bed of serpents. My face was cooling slowly; I rubbed the smudgings off my face; kept touching my cracked lips. I forced myself to sit very quietly by the sea, taking deep breaths to calm me.

The picture of them persisted before my eyes, no amount of disciplining thought could drive it away. I could not believe it: he had made me feel dirty. My body offended me, my mouth sickened me; I kept rubbing my hands in the sand to corrode my nastiness.

The melding of our bodies, then, was nothing singular; it could be done with anyone. It was a thing of the flesh and nothing to do with the spirit: my brother felt nothing for this girl, he hardly knew her.

I thought, my hands growing cold, then warm, by turns, that we had grown one into the other's body, slowly and painfully moving through the untidy span of childhood. But, no, we had not been children, not ever. Just unseen and all-seeing creatures, moving side by side towards the same spot in the sunlight. Now he had blotted it out by one simple act, an act that had brutally lost its meaning, its precious privacy, and left me in a void of questions.

O, the loneliness and ignorance of childhood – I would not wilfully inflict it on another human being.

I went home and tried to sit still, thinking how to face my brother when he returned.

He came into my room; I was looking out of the window. I sensed no distress in his person; the way he walked was jaunty, jubilant almost, there was none of the usual slowness in his gait. I turned towards him slowly, carefully adjusting my face; feeling it set like a gel. He seemed bright and animated; when he saw my expression he crumbled.

'You know, then.' The words dragged out painfully.

I could hardly speak, I was so angry suddenly, and yet like an open wound; and I knew I was about to stick my fingers in the wound and twist them around; I had not learned to protect myself from anything.

'I saw you,' I hissed.

He came and sat beside me. He seemed calm, austere now. 'I would have told you.'

'Why?'

'Because you'd have known anyway, even if you hadn't seen me. We: you and I, will not do it together any more. Today, with that girl, it meant nothing, it makes no difference to you and me.'

'How can it mean nothing with her if it *doesn't* mean nothing with me? what I mean is: if it means nothing with her, it cannot have meant anything with me ... just like animals, then.'

'No, it is not the same. Today I walked a long way, because I felt full of bad, nothing seemed good. I wanted things to go on the same as before, but I knew I could not let them. I wanted to know what would happen next. I don't know if I was looking for Nancy or not – maybe I was. At first I wanted to be gone from her, but she enticed me, and then I found myself thinking that maybe it would help – to prove to myself I could finish it with you, by having her.'

'And did it?'

'I don't know. I felt better afterwards, I did not feel bad about it, yet I wanted to be away from her as soon as I could.'

He seemed callous to me; I understood what he was saying, but I could not help feeling that it was all unnecessary. I only felt I was being replaced, and I could not comprehend why he should expect me to accept that readily.

'How would it be then, Christopher, if I were to do the same to you?'

'I should probably kill you.' A wan smile accompanied his words; it was not altogether a joke. A joke is another way of telling an unwelcome truth. I have never believed in jokes.

My tongue was caught in the snare again, no words would come; yet my mind raced on. I was so frightened: of things ending, of the sun setting, if he changed towards me. Like the dying strains of a song I wished they would sing again.

He was silent and sad, all the jubilation in him had died. He was being dragged under and I knew he did not know what to do. I saw myself through the blackness of his images. I wanted to bruise him, and yet I didn't. I had to injure him, yet injuring him was stabbing myself with the same knife.

'Did you like it, then, was it nice?' I did not want to know; he would tell the truth as always, and I did not want to hear it, but I had to ask.

'It was nice for what it was.'

I stood up, feeling my limbs kindly lifting me from the pain I had sunk into, and carrying me from the room.

From that moment onwards we could not bear to be in one another's company for a moment; yet I could not be far from where he was. I could not go to him; he had betrayed me with some slut of a girl; but if I did not see him for long hours, or if I did not know where he was, my desolation was unbearable. I knew with great certainty that he would not go to Nancy again; it was my only consolation.

Today, when I reflect on those days, I am amazed

that I did not for one moment consider that I ought to try to adjust my view. Christopher had made a decision, and he intended to abide by it, in spite of the pain it would cause us both. I could not agree to change; yet possibly if we had talked about it properly and if I had allowed myself to decide without the burden of the new emotional pain, I might have come to accept it. The only way he could fortify his resolution was by desecrating the purity of my ideal; he had done that for his own salvation. I had to find mine by other means.

We had one day left by the sea. I spent it walking down the lanes, and over the fields, past the little house of the content farmer and the field of the touch with the Frenchman.

I kept away from the sea and the cliffs because I knew he would be there; I thought he would probably go in search of our lighthouse lady.

Mamma was scurrying about, getting our things together; she was anxious to be gone. She had no patience with the in-between stages; she hated getting somewhere and only relaxed once she had arrived; and that, too, was short-lived relaxation, because as soon as she had settled she would seek out new diversions.

The day dragged by; I too wanted it to end. Everything saddened me: the peace and the loveliness of the place had dissolved into my gloom.

I went down to the sea for a last walk, after determining that Christopher was busily employed aiding Mamma to strap the trunks up securely. It was very sad to be there saying goodbye to the sea without the weasel. I sat down in the cove and looked hard at the place where we had first lain in the sand: not a trace. The sand only reminded me of the new eyes of my brother and their strange blanched expression.

The sea continued to eat away at the shore, disgorging tiny carcasses to whiten in the sun. Such blue emptiness, spreading, spreading and quite uncontainable; swallowing the sky and still unsatisfied.

32

In the morning we left the stone cottage with the passion flower and clematis. Mamma shut the bold green front door softly behind her and it was all closed out; I felt as though I'd left something of importance behind and wept a little under my bonnet as we drove to the station.

The train was unbearable: the heat stifling; the crowds, rushing back to the cities from the sea, glutted the corridors and compartments. The idea of this assorted humanity around us all the way to London filled me with melancholy. The journey was long and grim; children stampeded to the windows, blocking out the sluggish gusts of wind; the mindless chatter of two old ladies in the corner and the slow chugging of the train all added to my misery.

Christopher sat at the far end of our carriage, his face behind his book; I knew he was not reading it because his eyes were fixed in one direction and they never moved; moreover he rarely remembered to turn over the pages. His shoulders were bunched up and his brow was ploughed with worry. Finally he set aside the book and turned his face towards the window and away from my grey gaze.

I tried to sleep, but the busyness of my brain and the noise prevented it; in the end I adopted Christopher's trick and pretended to sleep.

How strange our house seemed after the weeks away; the Frenchman had sent flowers and Mamma was instantly cheerful. I walked slowly up to the second floor and hesitated; remembering I could no longer go up to my old room. Heavy-hearted, I walked back along the corridor and dropped my things with a low thud upon the floor of the old illness room next to Mamma's. I could hear her laughing up the stairs; chattering to Lucy who was carrying her trunk. She saw me sitting despondently on my bed and sat down beside me.

'What is it, Catherine, are you not glad to be back?'

'Yes, I'm always glad to be home – well, usually, anyway.'

'I'm glad you've decided to have a room of your own,' she said cheerfully ... 'you're thirteen now and quite grown-up, I thought I'd never get you out of Christopher's bed, funny to think of you turning into a young lady, you were always so thin and gangling.'

She got up to leave, but stopped at the door as a thought hit her: 'Ah – Cath, you can't really sleep in this room; better go up to the spare room next to Edward's.'

'Why may I not sleep here, Mamma?' I asked uneasily, not perceiving for a moment her desire to be rid of me.

'Well, it's better for you all to be on the same floor.'

'But I shall be so far from the rest of you (this room was almost exactly underneath my brother's, and the room she was suggesting was right the other end of the corridor where Edward hid himself away). Please, I don't want to sleep near Edward, he's so horrid to me.'

'O, don't be foolish. It's not good for you to sleep in this room, it will probably give you nightmares since you were so ill here ... I'll get Lucy to make up your bed in the other room.'

I dragged out after her as she flounced off to her bedroom, tossing me a stale smile, a careless caress. On my way up the stairs I passed Christopher coming down.

'Where are you going?' he asked tentatively.

'To the room near Edward's. Mamma does not want me to sleep next to her.' My voice was fluttering like a bird. He put his hand out to me, but I rushed past it, the idiotic tears beginning to fall.

O, how far away Cornwall seemed, and the gentle, changeless pattern of my old life! How easy it was to be felled by a word or a look.

The room was cold, and smelt damp and unused. I wanted to get some of my familiar things from the old room, and took advantage of Christopher's absence to sneak down the corridor and retrieve my best books, the pale blue vase, the silver-topped trinket box father had given me an age ago and my book of pressed flowers. I felt a little better once I had settled them in. I got into bed; my bed was not Christopher's.

The next morning the sky was the colour of a bird's egg. School was not to begin for three days, and I wondered how I would spend the time. Mamma was not at breakfast; I presumed she had gone to call on the Frenchman. Christopher went out soon after breakfast and did not appear again until tea-time. Mamma took tea with us, and informed us that she had received a letter from her brother.

'You've never met Jonas. He has a good-sized farm in Wales; and lives there with his wife and their three sons: your cousins, I've told you about them. Anyway, what has transpired is this: his eldest son, who is nineteen, has just left home to take up farming on his own, which leaves your uncle in the position where he needs help on his own farm. He thought that perhaps one of you two would like to go. He will teach you about farming, and pay you while you're learning, and at the end of the time you will know the land and can either stay on with him or branch out on your own. Of course Edward is too involved in his studies so he cannot go –

in any event he hates to get his hands dirty, don't you, Edward?' He glowered. 'I thought Christopher might like to go. You don't like school much, and you seem to like the country. Anyway, think about it for a while and let me know so I can write and tell him what we have decided.'

Christopher sat very quiet; his face animated and thoughtful. I thought he would say the whole idea was nonsense.

'I don't have to think about it, Mamma, I want to go.'

'Well, are you sure, Christopher? You should really stay on at school for at least another year. You might regret it later. And it will be hard work up there. My brother works like an ox and probably expects everyone else to as well. His wife is an elephantine lady, and works like one – terrible condition her hands were in when last I saw them. Yet she is a kindly soul and you will like her.'

'No,' he said firmly. 'I am resolved to go. It is exactly what I need and want. I must get away from here and see something different; begin again.'

The coolness with which he had decided to leave me filled me with anger and amazement.

He wanted to go immediately, but finally it was agreed that he would go in a few days' time, and Mamma would write forthwith and tell her brother that he was on his way. I was stunned, I sat dumbly and looked at him. He left the room.

The next few days were a flurry of activity; Mamma and Christopher went out to purchase stout clothes and boots. I would have gone with them, but I did not think I could maintain my smile. We could not speak of his departure at all. The days rushed by with cruel velocity; I woke up one morning and realized it was his last.

We walked together on the common just before he

was due to go. It was almost September and the cold was beginning to come through.

'When will you come back?'

'O, I don't know, I will have to work there for years before I will be wise enough to be a farmer, but I'm sure I'll be able to come back sometimes.'

'O.'

'I don't know what it is going to be like, Cath, but I'm going to have a good try to make it work out. Nothing ever has before. I think it is the best thing to do. I will be happy in the country and the peace and quiet.'

I thought bitterly that when we had talked of these things before our plan had always been to live in the country together.

'I will miss you,' I said numbly.

He stopped and hugged me so hard that my breath flew away.

'I cannot imagine what I will do without you, Cath: I cannot imagine a day without your face, or your sweet companionship. I do love you. But this must be for the best. I have written you a letter, it is under your pillow, you can read it when I have gone.'

He was weeping the silent tears, the ones that take the skin off your throat and make holes in your stomach.

We went home, very slowly our feet retraced our steps across the common. Mamma was waiting and in a hurry to get to the station. He brought his suitcase; Edward gave him a book; Mamma gave him father's gold watch, but he didn't want it and asked Mamma to give it to Edward. I had nothing for him so I gave him *The Old Curiosity Shop*, my favourite book, and hoped Little Nell would keep him company.

He said goodbye at the door. He was bundled up with so many things that he looked untidy, and a little lost and mournful.

'Be careful with yourself, Cath ... goodbye.'

'Goodbye.'

If I had not had the letter under my pillow to look forward to I could not have borne it at all. I fled to my room and opened the single sheet of white paper. It said:

Dear Cath,

Do not be sad that I have gone, though I shall be very sad. I know it is going to be very difficult for you without me here, but it will be just as painful for me. I know that it is best for me to go – I have to decide for both of us.

Cath, there is so much that we do not know, so much we have to learn. I cannot do your learning for you; you have to do it yourself. Where I am going will be so utterly alien and new to me, it cannot help but be good. I will have to work hard. I will have to accustom myself to those people. Mamma has given me some money, and I intend to spend it all on books; I want to fill my head with books, I want to drown in words.

And you, Cath, must force yourself out of the little corner we have lived in: you must make friends and come out of yourself. I'm sure I'm not the only person who can find you so lovely. You have been most good to me, I shall remember it all the time. I shall never be far from you.

I am going on an adventure and it excites and frightens me; you could not have come with me. The break had to come; I see that now. It is going to be very terrible for us both for some time, but in the end it will be better. I only want this to be true; I want you to be happy and grow up straight without me.

The W.

33

The trees were twisting in the cold September sun, twisting and turning yellow. The days limped by since he had left. I looked at his little bed and it saddened me. I talked to him constantly in my head; I was so close to him I did not miss him.

I was amazed at how lonely I felt without his company, without the hope of him turning a corner or walking into a room. It frightened me to realize how dependent I was upon his presence; how I relied upon him to look after me, but had always felt it was I who looked after him.

I talked to him all the time, and asked his advice on all matters; our conversations were long and made me happy, for a while. Each morning when I woke up, and every night before I fell asleep I thought very hard about him, his face moved in front of me, close enough to touch. Sometimes I would forget him for a while, but he would always re-enter my mind and fill the space he had left perfectly.

I knew he walked around with me, and went whereever I went. The closeness was nearer than my shadow. Often I would turn, knowing he would be there, and find an emptiness. But I knew how he felt, and what he was thinking all those miles away. I had dreams about him: often I would wake up almost crying his name, sometimes I woke with my body shaking and a wet and strange sensation in my stomach as though he had been inside me.

Even after I had heard nothing from him for a

month we were still touching, as close as air. Finally a letter arrived, thirty-eight days after he had gone. It said:

Dear Cath,

You did not think because I had not written that I was not part of you. It seemed unnecessary to write: I have nothing to say really.

It is nice here. The country is beautiful. The trees are losing their clothes, as you used to say when you were little. The reds and golds and browns are splashing all around. The air is so clean and good.

I work very hard and my body has got a bit bigger. Uncle Jonas is a strict task-master but he is teaching me well, and I think he is pleased with me. It is strange to have a kind of father again; when I see how much respect his sons have for him I realize I missed a lot in having a father like ours.

I have a small white room right at the top of the house. It is a great stone house, very old and rambling. The house is quiet after eight in the evening; everyone retires early to bed. I read on when the house is fast asleep. We rise at five every morning (I can see you shudder!) yet there is so much to do, and so much that can go wrong on a farm: the cattle let you down, so does the land, the beetles eat the crops and it rains too much. But I am very happy here.

I cannot tell you what it is to be apart from you bodily. It is like a new life completely on my own. Yet I know what you're thinking always; sometimes I lose the thread for a little and it makes me suffer, but it always comes back. I could not bear it if the thread were broken; I think I would begin to decay.

I would like to bite your ears and bundle you up in the bed. Nothing now is as clear as it was when I was with you. I am filled with doubts and misgivings. I feel I was a coward and treated you badly. I had no right to hurt you in that senseless fashion. I thought it would be simpler to be away from you, from the constant temptation. It is not. My nightmares terrify me, they are eating my brain. I don't know how long this can last. But I must not give in. I am trying very hard to forget, but this conscious effort only makes me remember. I am full of rubbish, effete and weak. I wonder how you had such patience with me.

There are a few strapping girls on nearby farms, but I do not want them. They have coarse skin and their manners are disgusting. O Cath, there is a purity about you I need, I want! It compensates for my own lack of worth.

Here everyone lives from day to day, and they never talk at all, except about the problems. My conversations are all with you. My head is full of you and the lovely things you did for me. It's not possible that anyone will ever understand and know me as you do. I am frightened at times because I think nothing really changes.

Please look after yourself for me. Maybe I can come back for a little while.

The W.

I was so happy, so happy. My felicity spread through all my life and everything around me. I began to look closely at things again; I played the old game of finding images in the trees and faces in the bumps on the walls. It was the same, then: nothing had changed, he still felt and thought as I did. He would come back, I knew he would, he would not be able to fill the void. And yet, the cracks were beginning to show in my armour; I realized I could not go on refusing to think about it. I still had not made my decision; I was insisting always, like a child, that nothing must change;

nothing must happen to destroy our life together. But what would he do if he came back? Even if he could find something to do, we could not live for ever in our mother's house. Would we go off and live together elsewhere? how could we? But I thrust all these incipient questions to the back of my brain; being concerned still only for the next day, the next summer.

The winter was coming; the autumn leaves lay in sagging bundles of rotting gold upon the common. The mornings started cold; the air was frosty on my way to school, the trees hid in a haze of mist. The eleven o'clock sun made everything look diffused and unreal. I saw a man wearing a winter coat. I began to feel a change in things: it was as if my brother had retreated from me; I no longer felt so keenly in touch with his thoughts. Either the distance between us was telling at last, or something new had occurred that I had no knowledge of.

A feeling of doom came over me. It caused me to be depressed and prone to imagining disaster at all times. In the darkness I felt sure someone would come up from behind and kill me: nothing and nowhere seemed safe. These sensations of threat and disaster advanced with the cold. My habit of sniffing increased. I could not bear to wear colourful clothes or the pretty things that had previously delighted me. I wanted at all times to look as inconspicuous as possible. My head swam with fantasies of blood and pain, nearly always my own. My loneliness was complete and utter. I could in no way approach another human being. I lived through my school days in a kind of terror: that people would ask something of me or make demands upon my person. I got through the days by doing everything that had to be done the best I could, like a machine. The other girls left me alone; they thought me a strange one.

Mamma was totally wrapped up in her own problems: the Frenchman had returned to France and she had no idea when he might return. She was bored and restless, and constantly impatient with me. Soon she too seemed to forget I existed. Edward ignored me. My isolation was total.

Then the affliction promised me by the dreadful MacDonald beset me with new terrors. I began to bleed for the first time: the silent menses had taken over my body.

My fear and ignorance of these matters dragged me even lower into myself. I could not tell Mamma and there was no one else to tell. At first I conjectured that I must be bleeding to death; that there must be some serious contusion within me to cause this great flow of blood. I looked hard for some cut and found nothing. For two days I lived in a red hell, unspeakably anxious, yet terrified to tell Mamma in case she call the apothecary I so disliked. I could not recall what he had said of this prophesied illness, but it had seemed fearful, and I could not admit to having it. On the second day Mamma found me weeping and white in the bathroom; red all over the white of the tiles as I attempted to wash the blood from the bandages.

'Good God, child, what have you done to yourself?'

I stood silent and numb, and suddenly she laughed and put her arm loosely about me.

'Of course, I should have told you: now you too are burdened with the curse?'

'But what is it, what is it?' I cried, hiding my head in my hands.

'O, it's a thing all women get, after a certain age, it simply means that they are not going to have a child.' She sat down, realizing that she would have to explain the matter fully to me, for my face was full of incredulity and fear.

'Well, at a given age, usually about fifteen, a girl

gets a flow of blood, coming from capillaries rupturing in the lining of the womb. This happens because girls develop much faster than young men and therefore more blood is being produced which has to be released when, at a certain age, the girl's rate of growth slows.'

Mamma seemed most taxed by this unusually long and rather odious conversation, for she then left the bathroom, tossing over her shoulder this last remark, which further confused me:

'It is also considered by the more extreme members of the emancipationists that when woman has the vote, the menses will miraculously cease ... I do not hold with that view; and even were it true, men would undoubtedly find some other means of preventing us from living a free life.'

I deduced then that in some inexplicable way men had something to do with the unfortunate condition in which I now found myself. It was very mystifying.

This new drama caused me to be melancholy for some days; it seemed in itself a bad thing, a changing thing, yet I could not say why. On a particularly gloomy day in late November when everything seemed to have gone amiss at school and when sadness was creeping into everything I saw, I received another letter from my brother. He said he would be coming home for Christmas; and this filled me with such joy. Yet the letter left me feeling ill at ease. He said things were not going well at the farm, that many disasters had taken place, and indeed that our uncle was actually considering selling up and getting out of the country altogether and starting afresh elsewhere. It worried me for days, but since I could not put my finger on the actual reason for my disquiet, I began to look forward to my brother's return instead.

I felt better again. The rain came and cleared the

air. The ground was squelchy and it smelt good and fertile. I began to plan what we would do when my brother was home.

The next letter said he would be back on 23 December; in only three days' time. My excitement knew no bounds. I was so happy, so happy that he was coming back. I painted his old room, our room, all white. I felt ten years old again, without a care in the world. I wanted everything to be beautiful, and nothing to upset him or make him sad when he came home. I resolved to be very careful not to utter any word that could make him feel burdened by me, or my needs. I wanted everything to be as simple as he wanted, and not to see the pale pain in his eyes any more. It was so lovely when he was cool and quiet; when he brought out the hidden threads of himself and lost himself for a while in the talking of it. My only wish was for him to be happy. For myself I did not care; my pleasure was in his presence.

He came back on a Monday. Mamma allowed me to meet him at the station at twelve o'clock.

I brushed my hair a thousand times, put some of Mamma's rouge on my mouth, folded my hair like a flower, and splashed Mamma's cologne of violets behind my ears. I looked carefully round the house before setting off alone for the station.

It was very cold waiting at the station; I stamped my feet fiercely to stop them freezing up. I thought the train would never steam in; I kept catching sight of my reflection in the windows. How nervous I looked! I determined to try to be composed, yet I could not stop myself from rushing backwards and forwards. The train came in at last and shuddered to a stop. I could not see him, and I had awful thoughts that he had decided not to come.

Then I saw him, right down at the other end of the train. He looked so small; his smile was so faraway;

from another place. He put his suitcases down with a loud noise and I fell onto him. The smell of the weasel: so familiar, yet forgotten. He held me away from him and looked at me; I looked at him. He had come back with a finished face, with the features settled and the expression formed. I kissed him many times, and it was such a warm, unlonely feeling again. He gave in his ticket and suddenly seemed so grown-up and independent. We had a cup of tea and he had some toast. It pleased me so to watch him eat.

He was full of happiness to be with me; he held my hand and smiled often. He kept asking me how I was, but I did not know how I was. There was too much to say and no need to say it. Somewhere in his face was tiredness, and something else, too, which I did not understand. But I did not want to spoil anything by enquiring.

He asked me if I'd found a love. It was such an absurd question I did not bother to answer it. Yet it was another little thing that perplexed me, and I tucked it away at the back of my head for later.

We went home and he unpacked lots of books he had brought me to read. He did not appear to want to stay in the house, so we went for a walk on the common.

'How dirty everything looks here, Cath. Everything on the farm was so quiet and clean.'

'What did you do there?' I asked.

'I started off just feeding the pigs and chickens and cows, and then learned later how to kill and butcher them. Jonas taught me all about the soil; it is becoming thin and infertile there now – it's one of the reasons he thinks we should move. We have tried many means of fertilization, but the earth is used up with too many harvests. People there are only just beginning to learn about feeding back into the soil what they've taken out ... I like the smells and the simplicity of the life. I wish my own head and body were so simple!'

We were happy that day. His hand was the right hand to be holding. I could not keep my eyes off him. I concentrated on his mouth, because his eyes would find me out. His hands were always on me.

'It is lovely to walk with you in the winter, and find that you have not changed. You do seem wiser, though, Cath. And your little face looks older. You are so thin. Your limbs are slim as these winter branches ... it is nice to be home.'

I wanted to know how long he would be staying; yet I could not ask, in case he would say he was not staying long. He wanted to go and meet Edward, who was at his music lesson; it surprised me that he should want to see Edward – the old impatience and dislike had disappeared for the time being. We waited in the cold for a few minutes and then Edward tumbled out from his class in a heap of grey; his head down. He saw us and walked warily in our direction, trying to form a smile with his lips. He and Christopher looked at one another but said nothing.

Mamma was not at home at tea-time, but then she seldom was: it was her hour of being somewhere else. I wanted to prepare tea and Lucy was quite happy to let me. I put on the kettle and began to cut the bread. Christopher was watching me with gentle eyes and the knife cut into my fingers: a red tear dropped slowly.

'How long are you staying?' Edward asked. I held my breath.

'I don't know yet, I have to speak to Mamma.' My breath flowed again: the answer was neither good nor bad. I would not allow myself to think about how long he might say; the thought was too painful.

The front door banged shut and a treacherous wind blew in. I could hear Mamma taking off her bonnet and wraps in the hallway. Christopher rose eagerly and went to open the door. Mamma turned towards him with her smile; it was such a lovely smile when she smiled it just for you.

'You've grown, Christopher,' she said lightly. 'Why didn't you write – all I got was one mean little letter ... now I want to hear all about it.'

'It's not so good,' he replied carefully. Mamma had a cup of tea with us and Christopher told her what he had told me about our uncle's desire to leave Wales. When he had finished, Mamma said: 'Well, we can talk about it later. In the meanwhile I am glad you are back. I hope you stay awhile.' It worried me that he did not answer.

I helped Christopher settle into his room; he liked the clean white walls. I sat on the bed and observed him closely while he put away his clothes and put the dirty things on the floor. They were all the same clothes; it was like looking in an old disused cupboard and finding last summer's memories.

The cold sky outside had turned sooty, and the moon sailed naked and hard, dodging the clouds. Christopher kept looking out of the window; he was nervous; something had to be said, I knew it. He took my face in both his hands and kissed one eye and then the other. A slow sadness began to distil. We sat very quietly, wrapped in each other's stillness. We remained thus for some time as the shadows crept into the corners.

'Just sitting here close with you, somehow it is all that I require today; sometimes I seem to need so much. Yet to be with you, close next to your body, it is all I want.'

My thoughts were troubling me sorely: I felt concerned that we should be sitting so close together in the darkened room; I was fretful lest someone should enter and find us so. A year ago such thoughts would never have entered my brain.

'Cath,' he said gently after a long silence, 'there is something I must tell you...' Just at this moment Mamma's voice rang up the stairs and a feeling of deliverance rushed over me, but he continued:

'Mamma wants us for dinner, no matter; perhaps it would be better if I told you all together ... though I had thought to tell you first.' He was tense and agitated, his words clipped; my anxiety grew.

Christopher hunched down close to the fire in the dining room; he shivered slightly. The flames threw dancing shadows on his pale face – rising and falling. The flames lapped the logs with the shuddering sound of a far sea. Once a log shrieked and Christopher started violently. Edward laughed low.

We had supper; Mamma had ordered all his favourite food: fish in cream sauce and syrup pudding. The fire hissed and groaned in the grate; it was cosy and warm. I began to feel a trifle reassured, hoping that perhaps the tenseness was all in my head.

We were quiet, and in the silence I could hear the beating of my brother's brain; I could feel him forming words in his mind.

'Mamma, Uncle Jonas has sold the farm in Wales. He will be writing to you about it. He has decided to buy land in the Cape, the land is fertile and plentiful; it is not hot, not like Africa, more like southern France. The French settlers and the British have made it into a lovely place to live.' The words flew out like birds disturbed in the bushes.

Mamma's brow puckered and she said slowly: 'Well, this is rather trying. Does it mean, then, that you will be coming back?'

The words rushed out of him: 'No. I am to go with them. This is my last chance to come home before we sail.'

'Nobody has spoken to me about it, Christopher; this is just like my brother. And pray, what am I supposed to do about it? It's all very well for all of you, but what about me?'

'Mamma, there is nothing you have to do, it is all fixed, and my passage paid. We shall be very happy there, I am sure. By all accounts it is a beautiful country, with great storms and a healthy climate. The Dutch influence is not so great in the Cape, it will be almost like home, but much sunnier.'

'Yes, yes, but will you ever come home again? You seem quite content to just go off and leave your family behind.'

'No ... no, I am not content with that. But we will become rich in no time, people are making grand fortunes out there. I will be able to come back. But Mamma, (and here his voice became pressing and desperate) you cannot understand, but I must get away from here, I must get *right* away, where it is too far ... where there is no hope. I must start again ... it will be like a new birth there.'

'No I don't understand, but have no fear, I shall not stop you going.' And then she remembered all the wealth and diamonds, and suddenly it was not such a bad idea after all. She chattered on, but Christopher was not listening. He was looking at me: his eyes sucking out the marrow of my bones. I could feel my face freezing up and my eyes glazing over. The noise of my heart thumped in my ears and my breath was heavy.

I could not bear to think about it, it couldn't really be true. Could he really be going away like this? Yet it was true, and I knew it. I had known something was wrong all the time and refused to admit it. Yet I didn't know it would be as terrible as this: millions of miles away, a vast ocean away. I would never see him again. He would never touch me again, look at me with that fierce and gentle face. He had said, as we walked: 'Whatever happens Cath, you and I have something which defies any definition; something which reaches across from you to me, however far apart we may be. It is something which will never change, however hard we try to kill it.' And that was what he was trying to do: to kill it, to kill me. He was going to the Cape to escape me, he couldn't bear to live with it: he had to put the greatest distance between our two bodies.

O, the selfishness of men! He was content to start a new life without any thought of my existence. He could run off on a fine adventure – how I would have loved to have been able to do that too! – and leave me to sort out my cold life on my own. Without any aid from him, or from anyone; without the slenderest thread of hope ... he would not return.

Mamma babbled on, her voice floating above me like the irksome hum of a fly. She was not aware of the oceans of pain that were sweeping across from Christopher to me and back again. I was going down, into my black core. Everything went dark, I could see nothing in the room. He slipped into the gloom and fell out of my eye. My arms clenched tight about me, holding me together. A shudder began at the pit of my stomach, it moved slowly upwards and stuck in my throat. O, the fierce pain in my throat as the tears were forced back. My teeth clenched; his eyes were on me, in me, stabbing me with their deep darts. My fingers bit into one another; my face became an ivory statue; something was dying.

Very slowly, out of the deep chair and the throbbing warmth of the room, I rose. I was aware vaguely of a huge well of pain on my right. I walked past it, it reached out to touch me, I moved away from it, and out into the hall, out of the front door and into the deep blackness.

It had just started to snow.

34

In relating my childhood I have felt a great relief, a new wholeness with myself. I have looked and seen things clearer than before. It is as if I have found my eyes, my fingertips again and I have been happy during the writing of this. I have touched my roots, my beginnings: the things that have formed me. I have looked at them and though they have shaken me, I have been able to face them – to put them down coldly on paper. At the back of my mind I have been excusing myself a little; I have been saying: 'You were young then, a mere child; can you really take responsibility for the actions of twenty years ago?'

The final 'sin' I have to relate does not uphold even this tenuous excuse. There is no way I can delude myself that I did not know what I was doing, or what the consequences might be. And perhaps the worst thing is that Edward has been able to use this incident to manipulate and injure me of late.

But today the sky is the colour of Jesus' blanket. A lethargic wind is pinned back against the glass of my window. How hot the day is! It is so difficult to breathe. The servants come and go, they serve me creams and puddings and light jellies; I taste the corners.

This fierce glare penetrates everywhere, exposing every raw nerve-end, drawing out pain like a poultice. I like best the dark things and silence. The noise offends me: the happy chirping of the birds, the maddening buzz of the bees draining the flowers.

To escape the sluggishness of my mind, and also because I heard the approaching clatter of wheels on the driveway, I determined to take a stroll in the orchards.

It is strange how Christopher and I as children always bolted at the approach of strangers; it is a disposition I am still unable to shed. Mamma certainly was not of the same inclination; I think the trait came from Father. He disliked people on principle, always seeking the fault and not the virtue in everyone he came across. Even the few friends he had were maligned constantly; and he would eschew the company of strangers entirely, or only bear with it with much reluctance. He only enjoyed people's company after their departure, when he would deride them heartily for some small or imagined short-coming.

I did not feel this way about humanity; nor did my brother, but we felt nervous and exposed in the company of others, and would far rather slip back into the solitary state we understood. For my part I still feel this way; and now that Christopher is no longer with me, I would rather breathe the air of my own thoughts than consciously seek out other atmospheres.

When I think about our father today, I realize that we have very little for which to thank him; he of course would dispute this hotly and quote all manner of benefits. Yet I resent him because he was never able to show us the beauty of anything, rather its flaw. I hate him for his wilful destruction of my brother's self-regard. I think if Christopher now is burdened by anything, it is not by me, but by the damage done him by my father: the years of taunts and jeering, the despoliation of his Self.

If I were to agree to Edward's theory that he killed his wife by wishing for it, then I dare say Christopher and I were responsible for our father's death. I wished most fiercely that he might die, or be mercifully taken from us by a hopeless war. And today I hope most fervently that Christopher has rid himself of my father's unmaking; may he dance on his memory and be glad!

Gnawing on these thoughts I wandered up to the orchard, taking care to don my bonnet to please Thomas, or perchance because Mamma's stern warnings were at last having some effect.

Lord, how hot! The swollen apples and pears basked in the sunshine; one light touch and they dropped, heavy, spilling their sweetness on the dry earth. The flying creatures gathered like vultures, their probosces sucking and gouging the over-ripe flesh. The trees have my weariness, their branches are laden down, they hold themselves ponderously. I cannot bear to tread upon the spilt fruit.

If I am a seed about to burst, if I am to flower, the old seed, my Self, must die. Some new thing will grow out of me; but I must perish. I cannot have it; I cannot allow it to happen. I must protect myself from this that would devour me.

Up in the cool cluster of trees it was dark and sweet. Little light penetrated the green curtains of the trees; I sat upon the cool earth and touched the moss, gently, as my brother used to do, so as not to bruise it. It was so peaceful and quiet; it calmed me. The flutterings inside me terrify; an animal trying to escape. Is it stronger than I? which of us will win?

Last night no sleep would come to me, the spirits were at work in my room. The chaste and lovely moon lit up my chamber, she smiled and bid me look again; but I know the evil of the moon and cast my eyes away. The sky a strange violet hue: a spread of altar coverings. The movements within me were strong, a sudden thrusting, a light kick of the heels, then a vicious plunge. I heard Thomas close the door of the library and walk slowly up the stairs. He hesitated outside my door, then on a sudden impulse he came in.

'Catherine, you are still awake? I thought you would be fast asleep by now. When I bid you good night some hours ago you looked most weary.'

'I have been watching the moon.'

'Do you not know it brings about madness?' he said with a small smile.

Suddenly a fiendish pang caused me to call out. He looked most concerned and was by my side in an instant.

'Shall I call the midwife?'

'No, it is nothing yet; these are not the birth pangs, just the stirrings.'

'Your time is near, Catherine, we must take great care —' He rose to go.

'No, do not leave me, Thomas. We can wait and see when the next occurs before taking any action, surely?'

'Very well, but I shall stay with you ... I am very nervous about this birth.'

'Why, Thomas, do you have evil premonitions?'

'No, of course not. It is merely that when I was a child my mother could never produce a brother or sister, and it greatly upset me to be an only child, to have no friend in that big and lonely house.'

'Was she barren, then?'

'O, no indeed not, she conceived twice. The first time, (I was told all this by Clara my Nanny many years after the events) the first time she was in labour for many hours, and according to the midwife she would not allow the child to pass out of her: her body locked shut and she began to scream histrionically. The midwife did not know how to act and my father became fearful for her life.' Here Thomas began to shift uncomfortably in his chair. There was a silence and I thought he might not continue but he managed, as always, to regain his composure. 'In the end they removed the child by Caesarean delivery; but it was dead. On the second occasion, I was somewhat older and I had watched my mother grow large with much interest on the rare occasions I was brought to see her. She always seemed calm and tranquil, yet at the time of the birth her screams could be heard throughout the whole house. This child, a girl, was actually born, but at great personal cost to my mother. The child lived a matter of weeks, and my mother refused to have any more children after that.'

This narration made me soften towards Thomas and aroused in me a new curiosity about him.

'And has this affected your view of child-bearing, Thomas? I think it must have, since you have been fretting greatly in the last months.'

'Yes, indeed it must. I find myself getting more and more nervous as your time approaches. The process of birth is a mystery to me, the idea of it is a terror. I have my mother's screams in my memory constantly.'

'Did your first wife never conceive then, Thomas?'

'No.'

As usual, I could not engage him in any conversation on these matters; I knew virtually nothing of his first wife, for he always answered my questions about her in this monosyllabic fashion. Yet, we had had a small conversation together and this was unusual in itself. He did not speak often of his childhood and I was interested to hear of it. It helped explain his fussing towards me in the last months.

'Should you not try to rest, Catherine?' he now said. 'You must have been sitting in that chair a good while, and your lamp is nearly extinguished.'

'Yes, I will go to bed now, Thomas.'

'You will let me know immediately anything happens, however slight?'

'Indeed I will, Thomas, do not fear.'

'You have not disrobed, Catherine, would you like me to help you?'

'No, I can manage; in any event my great size would doubtless alarm you.'

'You understand these things well; I suppose you, too, have your childhood horrors ... I will bid you good night, Catherine. Call if there is anything you require.'

His quietness left the room, and I felt a little sorry when he had gone. The small serenity I had been trying to maintain was breaking up; the night was dragging her feet like a somnambulist and I was uneasy. Thoughts of my brother ploughed through my mind; I wanted desperately to sleep but no sleep would come.

The wind rustled the pale blue curtains gently; the walls were the colour of spilt cream when the moonlight played on them. On the dresser the old vase held the daisies, their stems winking greenly.

The tiny lamp has flickered and fallen, rising blue and orange, then it gently died away. In a moment I shall go to bed. I am determined that my first action of the morning must be to relate the incident I have referred to, but up to now, have lacked the courage to reveal. In the morrow it will be done, and before this birth overtakes me.

35

I was nineteen and it was June. I know it was June because the rhododendrons were in full flower: a great mass of violet tumbling at the bottom of the garden.

It was a slow Saturday evening and I sat reading in the drawing room, trying to decide whether the chill in the air and the sudden blotting out of light by the approaching rain warranted the indulgence of a fire.

I heard Edward's voice in the hall, and wondered to whom he might be speaking in such a high-pitched manner. The door swung open on the heels of this thought, and Edward entered the room with a tall, dark-haired man. I did not recognize the man, for his head was well down and the dusk was shielding.

Swiftly he raised his head. My heart soared and crashed, then I almost seemed to feel it move and creak and ache. He stood there heavy-browed, eyes and jaw clenched in anger, his lips a white scar across the darkened face. He was so tall suddenly, with such a wildness in his face. I moved involuntarily in his direction.

Edward's low snicker penetrated my arrested brain: 'Look what I found outside, lurking about in front of our house. You know, I don't think he would have come in at all, Catherine. I had to force him into his own house ... of course, if we'd known you were coming it would have been the fatted calf...'

Christopher's knuckles were white beneath the staining of the sun; I could barely see his eyes, so fierce and tight they squinted out between the eye-folds. The electricity was racing between our two bodies; I suffered and felt as he did. Edward sensed this; and feeling left out he flung himself from the room.

It is strange how clearly I remember all these things, yet I cannot recall where I lost my hairbrush yesterday.

I moved towards him slowly; the eyes seemed to hold me back. I smelt the harsh dry scent of his hair, the force that leapt out of these eyes, and then the strange, flat and unfamiliar intonation in his voice: 'How are you Catherine?' His voice was not the same; the eyes and the face carried the same scars, the voice was new. It was deep and there was an odd twang, a level quality in it. My hands burned to touch him; there was no life between us without it. But I did not.

'I realize now how long a time five years is,' he said.

'O, yes; it is very long.'

I felt foolish and exposed suddenly. I wished I were wearing another dress; I was conscious of the hole in the heel of my stocking; I wished I had known he was coming.

'You are still angry with me?' he asked.

'You never wrote one word: I have known nothing of you all this time, except what I felt in my heart.' It was a rebuke. One half of me wanted to be rid of him, to be free of the scaring pain that his presence brought, to sever myself for ever from his terrible power. The other half wanted him to take me, to devour and ravish me like flowers under his feet.

Swiftly, his self-composure vanished.

'What could I say?' he stammered painfully. 'What could I tell you? I have thought of you constantly. If you suffered hell, believe me I did too. I regret every day leaving you so cruelly – but there seemed no other choice. It is the reason I did not write, or return.'

'Yet you have returned, Christopher, you are here. Why?' My coldness surprised me.

'That fiend Edward, he saw me and pounced upon me like a mad dog. I was walking outside, just looking. I came back, Cath, for no other purpose than to stand again in the same place, to feel old sensations, perhaps even to see you from afar. I have the feeling it might be the last time.' My heart recoiled as from a knife wound. 'I never meant to be here in this room, close to you thus.'

'Why do you not go, then?' How pained I felt, how the griefs fluttered in my throat like small birds in a hedgerow.

'I do not take offence at the induration in your voice; you have suffered greatly; it is your only defence. I cannot go because it is as if I have grown into this spot, taken root in this room. It is a happiness for me,' and then softly: 'Perhaps I did really mean to see you, and Edward's appearance was a lucky chance that I was relying upon. It is more than possible that I might not have had the courage if he had not forced me to face this, and you. I imagine his only pleasure was my discomfort, and yours. Do you wish me to go?'

'No.'

He smiled as though he was remembering far distant memories. His blackened eyes looked through and beyond me; possibly at a small girl and two boys wrestling together in this same house, in another time, another life, so distant now, yet all still present in these self-same bodies. Suddenly he came back to the moment.

'But of course you will have changed. Our dead childhood must be just a dream to you now,' he finished brusquely.

'It is as though it were yesterday.'

He moved forward, I retreated. The black mask lifted and then lowered again. The front door slammed; and I observed that the rain had begun to fall gently. I moved to light a lamp, and then left the room to ascertain whether Edward had indeed gone out. He had, and it surprised me that he had not come back, further to torment his brother. Yet he had an uncanny way of choosing his time carefully, with the cunning of a stalker; I knew he would be back.

When I re-entered the room, Christopher was staring out of the window at the fuliginous sky; the rain was falling loudly now. I stood behind him, placing a careful distance between us.

'Where does Edward go?' he asked thoughtfully.

'You ask me that? I have no more idea of how he spends his time, or where he goes, than we ever did.'

'Hm, perhaps he goes to ladies of ill-repute,' he pondered, 'it would seem to follow.'

'Do *you*?' I whispered.

He laughed gently. 'That is not a question a lady ever asks, and certainly one a gentleman never answers. But we are equals, you and I, and I will answer anything you ask. Yes, I have been to ladies of ill-repute.'

It did not bother me: it was of no consequence. He was glad I understood this at last.

'Are you hungry?' I asked.

'No.'

'When did you arrive?'

'I got into Liverpool last night.'

Suddenly we had no wish to ask trivial questions, and we were both aware of the smallness of time.

He walked past me to the big armchair by the fireplace, brushing my cheek lightly with his hand. We sat together and he told me how he had spent the last years.

'We had a rough passage to the Cape,' he began. 'I was violently ill most of the time. I felt the Cape rollers would shake out my stomach. It seemed a just punishment.' He smiled ruefully.

'We bought land in the Cape, near Stellenbosch, a

small village close to the sea. Our uncle bought a great gabled house, and we had vineyards and orchards, fat cattle, everything a farmer could desire. The land is so fertile and good, it is lush and green and most beautiful: I cannot begin to tell you how beautiful it is. The sea is soft and gentle at times; fierce as a lion at others. I loved the place from the start. There is a spiritual quality about it; as if the mountain contained some magic, some power to heal. I began to mend inside, slowly. I tried to stop reproaching myself for something I could not alter.'

'Are you speaking of us?'

'Yes ... you see, I felt I understood how it came about, and why, and yet I could never seem to prevent myself yearning for that same closeness. I was left with such an abyss, such a loneliness.'

I moved to a chair in a dark nook of the room: I did not wish him to see how affected I was by his words, and his manner of saying them. He went on, talking slowly and carefully, putting into words thoughts he had been gathering over many years.

How he touched my heart, with his eyes on fire and his face consumed with that unreal passion, that bloodless agony. We looked at one another in silence. Then the words tumbled out of him like flood-waters released from a long-locked dam.

'You see, Cath, I am still convinced of my own lack of worth. I have not sufficient confidence to attempt another love. You loved and believed in me totally. I don't feel another human being could do that again ... And you, what of you? Why have you clung to me, or rather the memory of me. For surely the memory is better than this twisted, pathetic creature before you?'

'I have found no one better,' I said simply.

He let his head drop into his hands: 'I do not know what to do,' he uttered low, so low I had to strain my ears to hear the words. 'Is there no respite from this pain? Must there always be this lack of hope, this beauty without fulfilment?'

Waves rolled over my head; blood raced my veins and pounded behind my ears. My hands were damp and chill, my mouth dry, and an old passion rose in me. I moved towards the dark figure by the fireplace.

'Sitting in the dark, are we?' A voice flew in through the door, smashing the sweet silence and rooting me to the floor.

36

How lonely it sometimes is to sit here fighting this cold white paper, forcing myself to face myself, here on this frigid and unscarred white landscape, with no relief save the knowledge that subjugation is a worse torment than this exposure.

No one spoke in the room and Edward was forced to continue, for it was as if he had never spoken.

'I see you have made yourself at home – how long are you staying, if one might ask?'

'Not long.'

'Well, in Mamma's absence, as master of the house, I will ask you to stay with us.'

'I intend to.' As an afterthought Christopher added, 'Where is Mamma?' (Indeed I had completely forgotten about her.)

'Mamma,' Edward replied mockingly, 'is at present in Oxfordshire. She spends many week-ends there now. There is a gentleman – more erudite than the usual gentleman Mamma encourages – she intends to snare him into matrimony.'

'Edward,' I said crossly, 'you are always most fawning to Mamma in her presence, yet you attack her once her back is turned. It is odious of you.'

'I am not going to remain with you, have no fear. I see that my brother and I have as little in common as ever. I will be glad when you are gone, Christopher,' he concluded with acrimony, and, turning on his heel, he vacated the room once more.

'He still cannot abide to be in our company,' I mused.

'I should pity him, I suppose,' Christopher said, 'yet he just leaves me cold.'

We talked long into the night and how the hours sped by! We did not stop for food or drink, and felt neither hunger nor fatigue. Edward kept looking into the room; he obviously found it impossible to sleep, and every few hours he would dart his head through the door with a snappish 'So you are still there,' and then hastily retreat once more. This finally disturbed us so much that we resolved to retire to bed, Christopher to the little familiar room we had shared in childhood, and I to my room near Edward's.

I could not sleep; thoughts tossed and turned in my fevered brain. I felt greatly comforted by my brother's proximity and much un-nerved by it. All the old feelings and fears returned, harder to bear now, being tempered with more knowledge and therefore a stronger terror.

I woke from a shallow sleep with the strange impression that I was not alone. I immediately imagined spirits and apparitions, and began to quake. As soon as my clouded eyes could focus properly I saw that someone sat by my bed, on a small child's stool I had kept since my childhood: it was Christopher.

'You frightened me,' I laughed nervously.

'Sorry.'

'Have you been sitting here long?'

'No, less than an hour, I imagine. You looked so lovely with your mouth slightly parted and your hair tumbling all over the pillow. I imagined you might be Eurydice, and I Orpheus come to rescue you from the Underworld.'

'That would be a fine thing,' I smiled.

'I have thought so often how you might look, and

imagined how you might speak and move.'

'Do I disappoint you?'

'The very reverse: you are very lovely. Your cheek-bones have sharpened like Mamma's and your mouth is just like mine. That is a funny thought, is it not? There is an old sage who says we are all really in love with ourselves and trying to find ourselves in other people. Yet you are the same as me: body of my body and soul of my soul.'

'You held our propinquity against me once, as I recall.'

'I see you forget nothing, as always. You were a true joy to me, Cath, all those lonely, ignorant days, and my days are still as lonely, and probably just as ignorant. It is the pleasure that turns to pain, as it always must. It is the pleasure that destroys.'

'You are shaking a little; are you cold?'

'No, it is not the cold that makes me quake.'

'Why don't you get into my bed for a little while,' I said lightly.

His eyes flew to my face in panic; trying to see if anything lay behind the words. I looked back at him with great calmness: 'You need have no fear of me.'

'I never feared you; it was always myself I feared.'

He moved over and climbed gingerly into the bed, I made way for him. 'You look humorous in that night-shirt,' I said. He scowled and looked exactly as he had at fourteen. I ruffled his hair and he moved back from me.

I thought I could probably go to sleep now and feel as safe and content as I had only felt as a little girl with his warmth beside me in the night. But, Christopher now was so long and large, there was scarce room to breathe in the bed.

'Christopher, if you would curl me up in your shoulder as you used to, I would fall asleep very soon and be very happy.'

I moved into his body and his arm wound around me. His body felt stiff and tense and I wondered whether I was doing him a dis-service. We lay thus for a few moments and my eyes began to close. I became aware of a coldness on my cheek which rested close to his and raised my hand to touch it.

He wept. And it ripped out the membranes of my heart. I gathered him into my arms and kissed him fiercely.

The door flew open and someone strode up to the bed and looked down at us. I sat up very slowly, an anger rising, rising, taking over my body.

'Edward,' my voice screamed, so loud that it shocked me.

He stood there, looking down at us triumphantly like someone exposing a great crime.

'I see you haven't changed,' he sneered.

Christopher reeled from the bed and lunged at him. Edward moved back very speedily and said: 'Not so fast, dear brother, it isn't all going to go your own way as it used to, you know ... I imagine you thought me very dumb and stupid, yet I used to roam about in the night and hear things I could not quite understand at the time. I was too frightened to do anything then. But not now.'

Christopher smashed him on the chin and Edward fell backwards for an instant. Then he righted himself, and, cursing hideously, he spat out: 'Now listen to me, for this is what you are going to do, unless you want my sister exposed and disgraced. You are going to leave this house now, and you are never going to set foot in it again, Christopher. Go back to your bloody farm in the Cape and never come near us again!'

I began to weep silently, not really because of his threats, but because he was making me feel unclean, and dirt was attaching itself to me with every foul word he said.

'Nothing has happened Edward, you fool,' I whispered, 'I don't know what you are talking about.' But he just smiled and I knew that he had trapped us. I felt hot and I trembled, for I knew full well that we could not have prevented it: it would have happened again.

'Get out,' Edward ordered. Christopher walked up to him slowly. I moved so that I could see his face. It was indeed fearsome. The dawn creeping through the window lit his face with a warm flush. He looked like a statue, every muscle in his face was rigid; his hands were clenched at his side and he seemed not to breathe. Edward understood that look and he began to shuffle slowly towards the door. He was fumbling for the door handle, trying to open it without turning his back. Christopher's fist whirled into Edward's face and a crunching sound filled me with sickness. Edward crumpled. Christopher raised him with his left hand and his right fist pummelled into the face again. Edward slumped and I rushed up to them, and pulled Christopher away from the room.

'I hate, I hate violence,' he said between clenched teeth. 'I never thought there would come a time when I had no other weapon to use but the one I abhor most.'

He looked at me with all the sadness in the world. I began to weep against him.

'I have to go, Catherine, I have to go,' he said into my hair.

'No, no, you cannot leave me here, you cannot. I need help; I must have you: I cannot live again the way I have lived these last years.' My words fell about him, I could not keep them to myself now to spare his pain.

'You cannot come with me, and I have to go. I am so sorry, so wretched that I came back. Edward has had his revenge at last. I have been most stupid.'

He pulled away from me, and went through the door, and down the stairs. I ran after him, calling, crying: 'Please, you cannot leave me, please do not leave me so. O God, I shall die.' I rested my head against the bannister and wept most bitterly.

He came back and helped me up the stairs and towards my room; his face ashen and his lips bitten and bleeding.

'I cannot do anything else. I cannot stay here now, and I cannot come back ever ... It is hopeless. You know it is. You have to face it.'

'Why, why did you come back, why have you done this to me again?'

The agony was splitting out of his eyes and mouth, and pain seemed to seep from every pore of our bodies. He looked at me very hard, for a long moment, and then he tore himself from my wild grasp and flew down the stairs and into the night.

'Christopher!' I screamed and ran back to the stairs. I could see Lucy rushing up towards me in her old red dressing gown, I felt myself slipping under, and I can remember no more.

37

Perhaps all my life I shall remember what I felt in my body and heart that night. The guilt scratches like sharp-clawed mice over my naked heart.

Now, after all these years, the hardest thing to bear is not my chagrin that we were accused wrongly that day, but the certainty I feel that we were accused rightly. There can be no excuse and no vindication; and I feel as guilty as though it had indeed happened.

My pain and grief at that time were so terrible that I could not move from my bed for many weeks. I said not a word to anyone; Mamma gave up in disgust. She had been told that Christopher had come, and left after he and Edward had fought. Edward told Mamma no more than that, I am certain, and the incident shook him enormously. He came nowhere near me, and very soon afterwards made arrangements to live away from home.

Now I feel exhausted, drained of everything. I have exposed all. I have dragged it up from the recesses of my mind and laid it bare. And I feel numb. I feel defeated strangely by the task. It is like a death.

And today, to my utter confusion, a letter arrived for me. Sent on from Mamma. It is from Christopher and it confirms my conviction that we have been strongly in one another's thoughts over these past months of writing. He too has been writing. I know the letter by heart.

Dearest Catherine,

I write this in the midst of a bloody war. I began it months back, sitting on the outskirts of a miserable little dorp (town, that is) called Mafeking. The whole world has heard of it now. I am now retreating with my commando up towards Pretoria – yet we are not really retreating, except from Mafeking, for we fight daily – out on the dry veld and wherever we see the enemy. The enemy in my case being the British!

I am trying to put together all the pieces I have written for you over these last terrible months. Some I have lost, but I will put what I have together so you may have a story to read as you sit in the placid sunshine of an Oxford afternoon. I think I had better start at the beginning. Bear with me.

I do not think even now that I can write what I felt upon leaving you that diabolical day in June. I did not go straight back. I went instead to Cornwall and stayed at Land's End for three weeks. Three most terrible weeks where I could scarce move, so great was my pain and sorrow. I remember most clearly walking along the cliffs by the little cove where we splashed that summer away. I lay on the turf and tore up the soil and clawed the grass to try to release my wretchedness. The lighthouse is no longer there.

Then I sailed back to the Cape, and the sight of the mountain was the most comforting thing I had seen since your sweet face.

Things were still going very well for my uncle, and in the years after we grew even more prosperous and bought more land and cattle. We made wine: the French settlers here brought their great skills with them and the wine is excellent.

I grew older and a little more settled, but there was something about the Cape that was not sufficiently alien ... not different enough for me. The English had brought their Englishness with them and planted it in the Cape. I wanted something quite else, I became restless. I had met some fine young farmers on the outskirts of the Karroo – great fellows they were, and when the rains came we would go immediately into the Karroo and watch the tiny flowers spring from the desert sand like jewels. I liked their company greatly, and finally we formed a plan that two of them and myself would go up into the Transvaal and buy land there. I had collected quite some money of my own, so I told my uncle, and went with his blessing.

The journey through the Karroo I must tell you of: I felt like one of the Voortrekkers marching away from the imperialism of the British. How desolate the Karroo is – there is nothing for hundreds of miles, just little milk-bushes and thorn trees and the occasional kopje (a tiny hill) and dusty beetles. How different it was to the lush and beautiful Cape. Sand, sand and cactus – nothing more.

We went through the Orange Free State and into the Transvaal, to Potchefstroom where my friends had an offer of land. Here again the terrain was utterly strange: dry and red and dusty. Yet, how happy I was to be there. We began to farm, and all the skills I had learnt in the Cape were of little use. It was like starting again, for the land was not good, and the place was an agricultural backwater compared to the farming methods and machinery that I had been used to. But we were young and strong and full of enthusiasm. It was here that I really began to love the Boers and the land. The Transvaal is independent, and the people were happy then. It was totally un-English, a new culture, a new way of life. These people with their intense love of the land, with their strong Calvinistic principles, their simplicity, generosity, bigotry – they accepted me as their brother, took me into their homes, their hearts, their lives. We led a simple existence, drawing out the land's goodness, tending the cattle, making provision for dry years. They have a fine culture: told me wonderful myths and fables, taught me their strange dances and jolly music. I felt at home, Cath; for the first time I felt at home. I began to feel that this land was mine, that this was my country ... and with the fierce fanaticism that perhaps is only felt by those who do not rightly belong to the country by birth – I gave myself to the land and to its causes, and most of all to the great cause of Boer independence.

1886 was the beginning of all evil, when the gold-eyed devil in the hearts of the British began to assert itself. We were quite far from the Rand, yet we could see all the foreigners rushing in to grab their bags of gold and carve up the land. Our little peaceful life could not go on for ever. The Jameson Raid, when a bunch of Boer farm boys sent the British Army packing, was the start of real hostilities. It made us feel, sadly, that it was an easy task to take on the might of the British Empire – after all, they seemed such a foolish bunch.

Catherine, I have tried with all my heart to forget you. Yet how could I? to forget you is to forget myself. It is not possible. If I lose myself, how can I live, and to lose you is to lose myself. I would to God you cannot forget me – I wish you the same bitter torture that has racked me every day since I left you. I cannot erase the look on your face that day I walked out of the house. I am amazed that I had the strength to abandon you then, though I suppose I had little choice. Yet it is not so, for we always have a choice. I don't think I could do it today, knowing what I know now, and understanding through this bitter war what a trivial thing life is and what a supreme force is love.

I dare say Mamma has had many combustions at the mention of my name, and I often wonder what Edward told her. Truly I do not care for that, but greatly I care for you Cath, and most deeply I regret all the pain I have caused you.

Cath, how lonely is my life, with only my small twisted thoughts to keep me company. I have tried, but I cannot recapture the sweetness of youth, the innocence, the passion of complete harmony between two souls, two bodies. I write this for you, in the same way that everything I look at I look at for you, every thought I have I tell you in my heart, I speak to you at all times. I remember everything, our house in London, the holiday in Cornwall, the terrible time you nearly died. The things you said I carry around with me, your eyes shine in my eyes as a constant rebuke. Cath, I am still laden with pain, full of selfishness and inactivity. I am cold, bitter, twisted, I feel nothing, only what I felt once.

There have been big Afrikaner girls, with generous bodies. I take and give nothing, and then no longer wish to take. I remember the sweetness of your small, thin form. Yet, touching you was almost a violation, was always that way. I think of you that way — full of purity.

You will wonder how I came to write this to you. Well, first I met a man, Hanwell, a soldier in Mafeking with Baden-Powell. He told me about you — recognizing my name. He had come from Oxford and though he had not seen you for some time he remembered you well. I did not tell him how close my connection with you was, but let him ramble on as my heart beat fiercely at every mention of you. He said you were a quiet, demure thing — regarded as cold by the gentlemen, and that you lived a secluded life with our Mamma. He had some vague notion that there was talk of you marrying some elderly gentleman in the country – but suspected it would come to nothing. He told me how you looked, Cath. It was a great joy to me to think of you sitting quietly in an Oxford garden, your hair parted neatly down the centre, your black eyes quiet and your hands folded in thought.

After talking to him my heart felt free for the first time. I knew at last that you had not betrayed me. I began to write to you this letter. I wanted you to know that nothing has changed in my heart. That I love you with the passion of our youth, with the strength of all these long, long years.

When the war began there was no choice for me. I would fight with the Boers and against my own people. The British in South Africa sicken me: their greed, their stupidity, their inablity to allow the rightful owners of the country to govern themselves. It was not a hard decision to make: I felt a fervent Boer. I loved the land with a fierceness and dedication I had only felt once before in my life. I surrendered all my desires, hopes and fears into the cause of freeing the country of the British.

We were sent immediately to Mafeking on the borders of Bechuanaland. The British at this stage were poorly prepared and full of ignorance, with ludicrous leaders. Our spirits were indeed high. We received dispatches from our brothers outside Kimberley. They had repulsed the British Army at Belmont, Graspaan, the Modder River and again at the superb victory at Magersfontein. The flower of the British Army was defeated by a bunch of Boer amateurs, who inflicted fearful casualties on the British and suffered few themselves.

Buller made an immense fool of himself in this country. His generals continued to make frontal attacks and exposed themselves to our accurate and deadly aim. Their officers fell asleep in the sunshine, and our farm boys were wiping out impregnable British positions all over the veld.

In February, when Roberts had cleared up the British military mess somewhat, and Kimberley was relieved, the tide was beginning to turn. I felt most bitter that that swine Rhodes, the richest and greediest man in the world, got out of Kimberley alive. Always remember, dear Cath, that 448,000 highly trained soldiers were sent out to conquer a bunch of 40,000 amateur Afrikaners: their spirit, their immense bravery in this unequal struggle will always be remembered.

Yet for me, and my friends at Mafeking, life was very pleasant. My one grief was that my dear friend André, with whom I had been farming all those years, had been killed in a skirmish on the way to Mafeking. Mafeking is a dreadful little dump, just a splattering of tin-topped houses sprawling over the veld, and of course there's the railway line ... The countryside is like a desert – bleak, boiling, dust-ridden, fly-ridden. The African sun scorches down every day without fail, yet it does not oppress me. I write mainly in the night, when it is cool, often cold, and the sky is a mass of silver lights, and the black silhouettes of the thorn trees creak under the moonlight.

Baden-Powell is regarded as something of a buffoon, indeed I think he would be happy enough with that description himself – he considers himself a great joker. He makes coy jests about an act I am sure he has never performed! He spends a great deal more time on amusements than he ever does on fighting us. The British continue their British life in Mafeking, with polo parties, teas, concerts, plays and piano recitals. We do not hinder messengers from getting in and out of the town and they have plenty to eat. There is no suffering at Mafeking – the British are having a whale of a time. And Baden-Powell is truly in his element. Just a few days ago a British soldier married an Afrikaner girl, neither could speak a word of the other's mother tongue!

So the round of sundowners and dances go on, their laughter rings out late into the night. We sit and wait, living on mean rations, but suffering no great hardships. There are very few casualties and we are succeeding mainly due to the enemy's cowardice. We play cards in the sand and try to keep our spirits up with stories. The real enemy is boredom. I am happy because I am writing to you and you fill my thoughts.

Cath, it is the beginning of June now and things are going very badly with us. Mafeking was relieved in May to great and ridiculous jubilation. We are now making our way towards the capital and Paul Kruger. We have no orders, but have spread ourselves over the veld and will not give in. We fight against small troops of the British, who are scattered thinly all over the land, trying to round us up. There is desperation in our people now and we are suffering greatly. The fighting is bloody and constant and I have little time to go on with this writing. When we are not fighting we have to sleep to keep up our strength. Food is scarce and so is ammunition, but we have much spirit.

It has now become quite appalling. I write with a kind of urgency and horror. I am entrusting this document to a few faithful friends, in case something should happen to me before I can send it to you. We are in the middle of nowhere, the sand stretches for ever, the sun scorches down mercilessly, there is no shelter, little protection in this wilderness. Yet I have my faithful and marauding Mauser.

If I am captured by the British I'll be shot. I can lose nothing.

They have began to burn down the farms of our people: the veld is on fire, women and children are burnt alive, the earth is ruined and they think that in this way they will starve the brave commandos into submission. Refugees are beginning to crawl out of the craters, and to seek livelihood from the British authorities. They are without homes, food or water, and have been placed in camps. I have seen these camps and they are most terrible: shacks stuck on the sand, without sanitation, with little food and water. Disease is spreading like wildfire: they have no medical attention. Thousands and thousands of women and children are dying in these concentration camps. I believe they are trying to exterminate us.

We are nearly in Pretoria. Perhaps I shall be able to post this letter there. I hear that the victorious British are on their way there. I do not think the place can hold out, Kruger's lot are much weakened. I will continue beyond Pretoria. There is nothing else I can do. I know now that there is no hope for me. Once again I have landed myself in a hopeless situation where there can be no respite from pain.

I cannot give up and I know that the band I am with will not surrender either. So we will fight till we drop. I will not get out of this war, my sweet Catherine. But I cannot say that it concerns me. I have been happier in this land than I have ever been, apart from the days without pain with you. Even then I was much burdened by the curse of our father and my own shortcomings. I have grown into this land, this red place; I would not be parted from it; I could live nowhere else, so it is perfectly acceptable to me to die here.

I hope you think of me, Cath. I want you to remember everything, to suffer what I suffer, to feel what I feel. I want you to know what I have known and felt here, as I am sure you do ... I am sorry so much of this has been lost and I can only send you these fragments of my life. Yet I hope that it will suffice.

Cath, tomorrow we will be in Pretoria. This is my last chance to speak to you, but I will continue to touch you with my mind. I am glad, I am glad you are not married. It is utterly selfish and wicked, I know, but still I am glad. My whole heart rejoices that you have not found again what we had, and what I suppose you and I have always been trying to recapture in other people. Yet we cannot. I have found it only in you. You could find it only in me. I accept this now. And I leave you with all love, Catherine. Do not forsake me.

The W.

P.S. In these parts they call a weasel a meerkat.

38

I write this now in a definite despair; there is nothing I can do but put it down. It has sucked the breath from me. I have betrayed him. He presumed that I would try to find again what we had before; he did not think I could settle for so little. I should have done what he did: be content only with the ideal. I have maligned him much in my thoughts: have considered him callous and weak. Yet these are my failings. I have not dared to connect with another person, and I have purposely chosen a husband whom I could never love, whose heart and body could never meld with my own. He remembers me a far better creature than I am; and how greatly this grieves me: not to have lived up to his view of me. If he knew what I have done he would shrink from me. I, who have always questioned his fidelity, find it greatly superior to my own. I did not know, did not know that he had suffered so. And yes, I am glad too that he has drunk from the same bitter cup as I.

I am full of grief; the air about me is heavy and without hope. He is not dead yet, I know it, know it most surely. But he has accepted his death already, and to do that is to be as good as dead. I have fallen from grace. I am hollow, clanging with emptiness; there is no solution. And all day outside the flowers bloom and open; all around me is life; I keep it away from me by my own deadness.

Now the day draws into evening; it has wrung me dry. My mind billows, spins, then slowly subsides into a calm. It is the calm before the calamity. My brother is near me, he has begun to grow back into my body. His words move before my eyes. Even if he saw me now in all my great bulk I do not think he would reject me. I am so close to it, so close.

Thomas comes in and out constantly. He does not know what to say to me; he has noticed my withdrawal and it frightens him. He smiles and leaves me; he is full of nervousness. I do not need him, I am self-sufficient. I am wrapped in a brown blanket, waiting. It will not be long. Slowly the tides are swelling, and I am filling, about to break open. This thing within; his hour has come; he knows his victory is assured. This is his moment and it is my time to keep perfectly still and wait to be overtaken. I have nothing to fight, yet the waiting is most terrible. The minutes tick by on the lovely French clock, the colours are darkening outside my window; my emptiness is spreading thickly about me. I will put this safely away now. I have nothing to do but wait. I have nothing to leave.

My scream frightened me: where did it come from? It leapt from my mouth without my bidding. Elizabeth came first and then Thomas. They began to do things all around me, they took no notice of me. The pains came and went: stronger and darker and quicker. The midwife came with scrubbed white hands; her sleeves held back with long white elasticated bags. All around me was the clicking of steel and instruments, like the butcher's shop. The mountain of my belly was alive and busy, heaving, contracting, gulping up my breath. Thomas looked grey and sick, he did not look or speak to me; then he left. Elizabeth rushed backwards and forwards with steaming water and towels; the midwife's clipped voice cut into me. It was too late to go back: I had to accept everything that was about to happen. No escape; all this had little to do with me, it seemed to continue in spite of me. I was not necessary here, they were using my body for a new life.

I do not remember any screams; I remember no noise save a small tearing sound below me, and the slimy slide of the placenta after the vicious thrust of that small body. How strong was his desire to be born into this wretched world; he was happy to survive at my expense. He had no thought for the tearing of my flesh. He was after life. I was most violently ill, and then my bed fell away and the faces: I had a vague idea of Thomas at the far end of the bed smiling with the women, as if they were in a conspiracy together and it had come to the right conclusion. Is it a birth, or a death?

I seem to have slept for a long time in a grey fog. I woke this morning with the sun behind my eyes. There is a small red form beside my bed: I look at it in wonder. It is so small. I do not want to touch it. Elizabeth, who is sitting quietly in my chair knitting, sees that I am awake: she rises and goes to the child, takes it out of the little cot and hands it to me. I wish she had not; yet it is so small, so helpless. I cannot feel anything for it; I cannot feel anything. The deadness is still here, it has not left me. The little eyes look blind, they don't seem to see me; but the face is full of wisdom. It is red and wrinkled like an old gentleman, and it seems triumphant, the smile is supine, tired but well-pleased. I hold it strangely, as if it were not my own. I am nervous; I hold it away from me. It is out of my body now and full of needs. O, I cannot shelter it from anything, not even from myself; I have no power to protect it from what lies out there. It is so little, so little, why can I not care for it? Why can I not feel?

I give it back to Elizabeth, I am disconsolate. She looks at me with incomprehension. She puts the child back in its cot and the sunlight plays on the red face and the delicate covers. How quiet is his breath: is he breathing, is he really alive? The colours above his eyelids are lilac and blue: silk colours.

Thomas comes in: he does not look at me, his attention is all on the little one. He is full of pleasure, his face beams. He says to Elizabeth: 'Is the mother all right?'

'Yes, she is awake now, Sir.'

He comes to me, smiles, then returns quickly to the child and lifts it.

'How lovely he is, a perfect child, how strong he will grow up to be. We will call him Thomas William. Look he smiles for me.'

He hands me the child reluctantly. I hold it stiffly. I have nothing to say to Thomas, he seems to have nothing to say to me. Until he remembers...

'Are you all right, Catherine? Do you feel well now? It was a good birth, she tells me, no trouble, the labour was not protracted.'

The baby is trying to wind its fingers around mine; it is trying to become part of me, to grow tendrils around my fingers so it may grow on me. I unwrap its fingers; they are so tiny, transparent.

Thomas says to Elizabeth: 'You must look in the village and find a woman to nurse the child. There is Mrs Williams, she has just produced, has she not? She will do well. Bring her up here, and make sure she is scrupulously clean. She is a big woman and she will have enough milk for two.'

Elizabeth turns to go, but Thomas stops her. 'Wait a moment. We must move the child into the nursery next to my room. He cannot stay in here, he will disturb my wife, she has her strength to recover. She must not be troubled by the child's crying.' Elizabeth nods and leaves.

Still I have nothing to say. Thomas takes the child and places it carefully in the cot. He looks down at it and smiles sweetly – O, so sweetly. Then he leaves, closing the door softly behind him with one last look at the child.

How red and bright the room is! I wish I had told Thomas to shut out the light: it hurts my eyes so. When I close them, great patterns form behind my eyes, pale orange splashings that slowly deepen to blood. They have not changed the water in the vase; the stems are swollen and soft. They seem to be growing a fur and the heads have flopped.

The air is thick with my thoughts, but I am tired of them. I am tired of this searching and searching and finding nothing. I am so tired of myself.

Some days it would be quite easy to die. I feel certain that Christopher is dead. There is some connection between this birth and his death. Why must he always desert me?

It is hard to go on. How can I escape this life, this round of boredom and other births? O, that I could be ten again and happy!

And yet something has been achieved. I have written the story of my youth, I have written the story of the weasel, and it is ended. But, perhaps it is just a beginning. I do not know. On such a harsh, red day it is hard to know anything.

I wish the night would come.